ARABESQUE

Aprilynne Pike

Books by Aprilynne Pike

Life After Theft
One Day More: A Life After Theft Prequel

The Kingdom of Versailles
Glitter
Shatter (2017)

The Wings Series
Wings
Spells
Illusions
Destined
Arabesque

The Earthbound Series
Earthbound
Earthquake
Earthrise

The Charlotte Westing Chronicles
Sleep No More
Sleep of Death

Anthologies
Dear Bully
Defy the Dark
Altered Perceptions
Side Effects (2017)

Visit Aprilynne online at AprilynnePike.com

ARABESQUE

Copyright © 2016 by Aprilynne Pike

All rights reserved.

Cover art copyright © Tomas Kriz
Used under license from Shutterstock.com

Cover design copyright © 2016 by Imaginary Properties LLC

No part of this book may be reproduced in any form or by any electronic or mechanical means including information storage and retrieval systems, without permission in writing from the author or as permitted by law.

This book is a work of fiction. Names, characters, places, and incidents are either products of the author's imagination or are used fictitiously. Any resemblance to actual persons, living or dead, events, or locales is purely coincidental.

Written in the United States of America.

ISBN-13
978-1-540522-64-1

To my readers

(that's you!)

who never stopped

believing.

ONE

"I CAN'T BELIEVE I'M GOING BACK!"

Laurel grinned and shook her head as Chelsea's voice broke the stillness of the forest. A lot had changed in twelve years, but not Chelsea—not really—and her response to being invited back to the faerie homeland of Avalon was much as it had been before. It was a once-in-a-lifetime opportunity none of them thought she'd get twice, not even with Yasmine as queen. Honestly there'd been a few years when Laurel wasn't entirely sure *she'd* see Avalon again. Fortunately for Chelsea, some things could only be accomplished by human hands.

Laurel held tight to Tamani's arm as he led them down a path now so familiar she could have traversed it in pitch darkness.

"Who's got Sophie and Zander?" Laurel asked over her shoulder. Chelsea's two adorable—if exhausting—young children were ordinarily in tow when Chelsea came out to the land. They loved visiting the forest and their *Uncle Tam*, but this was a journey they couldn't take with their mother.

"Jason's got them at home. As far as they know, Mommy's on a business trip," Chelsea said with a smile.

"It is business of a sort," Tamani said, with his typical unsmiling wit. "Faerie business. Besides, we won't send you back to Jason empty-handed and the pups will appreciate souvenirs."

It had long been the official position of Avalon that two humans could keep a secret if both were dead, but in the years since the renegade faerie Klea had engineered a trollish invasion, an unusually large number of humans had kept the secret surprisingly well. Among them, Laurel's adoptive parents and Chelsea herself—but Chelsea refused to keep secrets from her husband, who had once observed that even if he did try to tell others, nobody would believe him and he had no proof.

A lump formed in Laurel's throat at the thought of the other human who once knew the secret—but no longer. David was directly responsible for their return to Avalon today, making his absence all the more conspicuous. Laurel was glad to have Chelsea, but she couldn't help but wish both her friends had been able to come. *Willing* to come. The memory potion had taken a lot of convincing—mostly from Tamani, who was closer to David than anyone except, perhaps, Chelsea—but Laurel was certain she'd done the right thing. If only that certainty made the consequences easier to swallow.

Tamani whistled sharply, a warbling sound easily mistaken for a birdcall, and after a moment faerie sentries began to appear from behind trees. They were cautious, leading with their diamond-tipped spears and crouching low in the undergrowth, nearly invisible in their forest-hued clothing.

"This is Chelsea," Tamani said calmly, "our invited guest." The sentries straightened, making themselves fully visible. Laurel recognized only a few. Once, she'd known more of them, but most of the sentries who'd been guarding the gate during the summers she spent at the Academy had been killed.

Most, but not all. One approached now and Tamani reached out to grab his comrade, Aaron, by the shoulders, drawing him near with the gruff, backslapping hug universally utilized by males in both the faerie and human worlds. Silve followed, receiving the same treatment. They'd been brothers-at-arms even before bonding with their shared grief of Shar's death on their watch. Without the intelligence Shar died to obtain, Klea may have won, all those years ago. And even if she'd lost, Aaron and Silve wouldn't have been around to celebrate. Laurel watched their silent communication with reverence, the glimmer of sorrow that flickered across their faces resonating with her own. Even in victory, there was sadness enough to last a lifetime.

"It's a proud day," Silve said softly, and Tamani nodded,

though he didn't speak. "Shar would love to have seen it."

"He'd have been highly amused at the very least," Tamani said with a humorless laugh, settling back in beside Laurel and reaching for her hand. It was still hard for him to talk about Shar. He forced a smile, but these two hadn't listened helplessly to Shar's last moments from miles away. To this day, Tamani hated carrying a cell phone. "Shall we prepare the gate?" he said, and Laurel knew he wanted to leave that subject behind. For the moment.

Twelve green-garbed sentries gathered in a semi-circle around the tree that magically concealed the golden gate to Avalon. Chelsea took Laurel's free hand in her own, her breath catching audibly as the tree took on the gathering glow that presaged the blinding flash of its transformation. It felt so much like the day they'd all raced to save Avalon that Laurel almost looked over her shoulder to see if eighteen-year-old David was there.

"Ready?" Tamani whispered close to her ear, keying into her distress. He always did. He knew her so well it often seemed he could read her mind.

She loved him for that. She smiled up at him—a tight smile, but a smile nonetheless—and nodded. The golden gate stood shimmering in the clearing, sentries surrounding it with spears extended, ever vigilant, though at the moment nothing but darkness could be seen beyond the bars.

"Yasmine should be here any moment," Laurel said.

"Oh! I thought—"

Laurel gave Chelsea a quelling glance, then leaned in to whisper, "Much of Avalon knows that Tamani has the power to go where he pleases, but we're careful never to reveal how." Her eyes strayed to the nearly invisible lump beneath Tamani's shirt, where a golden key was strung around his neck on a claspless titanium chain made just for that purpose. "We summon Yasmine as often as we can."

Which was less often than it had once been, with Yasmine the only Winter faerie remaining in Avalon. In the wake of Klea's rebellion, Marion pursued a number of draconian reforms only to find herself thwarted, time and again, by the alliance between Jamison and Yasmine, as they slowly enacted their own reforms. When she finally tried to cast out both the very old and the very young Winter faeries, the faeries of Avalon had risen up *en masse,* Spring, Summer, and Fall, crowning Yasmine their new queen.

When Laurel had first learned of the revolution Jamison had planned, a vengeful part of her had craved some diabolical punishment for the selfish ruler who had abandoned her people to the trolls and threatened the lives of Laurel and her friends. But deep down she knew that Jamison would engineer a less destructive outcome, if he could, and so it was that Queen Marion moved to the Manor, in Scotland, declaring that she would only return when Yasmine and Jamison had ruined Avalon and came begging for her help. Marion's stubborn vigil was now in it's seventh year, allowing Yasmine the freedom to shape Avalon according to the wishes of her subjects rather than dreams of personal glory.

Early in Yasmine's reign Laurel was rarely called to Avalon to advise the young queen, but since Jamison had gone to the earth a few years ago, Yasmine had sought Laurel's counsel more frequently. It had to be strange, growing up as one of three all-powerful Winter faeries, doomed never to rule, to then suddenly find herself the sole Winter faerie in Avalon, and Queen besides. With no one to oppose her Yasmine could have done all manner of awful things. Or even simply lazy things—allowing a successful coup and the status quo to suffice. But she had embedded Jamison's philosophies deep in her core and now worked tirelessly to be the ruler she believed her people deserved.

But tireless and young though she was, there was still only one of her. Today she would be out among the fae, and it would be a small thing to come to the Garden and open the gate, especially to welcome an honored guest.

From the blackness just beyond the barrier, Yasmine's lithe outline coalesced. Her fingers slipped through the gold bars, and with a tug the gate opened, allowing Avalon's warm sunlight to tumble through as though from inches, not thousands of miles, away.

Yasmine smiled and beckoned them in. "Welcome. I'm so pleased you could come." She took Chelsea's hands and pulled her forward. "You, especially."

Chelsea was gaping at Queen Yasmine. The graceful ruler stood very still for a few seconds, then squirmed uncomfortably under Chelsea's appreciative gaze. "You were—you were this tall last time I saw you!" Chelsea said breathlessly, holding her hand out at about chest height. "And you're so beautiful!"

Yasmine laughed, rolling her eyes as she tried to slough off the compliment. Laurel hadn't considered how different Yasmine would look to Chelsea. Fae aged slowly, but at twenty-five Yasmine had reached her adult height—and was tall, for a faerie. The child-like roundness of her face had yielded to sharp, elegant features and her ebony skin was sleek, shimmering with some sort of cosmetic that made her look even more ethereal than usual.

"You turned out quite well, didn't you?" Chelsea said appreciatively, with her usual candor.

"I must say the very same about you," Yasmine said softly.

Chelsea's cheeks flushed, but Laurel was glad Yasmine had said it. Even the kindest of fae were sometimes dismissive or insulting when it came to matters of physical appearance. A side effect, Laurel suspected, of their long history of conflict with humans and, of course, trolls. And as the mother of two children, Chelsea had earned a more rounded figure than literally any of the tree-like fae could ever achieve. Laurel found her friend utterly beautiful, but she knew it couldn't be easy on Chelsea to be aging into her thirties while her best friend went right on looking like a high school senior.

Yasmine led the group into the garden and Laurel saw Chelsea suppress a cringe as they emerged from beneath the canopy—no doubt remembering the carnage they'd witnessed within these stone walls. Of that, of course, no sign remained. The garden was a haven of curated beauty. The towering trees were unscarred, the immaculate paths snaked through perfectly trimmed hedges and rainbow flowerbeds, the breeze was light and even a few birds deigned to chirp. Laurel couldn't help but smile.

A company of ceremonially-garbed sentries stood at attention in two lines, welcoming them. At their head Laurel recognized the captain who had refused to order an attack on Laurel, Tamani, David, and Chelsea when they were preparing to leave Avalon, and even stood—shield raised—in front of the foursome when Queen Marion lost her temper and attacked them herself. She gave both Laurel and Tamani a nod, but her eyes widened when she saw Chelsea. She took a small step forward and clicked her heels before saluting. "Welcome back," she said breathlessly. "Truly, this is an honor I'd never even imagined would come again."

With cheeks glowing, but a wide smile on her face, Chelsea murmured something Laurel couldn't hear, and continued on into the lush garden.

"The ceremony will start in a few hours," Yasmine said, "and I'm afraid I have much to do, but the two of you will see to our esteemed guest, will you not?"

"Of course," Tamani answered for all of them. He swept a low bow and Laurel followed suit, Chelsea right behind her. Laurel couldn't help but feel a flush of pleasure at the realization that Queen Yasmine was the only faerie Tamani had bowed to in almost a dozen years. He was a tiny microcosm of how far the entire kingdom of Avalon had come. Especially the Spring faeries.

They watched as Yasmine swept out of the garden in her glittering formal gown, her ice-blue train gliding over the grass with a gentle whisper. And though one *Am Faire-fear* trailed closely behind, it was a far cry from the retinue that had generally accompanied Marion and Jamison years ago. It said something not only about the peace that abided within the kingdom of Avalon, but the safety and kinship Yasmine felt with her people.

"Come on," Laurel said with a grin, pulling Chelsea along, feeling for all the world like she was sixteen again. "I have *so* much to show you!"

TWO

"AND ONE, AND TWO, AND JUMP, AND YES, VERY good. Higher, leaps, Rowen."

Rowen forced herself not to grind her teeth as her instructor corrected her once again. She didn't get noticeably more—or less—attention than anyone else in the corps, but often it seemed she was only called out for critique, and every five minutes at that. Her whole body ached from hours of practice and by the time the shadow of the sundial marked the end, she was ready.

The instructor clapped her hands and gave a few more pointers—none directed specifically at Rowen, this time—before setting them free. Any other day they would only have a short midday break, with sessions to resume in the afternoon, but today classes were cancelled for the ceremony.

Rowen groaned as she loosened the ribbons of her toe shoes and slid them off. She reached into her rucksack for a small pot of the Academy's healing and numbing salve and began rubbing it into her cracked, callused feet. The relief was almost instantaneous, but the massage still felt good. She needed to soak them in a bowl of fertilized water when she got home. Hopefully there'd be enough time. A few of the other dancers bade her farewell when they passed by on their way out of the studio, but Rowen scarcely heard them as she stuffed her shoes and shrugged on the straps of her pack.

Today was the day. She wished she were less nervous.

Opting to carry her sandals rather than wear them, Rowen headed out into the bright summer sunshine on tender bare feet. Her petals had finally fallen out last week, thank the goddess. As a Summer faerie she might have rendered them invisible, but her blossom was enormous and an illusion would only keep others from seeing it. Not feeling it. In the way was the least of what her huge petals would be. Besides, who wanted to spend all day concentrating on keeping their blossom out of sight? The timing was perfect and Rowen couldn't help but think of that as an omen.

The dance studio was in Summer, and despite the slow blending of the seasonal neighborhoods under the new Queen's reign, Rowen's grandmother, Rhoslyn, still lived in her big tree in Spring. So Rowen made the trek up the hill to Summer every day; at least when she was weary and spent she got to go downhill.

Grandmother. One of Tamani's words, borrowed from the humans, given to Rowen to ease her loneliness. *Uncle* Tamani—another human word. After the trolls had taken her parents, Tamani had given her the words so that she could claim her remaining family by names that marked them as hers. As far as she knew, she was the only faerie who used the human terms, but Tamani had been right—it did help her feel as though she had a place. She had a grandmother and an uncle; and she was a niece, and a granddaughter. It brought her a modicum of peace.

Many of the dancers streaming out of the large studio dispersed immediately to their homes in Summer, but others lined the path down the hill like ants, heading toward Spring. Almost half of the advanced corps were Spring faeries, now. There was even one Mixer who had opted out of her studies at the Academy and continued to pass all of her auditions to qualify as a full-time dancer. There were still many things only a Sparkler like Rowen could do—the Queen's putting an end to compulsory caste employment hadn't changed anyone's natural abilities—but no one was born with the ability to dance. Or, more importantly, the inability.

What surprised many of the Summer faeries, Rowen included, was how quickly some Spring faeries were able to match the skill of the Summer fae who had started training as soon as they were stable on their spindly sprout legs. Two years ago—the same year Rowen made it into the elite corps—the first Spring faerie had also passed. And last year the unimaginable became reality; three Summer faeries had been cut and replaced by Spring faeries. Most Sparklers accepted this as a challenge, a reason to work harder. But Rowen was already working her feet to their stems, trying and mostly failing to preserve the specialness of her personal life that had been slowly leeched away by circumstance. She put in more extra practice hours at open studio than any other elite dancer she knew. She wasn't at the bottom of the corps or anything, but she'd be blighted if she was ever going to let her status as a Summer faerie be torn away from her. Ever. Rowen would do anything—anything—to continue dancing.

At the edge of Spring Rowen caught sight of Lenore, standing in front of a memorial for all the faeries who fell in the war, and ran the last hundred yards to join her. "Hey," Rowen said softly as she approached. Her friend wore a conflicted, lonely expression—one so few people seemed to understand. One Rowen spent a lot of time trying to keep from her own face. It was one of the reasons Len and Rowen were so close—practically sisters. "What's wrong?"

Len looked up, forcing a smile and shaking her head. But Rowen just waited until Len gave a one-shouldered shrug and said, "Tamani's at your house."

"Oh." Rowen was torn, wanting to go to him, wanting to

stay and comfort Len.

"I snuck away. I didn't want to see him."

It wasn't that Len didn't like Tamani, in general, but he represented everything Len had lost. Her father, Shar, had been killed by the renegade faerie who started the war. Tamani had done his best to graft himself into Shar's place—and in her more intimate conversations with Rowen, Lenore confessed he'd done a pretty good job—but the main reason he was such a big part of her and her mother's lives was simply that Shar was dead. Rowen's own situation was sufficiently similar that she could empathize. Her uncle seemed, at times, to blame himself for all the damage the trolls had done. And to attempt to atone.

Lenore stared a little too intently up at the rows upon rows of names inscribed in the marble monument. "I don't think I can go to the ceremony today," she whispered.

"It's for your father."

Lenore scoffed.

"Not specifically, obviously. But it's for all of them." Rowen gestured at the rows of stone slab. She knew right where Shar's was—fourth column over, about a third of the way down. One name among hundreds and hundreds, despite the pivotal role he'd played.

"Not really." Lenore's voice was steady enough, but Rowen could tell she was holding back tears. "It's for David.

And Laurel. And Tamani. Oh, and all the other honorable mentions."

Rowen closed the distance between them and slipped her arm around Lenore's shoulders, bringing their faces close together. "I know they don't understand," she whispered. "I wish they did. Tamani wishes they did." Much of Shar's role in Jamison's scheme to bring an end to the caste system was still secret, and the parts that weren't were poorly understood by the average citizen of Avalon. Aside from the guardians on the human side of the gates, most fae had never even seen a human until the battle with Klea. They would never understand how close Avalon would have been to total annihilation without Shar. Tamani grew visibly uncomfortable in the glow of honor and adoration often beamed his way, knowing how much of it should have belonged to a faerie whose name almost no one in Avalon would have recognized.

Lenore's father.

"All David did was be human," Lenore said. "For one day."

Rowen didn't say how much of an oversimplification that was. How David's choices, not his humanity, set the tone for what happened after he left. They both knew it. Lenore was the one who listened to Rowen's irrational dissatisfaction with their new world, and today Rowen returned the favor with her silence.

"I should take my dark cloud off somewhere so I don't spoil everyone else's sunshine," Lenore said after a few more minutes of silence. She finally turned to meet Rowen's eyes for the first time, and Rowen didn't hide her own emotions. It was an exchange that required no words, and meant more than hours of conversation. "Will you tell him not to come looking for me?" Lenore asked, one tear escaping, only to be swiftly rubbed away.

"I will," Rowen said, her own voice shaky. This was the moment to say goodbye—if her plan worked, Rowen had no idea when she'd see Lenore again—but in this moment she couldn't bring herself to add to her friend's pain. A note would have to do.

Lenore turned and headed toward the forest surrounding the hill where the World Tree loomed.

Rowen turned and headed for her house, feeling every minute of hard work from the studio that morning. The conversation with Lenore had unearthed her own feelings about having lost her parents. That was appropriate; it was a day of mourning as well as a day of celebration, after all. Still, Tamani was here—and Laurel, she assumed. Of course, they would have other things on their minds. Just like everyone else in Rowen's life.

Rowen opened the front door to a wall of sound, a cacophony of voices coming from the great room. She dumped her bag at the foot of the narrow staircase that led up to her bedroom and peeked her head around the corner.

"There you are, Row, come in, come in!" Her grandmother beckoned warmly and Rowen grinned as Tamani crushed her against his chest in his usual ebullient fashion. Laurel gathered her in more gently—but when Laurel released her, Rowen caught sight of their third guest and couldn't stifle a gasp. The woman was middle-aged, sixty or seventy at least—but no, that wasn't right. Humans aged more quickly, and this was definitely a human.

The woman jumped to her feet, clasping her hands in front of her. "Oh my goodness! Rowen! You were practically a baby last time I was here. You've grown like a weed!"

Rowen's mouth fell open and the cheerful buzz around her fell into silence.

Laurel cleared her throat. "Um, it's perhaps best not to refer to a member of the plant kingdom as a weed."

The woman clapped her hands over her mouth, her eyes widening as the strangest thing happened to her neck and cheeks—they changed color in an instant, from pale peach to cherry red. Rowen took a step back, uncertain of what behavior to expect to follow the animal's display.

"Rowen," Laurel said, catching her by the arm. "This is Chelsea. I don't know if you remember her. You'd have met her very, very briefly, when Tamani brought her to Spring to gather all the fae."

"There's something wrong with her face," Rowen whispered frantically, trying to put more distance between herself and the human, even while not wanting to be rude to Laurel, who wore a concerned expression.

Laurel kept her tight hold on Rowen's arm, but looked back at Chelsea in confusion. "Oh!" she said, then grinned. "She's never seen anyone blush before," she said to the woman.

Then woman let out a hollow laugh. "And I imagine I'm doing even more of it now," she said, pointing at her own face which was, indeed, reddening again.

"Blushing is how humans show embarrassment," Laurel said to Rowen, clearly trying not to smile. "It not harmful. And she'll probably do it again. Chelsea's skin is quite prone to flushing."

Rowen continued to eye the woman warily, but stopped trying to get away. Hopefully, she wouldn't put a thorn in Rowen's plans.

Tamani made a choking sound; when everyone in the room turned to look at him he burst into peals of laughter.

No one joined him.

"Sorry," he said as soon as he had himself back under control. "It's so easy to forget how much I had to learn." He slung an arm around Rowen, which always made her feel a little safer in spite of everything, then pulled one of his incomprehensible human devices out of a pocket. "Not too much longer until the ceremony. You said you wanted to take Chelsea by the Academy, Laurel?" At Laurel's nod he looked toward his mother and said, soberly, "I'm going to Ariana's. It's been too long since I saw them."

Rowen felt a stab of guilt, remembering Lenore. She hated knowing what Tamani's eyes would look like when she told him, but she'd promised Lenore and today, of all days, she couldn't break her word.

Goodbyes were murmured all around and Rowen stepped up onto the first stair to let everyone pass by her in the front entryway. Tamani held the door for Laurel and Chelsea, but before he could leave, Rowen grabbed his sleeve. "Lenore isn't home," she said quietly.

"Pardon?"

"Lenore isn't home." Rowen repeated, then lowered her lashes so she wouldn't have to meet his eyes. "She doesn't want to be home today."

She felt Tamani's shoulder tighten under her fingers. "Not even for me?" he said, his voice a scratchy whisper.

"Maybe especially for you," she said, hating the unfairness of it, but needing to do her duty toward her best friend. She chanced a peek at his face and was unsurprised to see his jaw clenched and sadness deep as the ocean in his eyes.

"It's hard for me, too," he whispered, but this time Rowen suspected it was as loud as his emotions would allow him to speak.

"It doesn't have to make sense."

At that his shoulders relaxed and he swallowed visibly, then nodded. "You're right. The point is to help her—not me."

"I'm sorry," Rowen blurted, feeling the need to say something, even something so trite, so inadequate.

Her uncle reached a hand up and squeezed her arm. "We all paid a price for Avalon that day—but some paid a far greater price than others, and got less for their sacrifice. You know that better than most. And Lenore has been paying longer than others—even when she had him, her father was so often absent. He hated leaving them." Tamani's eyes were fixed on another time, another place, and it was several long seconds of silence before he came back. "When you judge it to be helpful, please tell her I send my love."

Rowen, tears gathering in her eyes for these wonderful people who couldn't seem to help each other in their shared grief, simply nodded. As she walked upstairs she considered what Tamani had said about sacrifice and hoped he would remember his own words later, when he was angry with her.

THREE

THE CLOSER LAUREL AND CHELSEA DREW TO THE Academy, the heavier their memories became, and their conversation dwindled like mist on the wind. The trolls brought suffering to all of Avalon, but as a group the Fall faeries had suffered more than most. More than three of every four Mixers had perished for Klea's pride.

Even so, the Academy changed little while the rest of Avalon changed much. Most of the tasks and roles traditionally held by Mixers couldn't be filled by anyone else. Still, small changes could have significant impact. No longer were Fall sprouts taken from their Spring parents and made children of the crown; that practice had been done away by Yasmine and Jamison a decade ago. Young Mixers still came to learn, but for the most part no longer lived in the Academy's halls. Far from seeming empty as a result, the Academy now hosted fae of all seasons, for though Mixing could only be done by those with the gift, anyone could make use of what the Fall faeries produced. Furthermore, anyone could imagine new uses for old recipes, and open communication between producers and consumers was generating something of an academic renaissance in Avalon.

So the grounds of the Academy still bustled with students, and if there were strictly fewer than when Laurel had been learning there, it wasn't by as great a margin as might have been. It would take centuries, at least, for Avalon to replenish its Fall faerie population after the madness Klea engineered. A decade and more had done little to dull the stab of anger Laurel always felt at the thought of the renegade Mixer and her vengeful dream of building her own twisted utopia on the island from which she had been exiled.

As they passed onto the grounds of the austere stone building, several students recognized Laurel and waved. It had been almost a year since Laurel's last visit—though Tamani came by a bit more frequently—and Laurel was excited to see whether Yeardley had made any significant changes. And then, as if summoned by her thoughts, he burst through the heavy doors to welcome them as they approached.

When Yeardley threw his arms around her, Laurel squeezed him hard. He was her favorite person in all of Avalon now that Jamison had passed and been buried amidst the roots of the World Tree. After the loss of most of the senior faculty,

Yeardley had taken over the running of the Academy; as his hair had taken on more silver in the last few years, Laurel couldn't help but think of him as a Dumbledore of sorts, with the Academy his own personal Hogwarts. Though in light of his often brusque manner and the fact that the Academy mostly produced potions, Yeardley was arguably more of a Snape.

The old Mixer drew back and favored Laurel with a smile before turning to Chelsea, his eyes dancing with delight. "Chelsea! I didn't expect to see you again." He extended a hand to her, but rather than shaking it, he brought it to his lips and laid a soft kiss there. "Honored. Delighted. I'm only sorry that both our champions couldn't be here."

Laurel knew Chelsea's face must have clouded at least as much as hers. There had been a time when Chelsea wouldn't, couldn't speak to Laurel—after finding out how she'd helped David give up his memories of Avalon. Laurel understood and had given her friend the space she needed; in time, they'd reconnected. But it still wasn't something they talked about. Today was not the day for that conversation. Maybe that day would never come.

"Foolish of me," Yeardley said, sobering. "I shouldn't have mentioned it. Of course it still weighs on you."

Chelsea turned to look down the hill toward Summer, averting her face while she gathered her emotions.

"I actually brought Chelsea to see the line," Laurel said softly.

Yeardley smiled softly. "Of course. And Fiona. You must take her to see Fiona—she'd never forgive me if she knew you were both here and I'd not given her the opportunity to see Chelsea again."

Chelsea put on a brave smile as Laurel led her indoors, returning waves and greetings from those who knew her. The Academy must be hardly recognizable from the near-rubble it had been when last Chelsea saw it. The splintered front doors had been replaced, the fire-blackened stones scrubbed clean or overhung with vibrant tapestries. Laurel knew from Chelsea's expression that she was seeing the death and destruction she'd witnessed here at least as vividly as she was seeing the life and creation that had taken its place. Still, it had to be healing to see how far the Academy had come.

"You're that girl," one dark-eyed faerie said, stopping them in the hall and reaching out a hand to touch one of Chelsea's auburn curls.

Laurel saw Chelsea's eyes widen as a tear slipped down the young faerie's face.

"You saved me. I never thought I would have this chance—you probably don't remember. You pushed me down when I didn't know—I don't—" The faerie struggled for words and Laurel saw Chelsea squeeze her hand. "I helped you build the barricade. I'd have never known to do such a thing. But then I never saw you again to say thank you. I've regretted it ever since."

Overhearing, another faerie approached to tell Chelsea what she'd done for him that day—and then third, a fourth. Chelsea smiled tearfully at their gratitude and responded with grace, but Laurel could feel her hands shaking as other faeries noticed the commotion, then others noticed the crowd. As a seventh faerie pressed in to express her personal thanks to Chelsea, Yeardley uttered a few soft words and the fae dispersed, though many stopped quickly to touch Chelsea's hair or shoulder.

"I always think of David as the hero who saved Avalon," Chelsea confessed softly. "I was too dazzled to accomplish much."

"You were here at the Academy for *hours* before David arrived," Yeardley said, not with emotion or even with noticeable gratitude. He may as well have been lecturing; it was a tone that simply conveyed *facts*. "Without your help, there might not have been an Academy left for David to defend."

"Come on," Laurel said, taking Chelsea by the hand when the silence grew heavy and leading her toward the open double doors of the dining hall. "This is what I wanted to show you."

They stepped through the tall doors into the spacious room where they'd once sought escape from the creeping death of Klea's vile red potion. "Look," Laurel said quietly, pointing at an irregular stripe of gold, stretching from one side of the room to the fountain in the center.

Chelsea examined it, her brow wrinkled, but Laurel was sure she'd remember in a moment.

"The sword," Chelsea said at last. "He dragged the sword when he went to wash at the fountain. He was … he was covered in blood. It left a score." She turned to Yeardley. "You filled it with gold."

"One of two marks he left," Yeardley said. "The other is there—the hole he cut, through which many made their escape." He gestured to the wall, where a roughly squarish gold outline stood out from the masonry. "A window was proposed, but this proved wiser, structurally. His heroism will never be forgotten while this building stands."

Chelsea stared down at the long gold line, and Laurel could see tears shining in her eyes before she spoke, voice trembling with emotion. "It broke him, Yeardley. To kill so many. He was a born healer. It went against everything he stood for." She paused and Yeardley laid a hand on her shoulder. "It would have broken me, too. They weren't human, I know, but how narcissistic would it be to believe that mattered? Hundreds, maybe thousands of *people*, dead at his hands. Who wouldn't that have broken, if they had any semblance of a soul?"

Laurel clenched her fingers, but Yeardley had never failed her and he didn't now. "I tell my students that true strength is not found in the taking of life, but in the giving of it. David shattered his soul to save us. It troubles you that his memory is gone, but by taking that weight upon yourself you have given him a lifetime as a human healer, to put those pieces back together. A noble gift on everyone's part. Don't forget that."

Tears were streaming down her cheeks, but Chelsea smiled and nodded.

Laurel smiled, too. Yeardley's gift for healing extended well beyond his mixings, as she herself had experienced.

"Well," Yeardley said, straightening and clearing his throat, "Let's seek out Fiona, shall we?"

Chelsea's gaze lingered a while on the long golden line before she turned and took Yeardley's proffered arm; he swept her from the room, as regally as any queen.

***

Tamani knew it was nearly time to get down the hill to the ceremony, but he never came to Avalon without visiting the World Tree. Because he and Yasmine could speak right at the gate, he found himself hovering on the precipice of his homeland—speaking across the boundary—more often than not, especially in the last year. Which meant he visited less frequently than he used to.

After a lengthy climb, Tamani crested the highest hill and felt the familiar ripple of power wash over him. He paused and closed his eyes, appreciating it for a long moment before moving closer to the twisted trunk, falling to his knees in the spongy grass as he'd done so many times before—in gratitude, joy, exhaustion. Today he specifically remembered the day he'd come and knelt in sheer despair after Laurel had sent him away and he didn't know where else to go. He'd been in such torment he hadn't been able to form a coherent question. Even then, the tree hadn't failed him.

He ran his hand over the vines that spiraled up a small silver marker that bore Jamison's name; the wise old faerie had given up his opportunity to truly join the World Tree in order to provide the mysterious service the tree had told him was his destiny—to open the gates of Avalon to two humans, who in turn saved the faerie kingdom. Yasmine thought it fitting that he be buried here—nestled in the roots beneath this particular spot.

Tamani lifted his other hand to the tree's roughened trunk, to the scar where Laurel had carved into the tree to get the answers she needed to save Avalon from Klea's terrible poison. Laurel still had a matching scar on her hand. She'd heard the tree speak, then, as Tamani lay dying, with the voice of a man asking her to save his son. Ever since, Tamani had felt a little closer to his deceased father by laying his land on that spot.

"Hello," he said, greeting them both, as he always did. He didn't know if they could hear him. His father was a tiny part of the consciousness of the tree, of course—but he had no idea what might remain of Jamison. The human world had a lot to say about spirits and afterlives; Chelsea had some particularly interesting ideas that he could hardly take seriously, except for the fact that she did. Whatever the truth ultimately proved to be, Tamani liked to think that somehow, Jamison could hear him. Or, at the very least, that maybe Tamani's father could pass along a message.

A tiny breeze tousled his hair and, though it was probably nothing out of the ordinary, Tamani smiled, thinking that perhaps it was his father greeting him in return. "Laurel and I did the math the other day—I've spent more time living in the human world than I have in Avalon," he said with a wry chuckle. "At this point, I'm almost as human as she is." And then he sat silently, hands resting on the marker and the scar, symbols of Avalon's brush with destruction and embrace of rebirth. There was plenty to tell. He'd been gone for almost a year and there were stories and events and *things*. But he sat in silence, letting minutes pass by as he considered the most important thing.

"I'm going to be a father," he whispered, surprised how hard it was to choke out those amazing words. "We planted our seed last fall, after Laurel lost her petals. A little seedling. *Little* … it's almost full-height. I'm hoping for an autumn arrival." He laughed. "Not for the reasons you'd think—just because that's the fastest it could bloom. I want … to see what kind of faerie Laurel and I make. My hair? Her eyes? Well, I'd be happy if it looked just like her."

He smiled ruefully. "Mother is out of her head with glee. She comes out to our home often to tend the seedling, of course. Won't let any other Gardener near it. Barely lets Laurel do the day-to-day maintenance." He hesitated, unclenching his fingers when he realized he was in danger of smothering the little vine snaked around Jamison's marker. "I'm terrified. Excited, but scared in a way I never felt in a hundred battles. This faerie will be split between two worlds. Very literally. We can't raise it in the human world—not for many years, at least. Too many oddities to explain. But it'll be the first faerie born outside of Avalon in thirty years at least, so it won't truly be a faerie of Avalon, either. Especially not with Laurel as a mother." He paused and let a sappy grin cross his face. "Laurel as a mother," he repeated. "Imagine that."

He looked down at his knees, feeling oddly ashamed. "Rowen's having a hard time. Mother talks about her frequently on her visits. Doesn't know what to do." He raised his eyes to the canopy of the tree, thinking back to that awful day. "One of the worst moments of my life was telling my own mother that her child was dead. My *sister*. I didn't tell Rowen—she wasn't in the room. But I think she already knew. Understood. Her mother, at least. I think she watched her die."

Tamani melted into silence again, remembering the nightmare of that terrible day, and fighting the guilt, the fear that despite everything, he hadn't done enough. "There was so much going on, and I had to focus on getting Laurel and David and Chelsea out of Avalon safely," he said, countering an argument no one ever made. Not to his face. He shrugged, feeling helpless all over again. "Maybe I botched it. Maybe things would be different if I'd taken the time, but … we always see our mistakes after the harvest, don't we?"

He glanced down the hill toward Spring; he could faintly hear the murmur of thousands of faeries gathering. "I can't stay long. This is a difficult day for Laurel. For Chelsea, too. They'll need me." His brow furrowed. "Probably hard for Rowen, too. I know it is for Lenore. I want to fix everyone, and I know I can't. But Rowen especially is my responsibility. She will be for a long time. Mother won't be around forever, and then it'll just be me. Me and her. And if I can't do right by her, how can I hope to do right by my own child?"

He shook his head. "I wish you were here. You were both fathers to me and I don't know how I'll ever be half as good at it as you were."

FOUR

"TODAY, WE PLACE THE CAPSTONE ON THIS monument, memorializing our human champion, David Lawson, and all those who fought for their lives and ours on that day."

Yasmine's voice quavered very slightly and Rowen studied her sky-blue slippers, changing their appearance from pink to sea-green and back again to distract herself from the uncomfortably somber moment of silence. The smooth sphere of white-and-grey-ribboned Calacatta marble behind the queen wasn't much to look at, and—thanks to her connection with Tamani—Rowen was seated close enough to see that the ceremonial stone wasn't carved with a single name. As capstones went, it seemed bland and inadequate, but Rowen suspected she'd make no friends by saying so.

The queen raised her chin, cleared her throat, and continued—a little louder, though even her whispers carried well; royalty certainly had a knack for tampering with acoustics. "I've personally read every name on this monument. I've run my finger along each and every engraved letter, and today—every day—I thank them for their sacrifice. We cannot, we must not, ever forget our fallen fae." She smiled momentarily, and the audience's mood seemed to lift a little—a ray of sunshine through darkened clouds. "Now, with the completion of the monument, I hope we can also turn our faces toward the future, toward brighter days to come."

Surprised murmurs rose like the buzzing of bees as a small group of sentries parted to reveal the human woman from Rhoslyn's house. Rowen didn't know precisely what this Chelsea's connection was to the fabled David, except that they'd come to Avalon together on the day of the battle. But they must have been close, because anguish was clearly splashed across Chelsea's face as she clutched the hilt of Excalibur. Tamani hadn't mentioned this part.

For most of Rowen's life, the sword had been right where David left it, a strange metal sapling sprouting from the center of the circle where Laurel's *viridefaeco* serum had cleansed a deadly poison from Avalon. Utterly untouchable by fae, the sword had been kept carefully free of weeds and vines, and it's incorruptible blade never failed to shine with a high gloss in the sunlight. A small shrine of sorts had grown up around it over the years, beside the path between the Academy and the

Winter Palace—nothing ostentatious, nothing with walls or a roof, but a place people could come to see the sword, were they so inclined.

Now it would be gone. Or rather, it would be *here.*

The curly-haired woman raised the sword, her hands shaking, though Rowen doubted many were close enough to see that detail. With no assistance—not that anyfae *could* help her—Chelsea carefully, with almost no force, laid the tip of the sword at the very top of the smooth sphere, then pushed the blade into the marble. When most of the blade was buried, she clenched both hands around the hilt and closed her eyes. Several long seconds passed with no sound but the rustling of leaves in the breeze. Then, the woman opened her eyes, peeled her fingers away, and stepped back.

The silence stretched until Queen Yasmine began to clap. Applause spread, as applause is wont to do, and Rowen lifted her hands as well, though she tapped her palms together soundlessly. She was grateful to David; without him, there would be no memorial, because there would be no fae alive and free to carve the names of the dead into the marble. There might be no Avalon on which to build a monument. But the fact was, before the revolution Rowen had two parents who loved her and a special place among the Spring faeries. Now she was an unremarkable orphan. She didn't begrudge anyone the vast improvement change had brought; she couldn't deny how much better life was for nearly everyone who'd survived the attacks. But it was hard to be fully joyful when her own life had been so trampled.

She almost didn't hear when Queen Yasmine concluded the ceremony and invited everyone to the revels.

The festivities became a blur of tasteless food and meaningless chatter as Rowen was careful to keep her quarry in sight. Len was nowhere to be seen, but that was both expected and helpful—Len alone might have seen Rowen's nervousness for what it was. She almost lost her courage when her grandmother bid her good night shortly before sunset. But she poured all of her gratitude into a sincere embrace and, afterward, found herself more determined than ever.

It had only been a year or so since Rowen was permitted to stay past feasting into the dancing and frolicking that followed, but even as her friends began joining hands in a circle, she wasn't tempted to stay. As food and conversation gave way to music and dancing, Rowen watched with interest as a small group made their way down the hill.

Shouldering the rucksack she'd kept hidden most of the day, Rowen turned herself invisible and padded softly after Laurel, Tamani, and Chelsea, stepping carefully around faerie parents who carried half-asleep sprouts on their shoulders and older fae strolling hand-in-hand toward their homes. But as she drew near, she discovered to her dismay that she wasn't her uncle's only stalker.

"Today of all days they're watching you," Queen Yasmine said, sounding breathless as she addressed Tamani in a surprisingly informal tone. "I'm certain at least some have noted your departure. It's best I accompany you."

Tamani shrugged and made a gesture for her to join them. It wasn't quite arm in arm … but it was close. How odd.

"Thank you for coming," Yasmine said. "I know it wasn't easy."

"Our schedule really isn't that tight," Tamani said, waving her thanks away. "We've been spending a lot more time at the land since—"

"I didn't mean for your schedule."

Tamani paused. He and the queen were of equal height, but watching them stand there, face to face, addressing one another, Rowen was struck by how utterly equal they appeared in, well, *stature*. She knew her uncle for a hero, but also for a mischievous trickster and even, on rare occasion, a gloomy old mope. The way he was regarding the queen, the way she was regarding him, was outside anything Rowen had ever seen or even imagined of him.

"A revolution has many costs," Queen Yasmine said. "Some are greater than others. I know that when you come to something like this, you're thinking more of the costs. You don't see the benefits the way I do."

"I know they exist, though," Tamani said, and his tone was fervid, rather than argumentative. "I'm so pleased with the changes you've made. Jamison would be, too."

"I know. But you paid much, and gained little. Chelsea, you, too, paid much in return for even less. Today can't have been easy. I want you all to know that you're appreciated."

"Thank you." The human woman spoke up first. "For myself, I think I didn't know how much I needed this. I needed to see that you understand what … what David gave up for you."

"I do," Yasmine said, with a decisive nod. "Jamison always did. And faerie memories last a long time." Yasmine looked up toward the lights of the festival. "The goal of today was to celebrate and move on. Move *forward*. But don't ever doubt that we remember. Even when he no longer can."

Chelsea nodded, but didn't speak, and her cheeks were doing that reddish thing again, though Rowen couldn't imagine why the woman might be embarrassed now. Humans were incredibly awkward.

"You're welcome to return," Queen Yasmine said.

Rowen barely suppressed a gasp. Friend or not, Chelsea was *human*. Avalon was no place for a human.

"Thank you," Chelsea said. "I'm honored, and I might even take you up on that, someday. But I have responsibilities elsewhere, and something about being here …" As her words trailed off, the human looked around and Rowen followed her gaze, wondering what she was seeing. To Rowen, it was Avalon as usual—green and growing. Did the human see it differently?

"Say no more," Queen Yasmine said softly, "I understand."

The entire group began walking toward the Gate Garden once more. Rowen followed quietly, grateful for her ballet training. She'd certainly seen the gate on occasion—a square of golden-wrought fencing, inlaid with flowers, surrounded by sentries—and as the queen pulled it open, Rowen moved as close to Chelsea as she dared. The woman smelled vaguely of flowers, which seemed wrong; Rowen was pretty sure humans never blossomed. But she suspected that the human's senses would not be as keen as Tamani's or even Laurel's, so she would be unlikely to realize she had a shadow.

Yasmine stopped Tamani and the two of them shared something in whispers. Rowen was sure she was somehow caught, but Tamani silently met the queen's eyes for long seconds, then turned away and gestured Laurel and Chelsea to proceed in front of him.

They trailed through the golden gate in single file; Rowen held her breath as Tamani greeted the gate sentries in the human world with a brusque nod. Excitement and fear made her tremble slightly and she was terrified she'd trip and give herself away before the gate was even closed.

The human world. She was in the human world!

And it was very dark here. Surely it wasn't dark all the time, but they had stepped from dusk to pitch-blackness and Rowen didn't like the fact that she was on unfamiliar turf without the ability to see clearly.

"Here," Tamani said, and abruptly a yellow-orange light cut through the darkness, shining from a smooth red cylinder in Tamani's hand. Rowen almost shrieked in surprise. Neither Laurel nor Chelsea seemed alarmed in the least, so Rowen pressed her lips together and continued to follow them, grateful that she could at least see the ground in front of her. It didn't look much different than Avalon. The grounds here were untended, but she'd heard how much bigger the human world was; maybe they simply didn't have enough workers to tend everywhere. Maybe Tamani would be more willing to let her stay if she offered to help with the tending here.

The path widened and a ball of light appeared through the trees. This light was more blue than yellow and Rowen blinked and squinted at it as they drew closer. It was shining from a building in a clearing, a building bigger than any she'd ever seen, save the Academy and the Winter Palace. It was a house, she was pretty sure. Laurel and Tamani's house. But it was *enormous*. Not like the cozy tree house she and her grandmother lived in. Not like the small cottage she'd shared with her parents when she was a seedling. Not even like the bubble house she'd only lived in for half a year before trolls smashed it to pieces.

She realized as they drew nearer, that it was actually two houses, with a path running between them and dozens upon dozens of planting boxes lining the entire perimeter. Trestles full of climbing vines lines the walls, and flowers in rainbow hues blossomed from hanging pots and ceramic urns. It was rather like the Academy, in fact, with only two floors, but with the same style of eaves and a sharply sloped roof with tiny windows in individual peaks all along the roofline. The yard was an expanse of grass, but there were little fruit trees and rows of furrowed soil everywhere. With a garden such as this, no wonder Laurel managed to survive in the human world.

Laurel, Tamani, and Chelsea had gathered in a tight circle in front of something very large, black, and shiny that Rowen couldn't identify—it had wheels, like a cart, but it looked too heavy to pull and pretty much useless for carrying anything.

Rowen noticed the sparkle of a Summer-wrought hair bauble nestled in the curls of Chelsea's hair—had that been there before? Then Tamani reached into his rucksack and pulled out a decorated gift box and a miniature bow and arrow; Chelsea laughed when he handed these to her. Rowen narrowed her eyes. She didn't like the idea of sending artifacts from Avalon into the human world, but if Tamani approved, then it must be something that wouldn't immediately give them away. Probably.

Chelsea tucked the parcels under one arm and hugged Laurel and Tamani and said something indiscernible as she swiped at her eyes and gave a small wave.

Rowen's eyes widened as something like lightning flashed out from two circles on the front of the black not-cart, and then Chelsea opened it, somehow, and crawled right inside.

Maybe she lived there?

Then a great growl sounded from the thing and Rowen jumped away with a shriek, tripping on something behind her and falling hard on her back, cracking her head on the corner of the building. Her hands flew to the aching spot, checking for sap, and she scrunched her eyes shut against the pain—and realized she'd let her illusions go. She forced her eyes open, but it was too late. Tamani hadn't fully turned to her, but he was glaring from the corner of his eye as he continued to smile and wave at the great black thing that moved—moved!—away from them down the wide path.

Once the black thing and its piercing lights were out of sight, Tamani shoved his hands in his pocket and sighed. "Hello, Rowen."

Rowen was still trying to untangle herself from the mess of what she could now see were gardening implements. Her knee hurt, and the back of her head ached like fire. She could tell there were a few other bruises and scrapes, but those would knit back together quickly enough.

Laurel rushed over and tried to offer a hand, but Rowen refused, struggling to her feet and then drawing herself up to her full height. Which was still a good hand's span shorter than either Tamani or Laurel.

"What are you doing?" Tamani asked. And Rowen was glad that at least it sounded like a genuine question and not a parental lecture. She didn't need that sort of thing from him, not now.

Rowen swallowed hard and tried to gather her courage. "I followed you."

"The queen mentioned that."

"I—I can't live there anymore," Rowen let out in a rush. She'd planned a whole speech, but now that nervous tension zinged through her whole body—not to mention pain—she couldn't remember more than a few words of it. "When I—wait, the queen did *what?*"

Laurel and Tamani exchanged glances and there was a communication between them that Rowen couldn't begin to interpret. "Are you seeping?" Laurel asked when Rowen reached up to touch the back of her head again.

Rowen studied her feet. "Yes."

"Come inside, then," Laurel said. "First things first, let's bind your cut."

Tamani was still glaring at her, but Rowen ducked her head and followed Laurel into the house.

FIVE

STEPPING THROUGH THE GATE INTO THE HUMAN realm had somehow failed to inspire anything like the trepidation Rowen now felt, facing the doorway to Laurel and Tamani's house. A human home, in spite of its inhabitants. The gate to Avalon went from one forest to another. *This* was a threshold between *worlds*.

Inside the first room it was dim—though the odd bluish light from outside poured through the windows, illuminating a smattering of chairs and tables, and Rowen could just make out paintings on the wall that were recognizably her grandmother's work.

"You knew I was following you?" Rowen pressed, trying to ignore the persistent ache at the back of her head.

"*I* didn't; the queen did," Tamani said, tossing the words over his shoulder. "One kind of faerie has the power to become invisible, and I only know one Sparkler who would do what you've done."

"Winter faeries can sense any plant's presence," Laurel added with a wry laugh. "We learned that the hard way."

"Indeed," Tamani said, a similar edge to his voice.

Rowen stared silently between them, but neither saw fit to enlighten her further.

"You didn't stop me, though."

Tamani shrugged. "Things are changing. More than you might realize. I didn't feel the need to air family drama in front of our guest or our monarch, and Yasmine seemed … curious, I suppose. Though it's hard to say; the Winter court has a habit of keeping its motives hidden."

Rowen was speechless. Weeks of preparation and practice and planning, and she'd only made it through because they *let* her?

"So you don't think we're lazy about defending the gate, your illusions wouldn't have gotten you past the sentries in any event," Tamani said. "You're awfully loud for a ballerina."

Rowen prickled, but saw the teasing glint in Tamani's eye and tried to swallow her anger.

"The kitchen is this way," Laurel said. "Come on." She turned toward a darkened doorway and Rowen followed, backed closely by Tamani.

It felt uncomfortably like being a prisoner.

As Laurel entered, the room exploded into white light.

Reflexively, Rowen gasped and flinched back, staggering against Tamani—Mixer lights only got that bright when they were setting something on fire. But the light made no heat, and Rowen lowered her hands from where they'd flown to shield her face. Did they already have a Sparkler staying with them?

Will I ever be special anywhere?

"Laurel," Tamani said rather sternly, giving Rowen's shoulders a reassuring squeeze. "Take it slow, Rowen's never seen electricity before. You're freaking her out."

"Oh." Laurel's hand paused on some sort of white panel on the wall. "Should I—"

"No," Tamani said. "Don't turn it back off. Just … take it slow." He chuckled low in his throat and Rowen had to suppress an urge to smack him. There was nothing funny about any of this!

"I'm sorry," Laurel said, and at least her voice was sympathetic. "This is just how we make light in the human world. You'll get used to it," she added, but she sounded uncertain. "Here, sit."

Rowen sank into a wooden chair that was—thankfully—perfectly familiar and peered around the kitchen with wide eyes. It looked a bit like the laboratories up at the Academy, but shinier, somehow; almost every surface was at least mildly reflective. There was an enormous black armoire, a silver basin beneath a night-darkened window, glass canisters and glossy boxes on nearly every surface—many with windows of their own, some glowing a sickly green that reminded Rowen of phosphorescing algae.

"Cradle of the goddess, but this is a strange place," she whispered.

"Human magic," Tamani said softly, lowering himself into a seat beside her. "More or less. You might come to understand some of it in time, but for now I think you'll adjust better if you think of it as human magic. But speaking of humans, you should—"

"You're home!"

An enormous animal, clothed in ragged fabric, hair standing on end like a madman, burst into the room. Rowen leapt to her feet, tangled her legs in the chair, and sprawled against Laurel's cupboards and onto the floor. She pulled her knees to her chest and, straining against the pain in her head, willed the light pouring from the ceiling-hung globes to flow around her rather than scatter off of her.

A great crash sounded and hot liquid splashed Rowan's leg along with the prick of something solid and sharp. She flinched away with a shriek, thwacking her aching head against the enormous black armoire, which—some detached part of her noticed with distant confusion—seemed to be *humming.* Not since trolls had smashed their way into the sugar glass house where her mother died had Rowen been so terrified. She had to *hide*, she had to get *out*—

"Everyone, freeze!" Tamani's commanding tenor was impossible to disobey and Rowen stilled herself with a whimper. Apparently the creature who'd just crashed into the room felt the same, because it was as motionless as a sprout playing frost-tag.

"Rowen," Tamani said, very softly, "become visible, and don't disappear again until I tell you it's allowed."

Rowen was almost too terrified to let her illusion go. What sort of animal were they keeping here, and why? Was it some kind of guardian? Is that why it spit hot liquid at her—because she was a stranger? Peering up through her fingers, however, Rowen saw that the crazed thing looked almost, well, *human.* Its face was too pale, too wrinkled, its gnarled fingers and wild hair a little on the side of *trollish*, but otherwise—

Hesitantly, Rowen faded back into sight.

"As I was about to say, you should know that Laurel's parents are here—Laurel's *human* parents—and you should expect to see them."

Rowen's gaze went back to the person standing in the doorway. Mortification made her feel like lettuce left too long in the sun. "I'm sorry," she mumbled, refusing to meet anyone's eyes. "I was … surprised."

"Me too," the man said, flexing his jaw a bit, as if surprised to find it working. But then he was grinning and moving toward her. "I can't wait to—"

Whatever he was going to say was cut off by Tamani's hand on his chest, so firm the man bounced back a few inches. "Hold tight," Tam said softly. "She's scared. I know you're excited, but you need to treat her like a skittish animal. At least for tonight."

The man nodded, but didn't take his eyes off Rowen. Or lose that sappy grin. Rowen, on the other hand, felt anger eclipse her fear, and glared at Tamani. "I am not an animal," she hissed.

Tamani let out a groan. "Hecate's eye! It wasn't an insult. It was an explanation that made sense to *my father-in-law*," he bellowed, this final comment somehow being the one that overwhelmed his control. Eyebrows low, he pointed a finger at Rowen's face as though *she* were in the wrong. "You need to simmer down in a serious way, Rowen." He stayed frozen in place between Rowen and the man, but looked to Laurel. "This is too much. Let's get her patched up. I'm taking her back to Avalon."

Laurel and Rowen protested at the same time, but Laurel's was the only voice that seemed to matter. "I don't think that's a good idea," she said, reaching up and tapping Tamani's chest. "Tomorrow morning we can call Yasmine and have her come down and open the gate."

Tamani grimaced and shot another glare at Rowen, then

nodded. "You're right. She can stay here tonight."

Laurel nodded and smiled. "I'll get my kit. As she left the kitchen she pulled her father after her, though the human man continued to smile and stare at Rowen until the doorway blocked him from view. Such a *creepy* species—they looked just enough like faeries to make the subtle differences stand out in the worst possible way. When they were gone, Rowen unclenched her fists and sagged against the strange humming armoire.

Tamani folded his arms over his chest shook his head.

"I'm not going back," Rowen said, rising slowly. She needed to make that clear from the beginning. She wasn't asking to stay—she was *staying*. If Tamani wanted to help her, great. But if he didn't, she was willing to do it on her own. Though that might not be anywhere near as easy as she'd thought, not if her experience so far was any indication—but Tamani didn't need to know that.

"Not tonight," Tamani said evenly once Rowen had managed to reseat herself.

"I'm not going back to Avalon. There's nothing there for me anymore."

Tamani just arched an eyebrow. "Your grandmother? Lenore? Your dancing *corps*?"

Rowen shook her head. "You don't understand. No one does. Well, Lenore does. But no one else." She looked up to where he towered above her with his legs wide, arms folded, and his jaw clearly as set as his mind. "Will you sit, please?"

He regarded her for a few silent seconds, then not only drew a chair close and sat, but also relaxed his shoulders and folded his fingers loosely in his lap.

He was listening.

"Try to see it my way," she said, rushing to get the words out while he was amenable. As amenable as he'd been since they left Avalon. "From the moment I was born, I was *special.* Not only did I have two parents who loved me, and family, but I was a Sparkler. Because of me, my parents got to come live in Summer. We had nice things and I got to go to dance lessons and illusion practice, and when I visited Rhoslyn, the faeries who passed paid attention to me."

"Rowen—" Tamani started, but Rowen a raised silencing hand.

"No. Let me finish. The trolls came, and I lost my parents. I …" She paused to gather her emotions, speaking words aloud that she'd hardly let herself think in quite some time. "I watched Mother throw her body over mine when a troll smashed our house in, and when Laurel rolled her off of me less than a minute later, she had no head."

"Earth and sky, Rowen," Tamani reached for her hand and she let him take it, needing some sort of contact to ground her, but she kept talking, words falling out fast and breathless. "I've never told anyone I saw that. It didn't seem necessary. But I did. And then you told me to look like a troll and run to Rhoslyn's house. We huddled together there and waited for hours, only to learn that Father was dead, too. And that was only the beginning. Within five years, I lived in Spring, no one paid any attention to me, and I was one of dozens of faeries of all types vying for spots in the *corps*."

"But you made it," Tamani said, reaching up to squeeze her shoulder with a pride she knew was unfeigned. "You've worked hard—you haven't rested on the fact that you're a Summer faerie. I know how many hours you've put in; your grandmother tells me about it all the time."

"Please look past that," Rowen whispered. "Yes, I've worked hard. And yes, I *am* proud of that. But that's all I am now. There's nothing special about me. The revolution took it all away. I'm not selfish," Rowen said loudly, talking over Tamani when he tried to interrupt. "I understand that things are better for almost everyone. I know that and if I had the power to take the changes away, I wouldn't. Not even," she swallowed hard, "not even for my parents. But it didn't help *me*. I lost everything." She studied her hands. "You can argue that I didn't truly deserve what I had in the first place, but the fact is that when I was young I had something wonderful and now I don't."

Tamani leaned back in his chair, Rowen's hand slipping

from his fingers. "Okay," he said slowly. "I see that. And you're not wrong. But what do you think you're going to do here? Running away won't solve your problems."

"At least I could swap them for different ones."

A laugh sounded from the doorway and they both looked up to see Laurel coming through with a healing kit in her hands. "I can't imagine anyone leaving Avalon just for a change of scenery," she said, pulling a third chair close. "But I didn't grow up there. The grass really is greener on the other side, I suppose." She opened her kit and began laying out healing serum and binding strips—blessedly recognizable to Rowen as *not* human things. "But why now?"

"It didn't really occur to me until … until my friend Tya lost her place in the elite corps. I thought we were both doing okay, but we had our yearly auditions and she got cut."

"Are you're in danger of being cut?" Laurel asked as she gently palpated the back of Rowen's head. And even when those probing fingers found the cut and the wound stung, Rowen found the process relaxing. Laurel had always been that way—soothing, calming.

"Not especially. I'm in the middle of the garden," Rowen said, wishing those words didn't tear at her core. "But I work *so* hard to stay there. I have to. If I let up—even a little—I'll slip and it'll be me next."

"But you can't be in the *corps* at all, if you're here," Laurel observed.

The numbing solution was kicking in, relaxing Rowen further. "I know ballet has leaked out of Avalon. Right into your city! You told me that, Laurel. You told me how they have ballet schools and companies right in San Francisco." Her skin pricked as she said aloud the words she'd been preparing to say for over a year. "I want to go to a human dance school."

Laurel and Tamani froze.

"You're the one who said faeries are naturally graceful in comparison to humans," Rowen continued through their oppressive silence. "I can do better among humans. I'll have a natural advantage."

Something passed between Tamani and Lauren and Rowen got the feeling that she'd be forever frustrated by the silent conversations they were always having.

"I'm not sure you understand just how much is involved in passing yourself off as human," Tamani said haltingly while Laurel got back to binding Rowen's cut. "Let's look at the last quarter hour." He held up a hand, ticking off fingers. "You injured yourself when Chelsea started her car, lost control at the flick of a light switch, and illusioned yourself invisible at the sight of a completely harmless, somewhat elderly human."

He wasn't wrong. It took all of Rowen's theatrical training to keep a bored expression on her face. "So teach me. I mean, you did it. I can learn."

That won her a strangled laugh. "I trained for *months* at the Manor, Rowen. It's already summer—I'd guess schools start in *maybe* six weeks? Assuming you get in at all, and—"

Rowen's stems snapped straight. "Of course I'll get in. I'm an elite dancer in performance *corps* in Avalon. What ballet *school* in the human world could possibly compare?"

SIX

"I DON'T LIKE IT," LAUREL SAID SOFTLY AS Tamani closed and locked the door to their master suite. They'd gotten Rowen settled into a guest room and extracted a very serious promise that she wouldn't so much as *think* about leaving their house until they'd spoken after a good night's sleep.

"I didn't say yes," Tamani replied, pulling his shirt up and over his head for the sole reason that Laurel preferred him that way. Even when her parents were in residence—which was about half the year, as Laurel couldn't persuade them to fully retire from managing their shops in Crescent City—Tamani usually went shirtless, blaming his photosynthesizing needs for the state of dishabille that was apparently unusual to humans. And technically, he enjoyed it for that reason too; he was a member of the plant kingdom, after all. "But I don't know what else I can say."

"How about *no*?" Laurel said acerbically, one hand resting on their intricately carved bedpost and the other fisted on her hip.

"And then what? She's a Summer faerie who lives with the woman we unlock Avalon's gate for once a week. I'm shocked she hasn't caught on already. How many more queenless unlockings do you think it would take? Honestly, I don't know which would be worse—if the sentries caught her and Yasmine was forced to impose some kind of punishment to maintain credibility, or if they didn't and Rowen ran off alone to do this thing she clearly thinks is simple enough for a sprout to undertake."

"You think Yasmine would punish her?"

"She might not have much choice. Marion's been pretty quiet lately—it would be nice if I could believe she's settled down—but if she got word of fae slipping out unsupervised, I'm sure she'd put pressure on Yasmine. And I don't know the sentries on the Avalon side anymore, any one of them could be feeding information back to Marion."

Laurel shook her head and Tamani could only mirror the sentiment. The idea that anyone might still be loyal to Marion after all they'd been through was not one she understood. Maybe some things were impossible to understand for those who grew up outside Avalon.

"She wouldn't make it ten miles," Laurel said. "You saw

how she reacted to my dad."

"How many fae secrets do you think she'd expose along the way?"

That won Tamani a skeptical look, but he could tell he'd gotten to her. Rowen was leagues past confident—she was arrogant and assured and she thought so little of humans that she'd be utterly unprepared for the first one she faced.

Tamani wadded up his shirt and threw it into the hamper in their closet before leaning down to pull a long knife from his boot and slide it into the sheath hanging from the headboard. It had been years since the last time he skinned anything more threatening than a pear, but as a sentry he knew that the best time to prepare for the worst was before you knew the worst was coming. "Even if she doesn't figure out we're opening the gate for my mother, at this point what are the chances she'll just go back to her dance school and behave?" He didn't turn to face Laurel, but stood with hands on his hips, staring into the darkened room where it seemed at least half his thoughts dwelt these days. "I wouldn't put it past her to stop training, get herself cut from the *corps*, and then come to us and say, 'Look, now my life here really is destroyed.'"

"She'd have no one but herself to blame," Laurel said without conviction.

"Don't you think she's been punished enough?" he

whispered. He blinked back tears as Laurel pressed herself to his back and twined her arms around his chest. Crying—well, almost crying—something else he hadn't done in years. Not until today, when every emotion that ever once felled him had come back for a second go. "Goddess above, she saw Dahlia beheaded."

"It wasn't your fault," Laurel murmured, her cheek pressed against his shoulder.

"Five minutes," he rasped. "If I hadn't had that stupid argument with you about whether or not you should come with me to the Academy—it could have made all the difference."

"Or it could have gotten you killed by the same troll," Laurel replied, always too sensible for her own good. "Remember how helpless we were in Summer? A few minutes' difference and maybe we *all* would've been dead."

He turned to wrap his arms around her and bury his face in her hair. Every moment he had with her, more than a decade later, was immeasurably precious. As though no amount of time could ever make up for those awful years when he was certain she was lost to him forever.

"I know you feel guilty about your sister," Laurel said, her murmured words a buzz against his skin. "And I know I've told you a thousand times that it wasn't your fault, but I'll tell you again. And again tomorrow, and the next day: *it wasn't your fault.*" She looked up into his eyes. "One of these times, maybe you'll believe it."

Tamani sighed, a deep and lasting sound pulled from his very core.

"Have you texted your mother?"

Tamani groaned and ran his hands through his shoulder-length hair—always green at the roots, these days. Once upon a time he'd grown it single-colored to blend in with the humans, but these days no one who gave him a second look was noticing his hair.

"We should at least let her know Rowen's here. She must be worried sick."

"Rowen's seventeen. Mother won't miss her until morning." He dug into his pocket for his phone. "But you're right—we can head off that concern."

"I'll do it," Laurel said. "I know you hate texting." She took the phone from him and retreated a few steps, thumbs already flying. Tamani hadn't been convinced a phone would even work in Avalon, but when Rhoslyn found out they were going to plant a sprout, she'd insisted on either moving in, or coming to their home weekly to Garden for them. Tamani and Laurel would both have enjoyed hosting Rhoslyn, but Tamani had argued that Rowen would feel abandoned.

He took no pleasure in realizing just how right he'd been. Would even be possible to keep Rhoslyn away, now? How many fae was he going to have to smuggle out of Avalon before this was over?

The solar-charged satellite phone they'd managed to get working in Avalon rarely took calls, but texts generally made it through. Rhoslyn's visits weren't a secret, exactly, but Tamani's key was, and keeping it that way was as much Yasmine's problem as it was his. Even now, Tamani didn't want Rowen to know about it, but he wasn't entirely sure how he was going to keep it from her if she was going to be hanging around on this side of the gate.

While Laurel texted, Tamani stepped through the doorway to the conservatory they'd added on a year ago to nurture their sprout. Its stalk was tall, thick, and healthy, nothing at all like the spindly batch of sprouts Shar had found in Klea's laboratory. Tamani still cringed at the thought of growing scores of seedlings so carelessly, their change of survival minimal.

Of course, Klea had never been after healthy faeries.

"Your mom's probably asleep," Laurel said as she joined him, distracting him from his morbid reflections. "But she should see the message as soon as she wakes up."

"Thank you," Tamani whispered. He always spoke softly in this room—it was hallowed ground, as sacred as the World Tree, as energized as the Winter Palace. With the Academy's Gardener for his mother, Tamani had been raised around sprouts, played and laughed among their planter-boxes. But this sprout—*his* sprout—was something else entirely.

He stared at the bud that held his growing child and a stab of longing jolted him so hard he lifted one hand to rub at his abdomen. "Rowen was only five when she lost them."

Laurel answered only by lacing her fingers through his.

"She has no idea what it's really like out there. She can't even comprehend the number of humans who live in San Francisco, never mind the whole planet. It's too much."

Laurel stood quietly beside him for a long time.

"Is it possible we owe this to her? Not us personally," he added when Laurel made a noise of protestation. "The natural world. A chance to reclaim some of what was taken from her."

"Maybe," she said, but he heard the skepticism in her tone. "But often what we're owed and what's best for us are very different things."

Tamani smiled. "Yeardley's rubbing off on you."

Laurel smiled, too.

"What if we let her stay?" he asked into the dimness.

Silence. Then, "She's really racist, Tam. Or specist, I guess. She thinks humans are naturally beneath her. *All* humans. I'm not sure how that ends well."

"Nearly everyone in Avalon thinks that way. Not so very long ago, I thought the same thing."

"That's true."

Tamani admired that there wasn't a smidge of condemnation in her tone. It was simply a fact—he'd once been like Rowen, and he'd learned and changed.

"But allowing her to think herself superior and then rewarding her with a chance to prove it seems … backward."

Her fingers squeezed his tightly, and he suspected she had no idea. "Maybe being among them would help her see them as equals. That's what it took for me. And Avalon can always use more faeries who appreciate humans."

"So send her to the Manor."

"You know they only train spies and sentries over there. And she wouldn't have a goal, like I did. I think … I think maybe she just wants to dance somewhere that isn't a constant reminder of everything she's lost."

Laurel was quiet again—processing. "Is she good enough to compete here? San Francisco is hardcore."

"Beats the hell out of me. I don't speak ballet."

"Don't curse in front of the sprout," she said, jabbing him with an elbow.

"It can't hear."

"Can't it? Then how does it bloom already talking?"

Tamani opened his mouth to retort, then realized he couldn't refute her logic. "Sorry," he said instead. He considered the training and preparation it would take to get Rowen through an audition in San Francisco. And that was without even considering her dancing, which he knew almost nothing about.

Laurel curled a hand around his arm and snuggled closer to his side. "If it's what she really wants, maybe you're right that she'll find some way to do it anyway. At least with your supervision it would be on our terms. Surely she couldn't do *too* much harm, with a warden keeping an eye on her."

Tamani shook his head and reached out to swirl a lock of her hair around his finger. *Warden* was the English word for Tamani's lifelong assignment to keep watch over Laurel, whose human identity protected the land surrounding the gate to Avalon. "Am I convincing you, or are you convincing me?"

Laurel raised one eyebrow in a semi-scold and made a sound that he couldn't even begin to interpret.

But he could laugh.

"You know," Laurel said, when they turned and Tamani began prodding her toward their bed. "Now that I think about it, a Summer faerie would have an easier time passing as human than any other kind."

"Mmm, totally," Tamani said, his mouth brushing the soft skin at her neck.

"No, seriously. Anything weird about her appearance, she could just cover up with an illusion."

Her voice was breathy, but not enough for Tamani. She shrieked when he lifted her to sit on their tall bed but kept saying something about illusions, so he pulled her strap off her shoulder and began kissing his way down her arm.

"Mmm," Laurel said, as his hands found the bottom of her tank top. "I mean, think about the food. She could eat her favorites and just make them look like burgers and fries."

She gasped when Tamani leapt up beside her and straddled her thighs, lifting her face to his.

"Tam! Are you listening?"

"Every word," he growled, his hand traveling to the bottom of her skirt.

"You're not," she said, laughing.

"Then you'll have to tell me again tomorrow," he said before cutting off whatever she was going to say with his mouth over hers. He held her body tight against him, kissing her with the same fervor he felt every time he held her. Like she was sunlight and air, and he simply couldn't survive without her.

She kissed him back eagerly for long minutes before he pulled away to divest them both of a few more articles of clothing. "We *are* going to talk about this tomorrow," she insisted with a grin as he tossed her sandal to the floor and ran a finger up the ticklish underside of her foot.

"Absolutely," he replied soberly. "And whatever we decided to do, we'll do it together."

"Like everything else," she whispered.

"I love you."

"I love you more."

"Impossible."

"Forever."

SEVEN

"WHERE ARE YOU FROM?"

"Scotland."

"Where exactly?"

Rowen lowered her eyelashes and gave a casual shrug. "A very small town. Near Perth."

"Good." Tamani tugged at the stick by his knee, which he claimed was used to control the *car*—Rowen knew what to call it now. "People might press you for more details. They like the idea of people from places they've never been. But keep to what we've practiced. And I'll fill out your paperwork for you so everything matches."

Tamani told her there were so many humans in the world that they kept track of each other with something called *paperwork*, and that he'd had special ones created for her at the Manor that would prevent the adults at the dance studio from asking too many questions. Or something. He told her this would make everything easier, but Rowen was rather appalled at the idea of so many humans they had to label them with papers. He assured her that the human part of the world was much, much bigger than Avalon, but really—how big could a world be?

Yesterday he'd handed her a small plastic square called an "eye dee" and said she needed to keep it with her at all times. It bore a horrifyingly yellowed, slightly fuzzy likeness of her face, but when Rowen complained Laurel had said that everyone's identification pictures were bad and that Rowen was already talking like a human. The way she said it, you'd think it was a *good* thing.

The talking *screen* on the *dash*—Rowen knew those words, too—blurted out that they'd reached their destination and Tamani said, "Now I just have to find parking." Then he gave an audible grumble Rowen didn't understand—didn't really care to understand. She'd already spent the last two weeks learning a million or so words that Tamani assured her humans used regularly. While not entirely a new language, it was close.

The crash course from her uncle was nowhere near as painful, however, as suffering through the barrage of questions Laurel's adoptive father insisted on asking at every meal. He apparently thought the fact that his daughter turned out to be a faerie was the best thing that had ever happened in the history of ever, and now he wanted to know all about growing up in

Avalon, since Laurel had missed out on that experience. Laurel kept the man busy most of the day, but dinner was family time. If Rowen showed any sign of not playing nice, she got exceptionally grumpy looks from her host and hostess. Rowen didn't know Laurel well, but she knew enough about Mixers to prefer to keep them happy.

Rowen would have preferred to keep her grandmother happy, too, but that was hoping too much. When Rhoslyn showed up at Tamani's house, Rowen had been a little afraid she was going to be dragged back to Avalon after all. But apparently Rhoslyn made regular visits and had neglected to ever mention it—ever. Rowen still wasn't entirely sure how to feel about that, except that it wasn't a nice feeling.

But after much "discussion" with Tamani behind a closed door, Rhoslyn had left, and Rowen had stayed, and now she was on her way to the Scazio Ballet Academy—one of San Francisco's finest ballet schools, apparently. And the only one still auditioning students, so late in the summer. The Academy guaranteed an audition for the San Francisco Ballet Company to all its senior students and that apparently was a very big deal. Or so Laurel claimed.

"Why can't I just audition for the company?" Rowen had argued. And Tamani had let out a short laugh, cut off rather precipitously by Laurel smacking his shoulder.

"You won't look old enough to dance in the company

until you're at least twenty-five," he finally explained, after regaining his composure. "You barely look old enough to dance for the school."

"I'm seventeen!" Rowen argued. "Laurel just said all these kids are thirteen to eighteen."

"Humans are born small but age quickly, at least by our standards. Most humans would probably guess that you're thirteen or fourteen. Human ballerinas who reach this level are generally shorter and thinner than others their age, though, so that helps you here."

"Do I have to dance with the younger girls then?" Rowen asked dismally.

"I suspect you're too good a dancer to pass for fourteen," Laurel said, and even if Rowen thought the words were a little grudging, it was nice to receive the compliment. "The senior ballet class is as close to a happy medium as we're going to come, I think. We'll say you're barely seventeen, a year ahead in school because you're from out of the country. I don't think they'll question that." She looked up at Rowen from under her eyelids then and asked, "Unless you'd like to spend another two years preparing in Avalon before you try this?"

That had been the end of that conversation.

While Tamani drove very slowly around a darkened cement grove filled with other cars and continued muttering under his breath, Rowen let herself admit that Laurel and

Tamani had gone to a lot of trouble to get her this far. She hadn't appreciated their questions about what she would do if she *didn't* get accepted into the school—she'd come this far and had no intention of failing now—but otherwise they'd been very supportive, and she was getting the idea that if she'd had to do this without them, it would have been much more difficult.

Not that she would've let that stop her, but help was nice.

Tamani finally found a place to stop his car and the two of them headed toward a large stone square. They emerged from the shadow of a dark overhang and Rowen marveled at the sight—it was like fifty Academies all squished together and stacked on top of one another. There was no horizon in view and she could hardly even see the sky without looking straight up.

And there were humans *everywhere*! It was as packed as any festival, except that no one was dancing and even the people with food were walking as they ate. None so much as glanced at the faeries as they passed by, talking to each other, near-shouting into cell phones. The humans were as oblivious as they were numerous.

A few did steal glances at Tamani, but it was always with furtive appreciation rather than the awe they should rightly experience. They were in the presence of a being who could, after all, magically command their total obedience, should he so choose. Rowen had never given much thought to the small magic her own parents once held—magic that Spring faeries ordinarily only used on the livestock kept in Avalon to fertilize crops, or managing the bee population. Here, now, that seemed like an oversight, somehow.

"This way," Tamani said, and Rowen's thoughts returned to the task at hand. They'd arrived at a rather austere building that—thankfully—wasn't as tall as many of the ones surrounding it. Rowen held her rucksack close and tried not to touch any of the humans thronging the hallway.

To Rowen's surprise, the humans inside the building looked very much like dancers. This should *not* have surprised her, perhaps, but she'd just walked past hundreds of humans and most of them had looked more like cattle in clothing than the creatures of ability and intelligence Laurel was always talking about.

Here, though, Rowen recognized the posture and poise that comes with years of dance training. It was in the way they walked, the way some were stretching against plain white walls, even the way they stood as they visited about … whatever it was animals visited about. One girl sat on the floor rubbing her feet, an unlaced pair of toe shoes resting nearby; a male and female were leaning on opposite sides of a freestanding *barre*, clearly flirting; a guy was spinning slowly in front of the mirror, working on tiny adjustments to his form. A smile tugged at the corners of Rowen's mouth as, for the first time in two weeks, she found herself feeling quite at home.

"Rowen, this way."

She hurried after Tamani's voice—just a few feet down the hall, but far enough to make her feel abruptly uneasy. Even dancing humans were still humans, and Tamani was more than just the expert on humans. He had power over them. That was a kind of safety she'd never before understood sufficiently to appreciate. He placed a hand on her shoulder and drew her close enough to whisper, "This one is your studio," as he pointed to a door with a sign attached to it that said SENIOR AUDITIONS. "But first, take a look around, and then go into that room and change." He pointed again, this time to a door labeled LES DAMES.

Rowen nodded and went back over to the window to study the dancers. Laurel had warned her about this—that what the other girls wore to dance in probably wouldn't match her. The pictures Laurel had put on her screen at home, with the help of some human magic called the *Internet,* had shown dancers in black suits and pink coverings on their legs. These Laurel had called *tights*, but Rowen could hardly believe that ballerinas would dance in stockings. But in fact several of the dancers in the studio were still wearing pants—jackets, even, though the temperature inside didn't seem low enough to justify extra covering. And the rest were, indeed, wearing something pink over their legs. How bizarre. Regardless, the outfit Rowen was wearing beneath her peasant top and shorts certainly wasn't going to blend in with what these other girls were wearing.

Wanting to be sure her illusion was convincing, Rowen turned to the milling crowd at her back and peered at the dancers still in the hall, hoping to get a closer look at these *tights*. Faking the need to check the buckles on her sandals, Rowen crouched, eying the legs of the girls who happened by. The tights weren't fashioned of a thick material, like true stockings—it was gossamer, similar to the sleeves of costumes they sometimes made in Avalon to tint their arms while still allowing the sun's energizing light to reach their skin. She could make the illusion today, but she suspected she could have something passable made for her in Avalon that would also do the job. Just in case anyone had any reason to touch her legs. Rowen suppressed a shudder at the thought.

She rose and gave Tamani a nod before pushing into the restroom to make her transformation. In an empty metal cage surrounding a toilet—which was convenient, but also odd—Rowen stripped off her outer clothes and looked longingly down at the two-piece, pastel green dancing outfit with a light skirt on the bottom and fun criss-crossed straps on the top. At least she could duplicate the straps. But black? How boring.

Still, when she emerged from the restroom with her newly

pinked shoes dangling from her hand by their ribbons, she was certain she looked just like everyone else. Tamani gave her a confirming wink, then pulled her close and whispered, "Good luck. I'll be right out here."

Rowen mumbled her gratitude and held her chin high, but she had a taste of true fear when she entered a room completely full of human girls and closed away the only other faerie in the building.

Eyes darted toward her as she sat to lace on her shoes, but Rowen was pretty sure everyone was looking at everyone else. There was an edge of fierce competition in the air, one Rowen was all too familiar with from her own auditions in Avalon. Though surely none of them could be half so concerned as Rowen had been at her last audition. Tamani had told her how many career paths humans could choose in their lives; if they didn't make it here, presumably they could just do something else. In Avalon, being cut was basically the end of your life as a productive Sparkler on the dancing track. The humans had it so easy.

Still, the atmosphere was surprisingly tense.

An older woman—surely over a hundred—walked in and clapped her hands. She was trailed by two more old women holding portable writing desks and pencils—quills were no longer used in human society, according to Laurel. The buzz in the studio snapped to silence as everyone gave the newcomers their full attention.

"Welcome to senior auditions," the woman said, with a hint of an accent that was different from any Rowen had encountered thus far. "Thank you for your interest in Scazio. The Academy has already had it's in-school auditions and this year we have room for only two ballerinas—one an open position and our one scholarship position."

There were some snickers around the room and Rowen followed the gaze of others to a tall young human with dark skin and black hair, standing to one side of the room with her chin raised high. She didn't return the gazes of the other girls; she only had eyes for the woman who was speaking. There didn't seem to be anything unusual about the girl, except maybe that she exuded grace to rival the very best of the dancers in Avalon's elite *corps*—a grace that showed without motion. Maybe they were all looking at her because she was the best? That made sense to Rowen. Maybe this dancer was her fiercest competition.

Still, there were at least fifty girls in this room, and the woman had said there were only two spots. Though Rowen didn't know what a *scholarship* was, so it might actually be only one spot. Maybe this wouldn't be quite as easy as she'd thought.

The girls were all directed to take their places at the *barre*, and the three women walked up and down the rows, leading them through stretching and limbering exercises—thankfully, not unusual to Rowen. The ladies gave no opinions nor critiques, only soft commands, and they all made copious notes before bringing everyone away from the *barres* to watch as they executed combinations diagonally across the floor.

The terminology was mostly familiar, and when Rowen was uncertain, she simply made sure she wasn't first in line. This wasn't the least bit problematic, as many of the dancers pressed as close to the front as possible. An amateur mistake proven when, after the first hour, about half of the dancers were invited to leave—mostly, those who always shoved to the front. Rowen smiled inwardly. An experienced dancer takes time to observe before rushing forward.

After another hour, a further fifteen girls were asked to depart, leaving only a handful, including the dancer everyone had laughed at earlier.

No one was laughing now.

Even Rowen was impressed. In fact, she grudgingly had to admit that this human girl might even have had a shot at the faerie *corps*. Not that she could ever be the best dancer in Avalon, of course—but probably she wouldn't be kicked out of the garden.

Soon only six dancers remained and Rowen was starting to get tired. The vast majority of humans were lumbering apes, no question, but perhaps these six had some latent faerie genes in them, somehow. For while Rowen thought she had an edge on them, they were undeniably skilled, and she was coming to realize that the benefit of being a perfectly symmetrical faerie was not only not very extreme, it might be the only thing keeping her at the top of the pack.

The three women kept the final six dancers for almost two more hours, until all of them were showing signs of physical fatigue. Then, rather abruptly, they said "we'll be in touch" and left the room.

"In touch?" Rowen grumbled. "What in the blue sky is that supposed to mean?" Why couldn't they just give her an answer? Still, at the very least, she'd made it to that final group, and she truly did think she was better than the others.

Except maybe that *one.*

The girl in question was passing by at that moment and, in a fit of bravery, Rowen reach out a hand and touched her shoulder. The girl turned and glared and Rowen was taken aback by the hostility in those dark brown, so very human-colored, eyes.

"What?" the girl said when Rowen didn't immediately speak.

"You—you're really good," Rowen said rather dazedly.

The girl only arched one eyebrow. "You sound surprised," she said. "Your kind always is."

My kind? Rowen thought in alarm. Had she been found out already?

But the girl just turned and walked away.

EIGHT

THE SKY WAS A MURKY EVENING ORANGE, BUT there was enough light to see the pale blue house—one in a long row of similar buildings, each a different color. Why were human houses always so *tall?* Rowen approved of the colors and pretty eaves each house sported, and many boasted sprawling vines and flowering window-boxes, but there weren't nearly enough windows. Human houses never had enough windows.

Still, Chelsea's home suited Rowen's personal preferences more than many of the dwellings she'd seen so far in the city. Chelsea herself answered the door with a cheerful exclamation and a hug for Tamani. She stepped forward as though to embrace Rowen as well, but Rowen took a step back without conscious intent and then felt bad when Chelsea's expression revealed hurt feelings. Before Rowen could cobble together some sort of apology—any words at all, really—Tamani was covering her gaffe by shuffling them all inside.

A large man stood from a chair at their arrival, and though Rowen had to swallow down a pang of fear at the sight of his furry, bear-like face, she managed to smile when Chelsea introduced him as her husband, Jason.

"Today was the big day?" Chelsea asked, directing the question to Rowen. But she sounded … hesitant. Probably because of the awkward moment on the porch.

Rowen nodded silently, feeling both exhausted and grumpy, while Tamani shook Jason's hand and smacked his shoulder. "We were at Scazio all day," he said in explanation.

Jason made a whistling noise between his teeth; Rowen was immediately jealous of the ability. "Scazio, eh? Good luck to you."

Rowen averted her eyes.

"Jason's sister used to dance," Chelsea said, pointing them through a doorway. "So he knows more about it than I do."

"She made it to the top six today," Tamani said, and Rowen couldn't help but smile at the pride in his voice. "They said they'll be in touch."

"Did they say when?" Chelsea asked.

"No, but classes start in two weeks, so it'll have to be soon, I imagine," Tamani said.

"Well, I'm so glad you two are spending the night," Chelsea beckoned them toward a couch. "We've hardly seen you since Laurel took leave this spring."

"All the better to fake a pregnancy, I'm afraid."

"She hasn't stooped to wearing a fake belly, has she?" Chelsea asked.

Tamani laughed as Rowen sank into the couch, utterly baffled but grateful to sit down. After sitting in the car for half an hour her legs somehow felt *more* tired rather than less. What kind of people made windowless dance studios, anyway? Rowen needed the sun.

"No, sprouts come in the season when they're ready, so there's no way to time something like that." Tamani leaned forward, grinning. "Imagine looking eight-months pregnant for six months."

But Chelsea snapped sober. "That would be a problem," she said very seriously. "What are you doing instead?"

"Only you would consider this a real problem." Tamani sat back and waved a hand in the air. "She's just staying close to home. Avoiding company, which is usually her preference anyway. Nothing to hide from her parents, nothing to hide from her best friend. And she's on the land—it was always easier to conceal things there anyway."

As they prattled on about things of no meaning or importance to Rowen, she pulled her knees up to her chest and studied the person Chelsea had introduced as Jason. It was so odd to see hair growing right out of his face. And he didn't seem embarrassed in the least.

Or maybe … as she watched him he started darting his eyes toward her in apparent question. Maybe he *was* embarrassed, a little. He certainly squirmed under her gaze.

She tilted her head. The hair on his chin went up along the side of his ears and connected to his hair. Maybe he considered it an extension of the hair on his head? She had seen a few other pelt-faced humans in the city, from a distance, but she couldn't figure out *why* some of them looked more like lions and gorillas and bears than others. There had been hairy trolls in Avalon, but asymmetry—like hair growing in odd places—was characteristic of their species. Did some humans also have fur on their backs, perhaps? Or their bellies? It was a disconcerting thing to imagine. Was that why humans insisted on wearing so many clothes all the time? To conceal how embarrassingly *mammalian* some of them were?

"Did you have a question for me, Rowen?"

Rowen straightened in surprise at the sound of her name. Jason was talking to her. "What? No."

Jason paused and for a moment Rowen thought he was going to return to the conversation with the other two. Instead he said, "You're staring at me."

"Staring?" She laughed. "Hardly. I was just watching you."

He locked eyes with Chelsea, who raised one eyebrow. "Is that not the same thing?"

The entire group was quiet for a long moment before Rowen heard something from upstairs and everyone's head turned toward the ceiling. Chelsea broke into a grin and said, "That'll be Zander. I'll get him."

Jason glanced at Rowen one more time, but as he apparently didn't like being observed Rowen watched Chelsea go, if only to pretend she wasn't intrigued. It really was amazing how much humans resembled faeries *and* trolls. It was impossible to breed a troll and a faerie, but if you could, the result would surely be something like humankind.

Chelsea came down the stairs a few minutes later, holding something wrapped in cloth. It was making snuffling noises. "Would you hold him while I make a bottle?" Chelsea asked, proffering the bundle to her husband.

A look of adoration spread over Jason's face and he took what Rowen could now see was a small human. He spoke to it in a high, affected voice, accompanied by some facial acrobatics worthy of the Summer stage.

"Let me see," Tamani said, holding out both arms. "It's been, what, three months?"

"You keep better track than I do," Jason said with a smile, handing the bundle over the low table between their seats. Tamani also made a number of shocking faces at the little human. The small one's hands flailed in tight fists and Rowen immediately understood. The poor thing was damaged. She wondered why no one had warned her.

Tamani rested the thing on his knee and turned it to face its father, making it painfully apparent that Rowen was right. The thing didn't look like it could even stand, much less walk. Its face was full of lumps and bulges and a clear liquid was dripping from its protruded lower lip.

Disgusting.

Tamani seemed determined to make the best of it and he rubbed its head and said, "He's got twice the hair he had last time I was here."

Was that an accomplishment? Perhaps for something so … *inadequate.*

"He sits on his own now," Jason said, beaming. No truly, beaming. "He'll be crawling in another month or so."

Sitting? Crawling? The poor thing really *was* in bad shape! To have one that couldn't walk at all must have come as a terrible blow to its parents.

Tamani apparently noticed her intent gaze because he grinned and said, "Would you like to hold him?"

Was this a test or…or…a joke? Rowen wasn't sure what her trickster uncle was up to. "Um—"

"Don't worry, it's easy." Tamani placed the lukewarm lump of blankets on her lap and wrapped her hands around its sides. "There, just like that. Bounce him a little if he cries."

Rowen stared in horror at the thing sitting on her thigh. It looked so nearly fae… and so very not. His rose-tinged cheeks were huge and he'd jammed a clenched fist into his mouth as though he thought his own body was a food source. His wide eyes were a deep, dark brown, like a cow's eyes, and when those eyes met hers, he grinned and revealed a mouth with only two teeth.

Where were it's teeth?

But Tamani went on spewing praises, and Jason continued beaming like he'd just put on the performance of his life. Perhaps this was a form of human politeness Tamani had failed to mention?

Well, she might as well try, for Tamani's sake if nothing else. "Are you well enough to speak?" she asked the poor thing softly, and when he didn't answer, she tried again in Gaelic.

He let out a sound at that that might have been a strangled laugh, and Rowen almost had time to wonder if he'd understood the language of the fae before a stream of white liquid burst from his mouth, splashing hotly over Rowen's bare arms.

"Gross!" Rowen yelled, shoving the thing away from her in disgust. The room exploded into activity as Tamani's arms shot out, almost too fast to see, and caught the human before it hit the floor. Rowen was trembling with fright, desperately wiping her arms against the upholstered seating. Lenore had once told her that some humans could spit acid, but Rowen had assumed it was a myth!

Somehow Tamani must have transferred the thing to Jason because now his hands were hard on Rowen's shoulders, holding her still, his face etched with a fury so intense it made her core shake with fear.

"I can't believe you just did that," he whispered harshly, and Rowen stared up at him in confusion until she caught sight of Chelsea, just over his shoulder. Chelsea was standing in the doorway, something in her hand, her face so white it could have been ash bark, tears streaming down her face.

The next few minutes were a blur; Rowen stood silently in the entryway as Tamani hugged Chelsea, whispered something to her and Jason, then practically shoved Rowen out the door and into the car.

"Tamani, it—he—"

"Don't," he said, his hand slicing sharply through the air. "I can't—I'm so angry I can't even talk to you."

Rowen wanted to argue, but she had never seen her uncle like this—and she had seen him in some terrible, terrible times. They stopped to feed the car only once the building had thinned out a little. Without a word, Rowen found her way to one of the human's odd tiled lavatories and used a huge handful of coarse linen—seriously, it was practically *paper*—trying to wash away the sour smell that lingered from whatever had come out of the little human. Not acid, apparently, but

Tamani didn't seem in a mood to explain. The water did little to purge the smell but Rowen didn't dare try the harsh chemicals that passed for human cleansing serums. Laurel had warned her about those.

Rowen thought Tamani might be ready to talk about what had happened once they got back on the road, but two hours passed without a word. The sun was fully down and it was so dark that Rowen could barely make out the surroundings flashing past her window until Tamani bumped the car slowly off the road and onto a ragged dirt path that didn't seem to lead anywhere.

"Follow me," he said softly.

He lead her along a darkened but well-worn path, into a forest of giant redwoods. Rowen trudged after, trusting but confused, exhausted by the emotions and events of the day.

When Tamani abruptly stopped in a small clearing, Rowen almost bumped into him.

"Do you have any idea what you did?" Tamani asked, his back still to her, hands on hips. His voice was a whisper so quiet she wouldn't have been able to hear it if they'd been any closer to the road where other cars occasionally flew by, roaring their mad roars..

"What *I* did?" Rowen said, aghast. "I was afraid I was going to lose an arm! *You're* the one who handed me the poison-spitting thing without a single word of instruction.

Without—"

"Thing." Tamani laughed, low and quiet, and Rowen felt a chill creep into her core at the sound. "What do you think that *thing* is, Rowen?"

"It's clearly a bad sprout," she said, needing to defend herself. Tamani was a faerie! He'd understand if she could only find the right words. "Or whatever humans call it. It's a little human that's obviously damaged and I feel a great deal of sympathy for it. I do."

"It's a *baby*," Tamani said, his voice still that scary quiet that made her insides quiver. "*He* is not damaged at all. And *he* is as precious to Jason and Chelsea as any sprout could be to any faerie couple."

Rowen felt like snorting at such a dubious claim, but the anger still simmering in her uncle's tone held her back. Some. "It's clearly under-developed. It couldn't walk, or talk, it didn't even have *teeth*."

"That's how human babies are. They don't come into this world as developed as faeries. They need more help." He turned to her and Rowen was glad she couldn't see his face clearly in the dark. The waves of fury coming her way were almost palpable. "That infant is one of the very best parts of Chelsea and Jason's life and you *threw him on the ground*."

Rowen was struck utterly still by the violence in Tamani's voice. "You caught him," she whispered.

"Thank the goddess. You could have killed him, Rowen."

They were quiet for a long time.

"I should have treated it with more care," Rowen mumbled.

"*Him*. His name is Zander and you should have treated *him* with more care."

"Him, then!" Rowen shouted. "But it all turned out fine. I'm sorry I acted without thought. I was *scared,* okay? Why are you so angry?"

Tamani stood with his arms crossed over his chest, studying her until she had to look away, feeling guilty for reasons she didn't understand. "You feel faeries are superior to humans, yes?"

"Everyone knows that."

"Why?"

"What?"

"Why?" Tamani repeated, his voice piercing.

"Because we're faeries."

His hand cut through the air. "Not good enough. Why?"

"We're plants."

"And plants are just better than animals? Your potted plant at home is better than the bees that make your honey?"

She considered that for a second. She loved honey; she'd trade her honey for her potted plant any day. "Perhaps not that precisely, but we're special."

"What makes us special?"

"We have magic."

"You've seen the technology, the human magic, in my home," Tamani replied. "And that's only the stalk above the soil. Humans can send messages across the world in seconds, create chemical solutions that would make a Mixer weep, and launch a team up into space to walk on the goddess-blessed *moon*, Rowen." He lifted his chin and looked down at her. "You can change how your clothing looks. Tell me whose *magic* is better."

"I—" No one had ever insulted her magic. It couldn't have stung more if he'd thrust one of his knives into her core. "There are so many of them."

"Oh, so numbers are important," he said. "That means that you're better than me, because you're a Sparkler and I'm a Ticer."

"What? No!"

"And as a Mixer Laurel's better than both of us. Is that what you're telling me?"

"Of course not. You know I don't think that." The hot burn of shame swelled in her chest that her uncle would think she was so elitist.

"Then what, Rowen?" Tamani shouted, his arms spread wide, his voice echoing off the enormous trees. "What the hell makes you so special that you can look down your nose at seven billion people who have complex lives and feelings and emotions *just the same as you*?"

"I—"

"You couldn't even hack losing your special Summer faerie status in Avalon, how do you think you could survive in a world where you're literally one in a *billion*?"

The tears were on her cheeks before she could choke out another word. She was so furious, so hurt, she couldn't even speak. She would have been less surprised if he'd slapped her face instead.

"You asked this world for help. Not me," Tamani hissed. "Not Laurel. Not really. You asked this *human world* to help you find yourself, rediscover your self-confidence, whatever it is you couldn't do in Avalon, and you have the audacity to treat them like they're the dirt beneath your feet?"

Rowen opened her mouth to retort, but couldn't find any words to speak. So she closed it again. Long minutes passed with nothing but the sound of their breathing.

"Come on," Tamani finally said, putting a soft hand on her shoulder and turning her back toward the car. "I'm not going to lecture any more tonight—we've got a few more hours left to drive and you should sleep. Just understand this," he said, looking down at her, his face so close she could see every detail, the depths of the sorrow in his eyes. The pity. And she didn't think it was pity for his human friends. "If you can't let go of this, this *arrogance* you have toward humans—I can't let you stay. I won't do that to *them*."

NINE

AFTER THAT AWFUL SCENE WITH TAMANI, THE call from Scazio had been anti-climactic. Their acceptance didn't much matter if Tam sent her home.

So she promised herself to be as accommodating as possible when Laurel handed her a glassy black slate that projected light from one side—like a slab of obsidian imbued with rudimentary Sparkler abilities. By touching the proper runes, a spell called *Netflix* could be invoked, which enabled the device to depict a variety of stories, several of which Laurel insisted Rowen watch from beginning to end.

These proved *fascinating*—much like the theatrical plays Rowen had been putting on in Avalon since she was young. Except the view stayed so close to everyone's faces, even though the size of some of their sets put even Avalon's biggest stage to shame. Close, then unimaginably far. Laurel told her there were "shows" about faeries too, but that humans got it so backward that it was entertaining for all the wrong reasons.

The point was for Rowen to learn to respect humans.

Rowen was wary of Laurel's plan at first, but the stories in these "movies" proved astonishingly engrossing. The humans portrayed odd mannerisms, did and said things Rowen could hardly understand, but most of the time their actions and feelings resonated within her on such a deep level that she was shocked and a little disgusted with herself.

Though she tried to squelch that particular emotion.

She spent hours each day watching human stories on the enchanted tablet. At dinner, instead of being peppered with questions by Laurel's father, she had questions of her own—questions, which Tamani insisted Rowen addressed to Laurel's parents.

This proved embarrassing—like discovering her undergarments had been peeking out during an entire performance. She knew that Laurel and Tamani must have talked to them about what happened at Chelsea's. Asking questions—favors, really, albeit small ones—of people who knew she considered them inferior, who she had to please if she was to be permitted to stay, was … harrowing.

It was a tremendous relief when Tamani finally told her to pack for San Francisco.

"You're almost late," he said, scanning the street as he pulled to the curb in front of Scazio Dance Academy. "My apologies. Six months away and I forget how crowded the streets get. Oh, don't forget this," he added, proffering a golden-yellow envelope, thick with papers. "Give it to the secretary. She'll call me if she needs anything else."

Rowen accepted the envelope, marveling once more that there should be so many humans as to justify their complex rituals of identification—in Avalon, a name was always enough. Occasionally the matriarchal surname if one was visiting a seldom-frequented neighborhood. But she reminded herself to think of it as a simple fact, not inferiority. It was no one's *fault*; it just *was*.

"Got it," she said, sliding from the car and swinging her rucksack onto one shoulder. Laurel had offered a more human-styled bag—something called a duffel—but Rowen wanted a memento from Avalon and Tamani had argued that it looked European enough to escape notice. Whatever that meant.

"Right here at five-thirty," Tamani said.

Rowen froze. "Class gets out at five."

"Guess you'll have to socialize for a while."

"Tam—"

But he was already driving away, grinning and pretending he couldn't hear her even though the convertible's top was down.

Rowen fought the urge to scream—or maybe just cast an

illusion to interfere with his vision so he had no choice but to stop. But though it would make her feel good, it would hardly be productive. She had a dance class to report to.

Something like stage fright made Rowen queasy right down to her core as she pulled open the heavy, metal-framed door to the dance school. It was a relief to see that the halls weren't nearly as crowded as the last time she'd been here. She supposed that made sense, considering how many dancers had shown up to audition for what ended up being a single slot. Other than the scholarship spot—whatever that meant. Of course there were fewer people here on a normal class day.

Rowen dropped off the envelope with the secretary, who made an incongruous comment about the studio's hours of operation. Rowen tried to think of an appropriate response, but after an awkward moment of silence the woman covered up what looked like a bug near her face and said, "Studio F, right down that hall. Hurry."

Apparently the woman hadn't been speaking to Rowen. But neither had she been holding one of the smaller screens—the *phones*—to her ear. What was the insect? Not five seconds past the doors and she was already accumulating questions for Tamani. *Technology* seemed mystifyingly diverse, as magic went.

Rowen edged into the well-marked studio scant minutes before class was scheduled to begin and nearly tripped over one of her classmates, who was sitting on the ground, lacing up.

The tall girl, from auditions.

"It's you," Rowen said in surprise, trying to remember the girl's name. Or had she even given it? The girl narrowed her eyes and Rowen knew she'd already botched the encounter. The silence seemed to demand *something*. An explanation, perhaps, for entering in such haste as to almost kick her? Rowen decided to try that. "I didn't expect you to be here."

"Why not?" she snapped back at full volume.

"I—" But when the girl rolled her eyes Rowen clamped her lips shut.

The girl looked down at the ribbons wrapped tightly around her ankles and grumbled, "Three years I've earned this position. I don't know why everyone thinks I'm going to fail now."

"Oh! I don't—" Rowen paused. She meant *here* as in on the floor just inside the classroom door. The girl had clearly thought Rowen meant at the school at all. No wonder she was angry. Rowen straightened and thought of an excellent compliment to smooth things over. "Are *you* the scholarship?" she asked with forced cheer.

It hadn't been easy for Laurel to explain scholarships to Rowen, who first had to learn what *money* was, and then learn why some humans didn't have enough. But class divides translated well enough. If this girl didn't have enough money to attend the school, then she had been auditioning not just for a competitive spot, but for *the* competitive spot—the one that she didn't have to pay to take. And had won.

But the girl huffed and jerked to her feet so quickly Rowen took a step back. "Meghan. I'm a person; I have a name. And the fact that Daddy doesn't write me a check doesn't make me any worse than you." She eyed Rowen from soft slippers to ribbon-bedecked bun. "It probably makes me better."

Near choking on indignation, Rowen opened her mouth to say—what? That she had no father? That she didn't know what a check was? That she was better than Meghan by the height of the moon and the span of the seas and the depth of the Goddess' love for the trees?

She never got to find out. The door opened behind her, sending her sprawling straight into Meghan. Meghan grunted and tried to push her away, but it was too late. The three women from auditions, along with two men Rowen hadn't seen before, stared at the two of them like they were ... well, the way Rowen generally stared at humans. A stab of shame pierced her chest when she experienced for herself how embarrassing it was.

"My fault," she blurted, not wanting Meghan to like her even less. "I shouldn't have stopped in front of the door."

"Certainly not," one of the women said, one eyebrow raised. The adults all turned their attention away from Rowen and Meghan and the leader clapped her hands for attention, but all Rowen heard was Meghan's sharp whisper of, "Thanks a lot."

Rowen ducked her head and moved a few feet away, then sank to the floor to hurry and lace on her shoes as the teachers, luckily, spent a few minutes welcoming the students to a new year at the Academy. Rowen still felt critical eyes on her as she tied her ribbons and shed her blouse and shorts just in time to be called to the *barres* in the center of the floor.

Falling into the rhythm of stretches and positions helped relax Rowen's thoughts and she gazed around from beneath her eyelids as she went through the motions by rote.

At least she looked like everyone else. After a long discussion with Rhoslyn about how they were all going to explain Rowen's absence, Rowen's grandmother went back to Avalon with a list of requests for the costuming department. As a result, Rowen now had a dozen midnight-black leotards, as well as those awful pink tights. A few skirts and short-sleeved jackets finished off her disguise—all made of fabrics that let sunlight through better than human garb, while keeping Rowen inconspicuous. The other students were still eyeing her—she'd caught a few embarrassed gazes—but at least she knew it wasn't because she was dressed wrong.

After pushing the *barres* to the side, across the floor came next, just like in auditions. This time no one crowded to the front of the line. There appeared to be a sort of unspoken order and Rowen was nudged to the very end.

Meghan, however, was at the head of the line.

No one was better than Meghan.

The others were good—very good. Far better than the dancers Rowen had auditioned against. But Meghan had that extra grace that set the great apart from the good. While the looks Rowen got were curious, sometimes shyly welcoming, and even—after a pass or two across the floor—impressed, Meghan got something else entirely. At first Rowen thought it was jealousy, which seemed foolhardy. It was the simplest of emotions to fall into, but a well-trained, disciplined dancer knew to treat someone better than them as an opportunity to learn. And it was clear from the quality of these dancers that they were all both well-trained and disciplined. Every single one.

But slowly Rowen decoded their pinched expressions, the way they averted their eyes as soon as Meghan might catch them watching—they weren't jealous. It was worse than that. They resented her. Her skill was taken as a personal affront.

After about an hour, Miss Sylvia, the woman who had led Rowen's audition, clapped again and said, in that odd accent, "*Pas de deux*," and Rowen froze in terror. She had hoped to avoid dancing with a human male for at least a few days.

No such luck.

Rowen wasn't the only one surprised—murmurs rose from the other students as Miss Sylvia continued, "I know we typically do pairs in the afternoon, but with a new year and new students comes new partners. No sense putting it off."

She held out her hand without looking, and one of the other women—a younger one who hadn't introduced herself but was clearly a subordinate—put one of those odd portable writing desks into Miss Sylvia's hand. The woman glanced down and then began calling out names in pairs. As with the line to dance across the floor, Rowen came last.

"Rowen Dale." Tamani had selected the second part—close to her mother's name, Dahlia, but not so obviously a first name. Unlike fae who simply took the name of their mother, humans had something called a last name that Tamani assured her sounded different from given names. "You're with Mitchell Sears."

There were whispers around her as a boy with a huge grin and the same tight black pants all the danseurs wore stepped forward, sketching a low bow. "Miss Rowen, I'm ecstatic to meet you." And before Rowen could protest, or pull away, the boy grabbed her hand and began laying kisses up her arm with loud smooching noises. Rowen's feet felt rooted to the floor with horror and disgust even as she tried to remind herself that humans weren't gross. But this! What was this?

Clearly unaware, Mitchell kissed just below her shoulder

and then yanked on her hand, spinning her and catching her against his chest in a very low dip. Instinctively, Rowen bowed her spine so he didn't break her, and Mitchell, holding her so her head was completely upside-down, whispered in her ear, "Don't worry, you're safe with me." He jerked his forehead to a spot a few feet to the right, and even with the world inverted, Rowen's eyes followed the motion to another boy with moppy brown hair, watching them and grinning with his arms crossed over his chest. "I'm dating that gorgeous hunk of meat over there."

Rowen barely felt Mitchell lift her back up and help her stand. She gaped at him, wide-eyed, every emotion within her jumbling like dandelion fluff in the breeze.

Hunk of meat. That's precisely how she would have described a human, two weeks past. Was Mitchell confiding in her that he, too, was fae? She knew there were other faeries outside the gate—the Mixer, Callista, had brought both renegade fae and trolls into Avalon twelve years ago. And there were the Unseelie—Lenore's grandmother was one.

Rowen peered closely at Mitchell, and dismay rose in her throat when she realized she couldn't tell. Even after two weeks of trying to understand humans, of watching them on Netflix, she hadn't imagined meeting one who could pass as fae so convincingly that she couldn't tell the difference. He was so handsome, his features so symmetrical.

But if he was, then—Rowen glanced over at the boy Mitchell had indicated. They had a romantic relationship. The other boy had the weird stripes of hair on his face that came down beside the ears and all the way to the bottom of his jaw, but no further. And although he was *clean-shaven*—another phrase Rowen had learned from Laurel's dad after a stammeringly awkward conversation—there was a smudge of dark shadow that indicated the hair was coming back. *That* boy was definitely human.

If Rowen's partner was fae—and what an enormous coincidence that would be—then he was romantically involved with a *human.*

Rowen didn't know which was more difficult to believe. The other boy—the for-certain human one—reached out a hand to Meghan and Rowen pretended to look away when Meghan put her fingers in his and he led her into a spin and smiled at her.

Meghan smiled back. She was awfully pretty when she smiled. It was the first time Rowen had seen it. But before she had time to contemplate any of this, Mitchell took Rowen's hand, rather formally, and led her to a spot near the front of the class.

"Not gonna lie," Mitchell murmured, his smiling face close to hers—so close Rowen felt like drawing away and then forced herself to stay steady—"you should feel complimented to be paired with me."

"Should—should I?" Rowen asked, her voice coming out strained and raspy.

"They always put the top handful of dancers together and last year I was Meghan's partner."

"Oh," Rowen said, not knowing what else to say. "Will Meghan be angry?"

"Ahn-grrrry," Mitchell said, mimicking Rowen's brogue and lifting both of her hands to his mouth and kissing her knuckles, right then left. "I love it! Your accent is exquisite. No, no, she won't be angry because she's got my Thomas, who I have no problem admitting is the best *pas de deux* partner in the Academy." He waggled his eyebrows. "And *out* of the Academy too."

Rowen could barely follow Mitchell's rapid-fire exposition, much less the thoughts and motives behind them, and it was a good several seconds before she let out a bark of laughter at his *entendre* and then clapped a hand over her mouth.

"Charmed," Mitchell said with a grin. "Now, let's see how *we* suit."

He led Rowen through a set of rudimentary turns and lifts and she was surprised how quickly she grew accustomed to his hands on her. It truly didn't feel any different than partnering the danseurs in Avalon. Although she did have to admit that knowing his affections were entwined elsewhere made her feel better right from the start.

What a mess *that* could be.

If he *were* fae, of course.

Not that there was anything *wrong* with being human. *Of course.*

She would repeat it to herself a hundred times a day, if she had to.

And she was glad that she'd gone ahead and had Avalon construct her some tights rather than using an illusion, because Mitchell would have known from first contact that he was touching bare skin. There was a lot of touching in *pas de deux*. Not simply because of the dance moves, but because Mitchell was apparently the touchy sort. With everyone.

After two hours of *pas de deux*—when Mitchell embraced Rowen and kissed her farewell on both cheeks before heading off to work with the other males—she hadn't seen him blush a single time. His skin was smooth, his features symmetric. If he had a heartbeat, she'd caught no sign—though belatedly she realized she wouldn't even know where to look.

Rowen still wasn't sure whether he was human or fae. And that niggling doubt shook her more deeply than any experience she'd had in the human world so far.

TEN

"THE TALL GIRL I TOLD YOU ABOUT IS THE scholarship," Rowen said when Tamani finally picked her up. "Her name is Meghan and she's the best dancer in my class." It almost hurt not to claim an exception for herself, but Rowen knew better than to think something became truth simply because she said it.

"She *has* a scholarship," Tamani corrected. "Not she *is* a scholarship."

Rowen tucked that away for later. "The other girls look at her like she doesn't deserve to be there, even though she's better than them." *And she really doesn't like me*, Rowen added in her head.

"Oh," Tamani said, as though suddenly realizing the conversation had a point. "Okay. They resent her because she isn't rich." He hesitated. "She doesn't have as many things as the other girls. Scazio charges very high tuition. It's no problem for Laurel and I to pay it for you, thanks to Avalon, but for many humans it would be impossible. Sounds like that's the case for Meghan."

"How does that make her unworthy?" It was the only word Rowen could think of for the way the other dancers looked at Meghan.

Tamani snorted. "Why don't you ask them? Do you think they'll have any better reasons than the ones you were able to give me when I asked why you thought humans were unworthy?"

He didn't say it in a critical tone of voice, but Rowen felt reprimanded just the same. She bit down the rest of her questions and tried to puzzle out the answers he'd already given her. Paying for things was something Laurel had spent a lot of time practicing with Rowen. The idea that people couldn't simply request the things they needed was very strange. No one paid for dance school in Avalon—nobody *paid* for anything. They just auditioned, and then attended if they made it. Maybe that meant everyone in Avalon had a scholarship.

"Home, sweet home," Tamani said a few minutes later, pointing up at a building so tall Rowen was afraid it was going to topple over right on top of them.

"You *live* here?" Rowen asked in amazement, staring up at the tower.

"Off and on. Most off, at the moment, but we hold onto the lease." With the car's top down Rowen was treated to a completely unobstructed view of the huge glass structure—humans seemed to like glass almost as much as Sparklers. She leaned her head all the way back and was assaulted by a wave of vertigo.

A strange feeling built up in Rowen's core as Tamani turned off the street and drove down a steep ramp into what looked like a deep cave. When she saw rows and rows of other cars, she felt a little better. She knew what this was: a parking lot. Like at Scazio. Except this one was under the ground. Under the *building*. Like a badger's hole. Or a troll's nest.

That thought made her more than vaguely ill.

The ceiling of the parking lot was the same drab grey as the walls and even the floor, and it was lower than most of the structures she'd entered so far. That, combined with the knowledge of the veritable sequoia towering above them made her feel like she could actually see the roof sinking lower, creaking down under the weight of the structure.

"Can we leave this place?" Rowen asked, fighting the urge to duck and cover her head. "It's too small."

Tamani paused and a crinkle formed between his eyebrows. As if making some kind of decision he nodded and pointed at what looked like two metal squares mounted on a wall. "Those are elevators," he said in whisper, his eyes darting about and taking in the three or four people within sight. "Try not to freak out, but you're not going to like how they feel."

"Will it hurt?" Rowen felt all knotted up inside.

"No, not at all," Tamani hurried to reassure her. "Just weird. A sensation that you're being tossed upward and then pulled down."

At the expression on her face he tried to hide a grin, but wasn't quite successful. Which only made her angry.

"Don't be mad," he said, reaching out to push a button with an arrow pointing up. "It really is impossible to describe. It just takes you up. It's not a big deal." He was back to his soft whisper. "I'll try to get us our own, but if someone gets on with us, you'll have to hide how you feel, because most humans have been riding elevators since they were children."

After a loud *ping!*, the big metal square split down the middle, then opened to reveal a small box just big enough for perhaps a dozen people. It held three women, dressed like they were going to attend a festival.

Wait, no, she remembered this from Netflix: a *party*.

Tamani held on to Rowen's arm as the women got off and two men took their places.

"Coming?" one of the men asked, his hand over the hole in the wall where the metal panel had receded.

"I'll wait for the next one," Tamani said, giving a casual wave.

The man shrugged and moved his hand, and a few seconds later the metal had closed the two men inside.

Rowen was trembling now, not sure where those two men had gone or what was happening behind the metal panels. And the fact that she was about to find out wasn't making her feel better.

Another ping sounded and the second metal panel split open. Tamani steered her to the empty box and immediately started pushing a button with two arrows pointing at each other. "Come on, come on," he said, scanning the parking lot. This was definitely near the top of Rowen's list of strange experiences in the human world.

The metal portal finally closed and Rowen and Tamani were alone. "Ready?" Tamani said, and he wasn't laughing at her anymore. He was quite serious and that made Rowen more frightened. But she put on her best neutral stage face and nodded. Tamani pulled out a small rectangle that looked rather like the identification card he made her carry, except that it was silver. This he inserted it into a small slot. Then, after a glance at her, he pushed the number fifty-two.

The floor shifted beneath her feet and Rowen was immediately glad no one else was in the elevator because she couldn't hold back a shriek. Her midcore jumped within her and then, just as Tamani had said—but in a way she could never have comprehended prior to this moment—she felt as though she were being dragged down. Her knees were already weak, but at the sensation that she was growing heavier and heavier, they buckled and she slid down the wall, too terrified to make another sound.

She tried to remind herself that this was Tamani. That even when he was furious with her, he would never, ever harm her on purpose. But she couldn't even look at him; she squeezed her eyes shut and tried to clamp her teeth down to stifle a whimper. The roaring in her head was so loud she couldn't tell if she'd succeeded.

After the shortest twenty or thirty years of Rowen's life, the elevator shuddered to a stop and Rowen felt as though she was hanging in midair. She cracked her eyes open just to make absolutely sure she was still touching the floor. Another loud ping sounded and the elevator opened to reveal a small, sunlit room smattered with chairs and short tables, covered in blue and green fabrics, and a fewpots all around with green plants sprouting from them.

It looked like paradise.

It looked so much like paradise, Rowen almost forgot the hellacious journey that brought her here.

Almost.

"Luckily," Tamani said softly from where he stood with his back to the open metal doors, as if to hold them in place, "the elevator goes right to our suite, so there's no chance of running into anyone up here."

Rowen wasn't completely certain why that was good news. Her thoughts were too jumbled.

"Come on in," Tamani said, still holding the doors open. "Crawl if you have to. No shame in that."

Rowen felt a jolt to her pride, but in the end, she took one long, slow breath, and did just what he said: crawled.

When she reached the line that separated the elevator from the beautiful room beyond, she was glad she hadn't risen to her feet when she realized the line was a thin crack with a slight breeze rising up through it. She clenched her eyes shut again, tried not to think about it, and skittered the last few feet, thanking the Goddess, the Universe, and Mother Nature herself for getting her out of that box of death alive.

With solid ground beneath her feet, Rowen felt instantly better and pushed upright on the plush carpet. She wasn't quite ready to get to her feet, but she could open her eyes and take in her surroundings. A glance behind her told her that the metal portal was closed and Tamani was jingling a key in a white, paneled door Rowen hadn't noticed before.

"Come in," he said, gesturing.

Rowen shakily got to her feet and hurried through the door into a larger room that looked much like the small lobby with matching chairs and a chaise, and a long coffee table in the middle of the area rug. A mirror and a few hooks were attached to the wall—one with a pink cardigan hanging from it—and Tamani was taking things out of his pockets and depositing them into a dish, just as Rowen had seen him do a dozen times at the house on the land. That bit of normalcy helped her shake away the rest of her terror.

She peered around at a room that practically shouted that Laurel had decorated it. Rowen had been to Laurel's room at the Academy a handful of times over the years, and the pale colors and delicate touch of feminine frills were identical, even if the actual décor wasn't. Rowen shakily rose to her feet and saw there were two hallways branching off from this spacious greatroom that probably led to bedrooms. Small openings in the walls showed glimpses of a kitchen. It was so bright! Rowen intuitively looked up and saw that the ceiling was checkered with broad skylights in addition to the tall windows set into the walls.

"It's almost like being outside," she said.

"That's why we moved here," Tamani said. "Laurel is a … well-funded Avalonian ambassador, so to speak, so we had our pick of apartments. Looked for almost a week before we found it." He grinned, his voice turning wistful. "She walked in and immediately told me this was the place."

While the outer walls were entirely windows, the ones that divided up the living space were hung with dozens of pictures—some clearly *photos* produced by human technology—including many paintings that Rowen recognized as her grandmother's. She rolled her eyes at one she could hardly *not* recognize, since she was the subject. "This won't be weird at all," she said dryly.

"That's precisely what I said when Laurel hung a big picture of me in our bedroom," Tamani replied, equally self-conscious. "But at least you're one of a big handful out here. There's only about four pictures in our room and one of them is me." He smirked. "A very large me."

Rowen reached out to touch a picture of Lenore and her mother, Ariana. "Is that Shar?" she asked softly, pointing at the male faerie in the painting. Lenore remembered him, but Rowen didn't.

Tamani nodded, saying nothing.

Even though Shar would have been long-dead by the time Len reached the age she was portrayed as in the picture, that was the magic of paintings; anyone could be added in. Rowen couldn't decide if it was tender or macabre.

"I didn't like it at first," Tamani said, as though reading her thoughts. "It felt wrong, putting him back into a family he'd been ripped out of. But Laurel hung it there, and I saw it every day when I walked by, and soon it felt so right that when she offered to switch it out, I refused."

Rowen's eyes traveled to another painting of a young, smiling fae couple and her throat felt tight when it took several seconds to recognize her own parents. The artist's skill was of noticeably lower quality and Rowen couldn't help but feel a little insulted on their behalf. "How old is this painting?" she asked, and Tamani must have heard the edge in her voice.

"Almost as old as you." He ran a finger along the top of the frame. "It's incredibly hard to lose a child. Mother has refused to paint Dahlia since her death. I could ask her to paint a new portrait of Jade, but it seems tragic to separate them. Even in a picture."

Rowen instantly felt guilty for having doubted Tamani. Or her grandmother. She wouldn't exactly say they loved her mother more than she did, but they had known her longer. Obviously the cut would be deep for both of them. "Who's that with you?" she asked, gesturing to a large photograph, as much to distract herself from her dead parents as anything else. She recognized Tamani, but he had his arm thrown around someone's shoulders and they were both smiling so brightly they must have been caught mid-laugh.

"David," Tamani said shortly.

"Oh." She turned back to the photo, taking in the wavy brown hair and sparkling blue eyes and trying to reconcile them with the fleeting memories she had from so long ago. "He looks … different than I remember."

"Less covered in blood, I imagine."

Ignoring her uncle's prickly tone, she reached out to touch

the picture, but stopped just before her finger made contact with the glass. "Happier, too. When was this?"

"Just after graduation. About six months after the attacks in Avalon." He folded his arms over his chest. "Sometimes I just stand and look at this picture and wonder if I can see any evidence of how haunted he was. If that smile really does reach his eyes."

"You could do the same thing as with Shar," Rowen said. "Have Grandmother paint a new picture of him."

But Tamani was already shaking his head. "He looks different now. Humans age a lot between eighteen and thirty. Besides," he said, his attention back on Shar's family portrait, "he's not dead. He's just … gone."

They stood there together in silence for several minutes, taking in the paintings and photos of all the people who were important in both of their lives. Dead and alive. It was strange how many of the people in Tamani's life were the same people in her life. Not for the first time, she considered how much more Tamani felt like a brother than an uncle.

"Well, enough of this or we'll both be hopelessly maudlin," Tamani said, a little too cheerily. "Come see my favorite spot."

Rowen followed him to a crème-colored, semi-sheer curtain that he pushed back to reveal a big sliding glass door like many Laurel and Tamani had at their house by the gate.

Tamani unlocked the door and she saw his hands flex on the handle, then he paused. "We're very, very high up," he warned. "I keep forgetting this is all so new to you." He hesitated and then said, "This is the balcony. Think of it as an outdoor room with short walls and no ceiling."

Rowen nodded and followed Tamani out onto what did, in fact, look just like a small room. There was a big, round chair that looked rather like a small bed—complete with colorful pillows and a rumpled throw—on one side, and crawling vines trailed along a metal railing as well as up the sides of the building where the balcony attached. Despite the horrific experience of the elevator ride it took to get there, Rowen felt marvelously free as she stepped into the open air so far above the noisy city. She could see what seemed like miles upon miles out into the ocean—which was a blessedly familiar sight—and to her left clouds were rolling in as the sun started to turn the horizon pink. There was nothing above her but the open sky, and though she didn't want to step too close to the edge and look straight down, seeing just how high they were didn't bother her very much.

"It's lovely," she said, quietly, as though she might break a spell by talking too loud.

"I … I sleep here, generally, thus the …"

Rowen turned when Tamani's voice trailed into silence and it took her several seconds to recognize the emotion she was seeing in her uncle's eyes, because she had never—ever—seen it in him before. He was embarrassed.

He gestured aimlessly. "You know, pillows. And such."

She stared at the round lounger that did look quite comfortable, but didn't understand. "At night?"

A short shake of his head. "During the day." He pointed at the sky. "Sunlight."

Of course. "But why don't you sleep at night?"

He shrugged. "I sleep some. When Laurel's here. I like to retire with her and wait until she's drifted off before I leave."

"Leave?"

He stopped shifting his weight from foot to foot and finally looked her in the face, his eyes serious, brow furrowed. "That's what I wanted to make you aware of. I'm Laurel's *Fear-gleidhidh.* Her warden. My work for Avalon is to make sure Laurel can do *her* work for Avalon. I keep her safe. At night I generally go out and … make San Francisco a little safer for her."

Rowen blinked several times. "I don't think I understand what that means."

He threw up his hands. "I fight crime in the streets, all right? I protect people and stop bad things from happening. It's not much, but I think every little bit helps." When Rowen's face still reflected blankness he added, "Plus, it keeps my stems supple. If anything were to happen that threatened Laurel or

… or our sprout, I need to be able to work at night—with no sunlight—and that's not something you can just jump back into. I need to stay quick. I need to stay sharp. And this place … well, let's just say it's hard to think like a sentry when you're living like a King."

"Oh," Rowen said, because she didn't know what else to say. Her uncle apparently went out at night and protected human beings from themselves. For fun. And exercise. It was hard to twine her mind around. "How long have you been doing this?"

"Years. Almost since the beginning." He shrugged. "I'm a very busy, active person. Always have been. It's what I was trained for. And following Laurel around to classes and just sitting there? It wasn't enough for me. Not mentally, and not physically." He grinned at her now. "So I took up a hobby."

She barely restrained herself from rolling her eyes.

"But it's more than that. I try to spot real threats before they grow serious. And that might be precisely what's happening now." He leaned over, his forearms braced on the railing. "I'm going to stay here, in the city, for the next week or so, to help you learn how to use public transportation and get you settled. After that, I'll make the drive at least once a week. I want to be home when our sprout blossoms, but I've been hearing some troubling things that require my attention here, too."

“Troubling? Troubling how?”

Tamani met her eyes and they were dark and shuttered. “Troubling like perhaps the trolls are trickling back in.”

Rowen’s limbs felt weak. The nightmares about trolls destroying Summer—killing her mother—they’d never gone away completely. “What makes you think it’s trolls?”

“I’m not sure,” he said softly. “Well, no, that’s not entirely true. There’s been a rash of drownings, weird ones: people who don’t seem to have any reason to be in the ocean, fully dressed, phones in their pockets. Half of them have had their throats ripped out. Very trollish. Also, since Klea cleaned out the trolls from the Pacific Northwest, it’s possible they could maybe migrate from other countries by boat …?”

Rowen heard the question at the end of the supposition. It wasn’t a strong suspicion then, merely a guess. And knowing Tamani, one of many.

He looked down and brushed a dead leaf with his toe before saying, “Well, it could be something else. Drugs. Human trafficking. That’s—never mind, maybe we’ll take about that some other time. It’s sometimes dangerous and I had hoped to keep this part of my life from you by having you stay with Chelsea. But—”

“—but I rather spoiled that, didn’t I?”

“You rather did,” Tamani said.

“I’m sorry,” she whispered.

"You'll be sorrier." When she darted a glare at him he continued, utterly nonplussed. "Right now you recognize that you legitimately did something wrong, and you're sorry about the fallout. But in time, when you really see humans as people, you're going to be devastated, and that's when I'll take you back to apologize. That's what Chelsea deserves."

"But I—"

"Have been trying. I know. If I hadn't seen very genuine effort, I'd have never let you come here." There was kindness in his eyes, but his words still made Rowen feel small. "But you can't reverse a lifetime of bias in a fortnight." He laid a hand on her shoulder. "Keep trying. It'll come."

She nodded, not trusting herself to speak without emotion strangling her words.

"Anyway, I stocked the fridge while you were at dance class, so let's have something to eat. Whether you admit it or not, I imagine you're very hungry after your long day. Afterward," he looked up with a sparkle in his eye, "I think you should practice riding the elevator again."

ELEVEN

TAMANI SLAMMED HIS KNUCKLES INTO THE punk's face—it was always satisfying to start his night out with a good, old-fashioned fistfight. When the thief was lying on the ground moaning and Tam's hands were striped with blood, he wrenched the small black purse out of the jerk's loose grip and turned to the woman curled up against the wall. Tamani handed back her purse, then offered a hand to help her up.

"Do you live near?" he whispered, knowing she would be skittish. He didn't know how many times the man had struck her, but his hand was raised in the air when Tamani had darted around the corner, and it was her screams that had drawn him in the first place.

When the human woman didn't respond, he added, "Maybe I can get you a taxi? I'll pay—no matter how close or how far. The point is to get you there safely."

As he spoke, she finally relaxed a bit. Something about his

vaguely British accent seemed to make people feel safer. He blamed the BBC—that Doctor fellow, or Poldark something-or-other. Of course, he could simply Entice her, but he tried to avoid stripping humans of their independence whenever he could. Unless the criminal element was truly overwhelming, it felt like cheating—and with their victims, it usually seemed like a pointless indignity.

"I was almost home," she whispered. "I was walking from the bus stop."

"If it's all right with you, I'll follow at a distance and see you through the door. Are you in an apartment?"

She nodded.

"Just the front door, then. I won't follow you to your place; I don't care about that."

"Th-thank you."

He let himself smile, judging from years of experience that she was ready for that. Small, without teeth. "I'm just glad I was here." And it was true. He knew that for every person he saved, there were a dozen—a hundred—he didn't.

But he was only one fae.

"Just a sec," he murmured as the woman started taking shaky steps. He pulled a zip tie from his back pocket and latched the groaning man to the bottom of a fire escape before he could wriggle away into his hole. As soon as the woman was safe, Tamani would call the cops. He was the master of the anonymous tip.

Twenty minutes later, citizen delivered and authorities notified, Tamani continued his walk toward the beach. He adjusted his hoodie to keep his face shadowed and stuffed his hands deep into the pockets of his black cargoes. Though every article of his clothing, right down to his heavy black boots, was faerie-wrought with light, sun-permeable fabric, he looked exactly like the thugs he fought nightly—absent their occasional firearms. The weapons Tamani did carry were nothing that would make most cops blink, should he ever have a face-to-face conversation with local law enforcement. Not that such a thing had happened in the decade he'd been playing vigilante. If there was one thing a faerie sentry learned, it was stealth.

But of course, faerie sentries learned many things—things some of the younger sentries had surprisingly little opportunity to put into practice. Enticement. Combat—armed and unarmed. How to use globes filled with fae defense potions that Tamani carried on a utility belt, concealed by the rumpled bottom of his sweatshirt. Even here, playing vigilante in a densely-populated human city, Tamani didn't often get himself into a tight enough spot to need those. But he would, surely, the one time he didn't have them. Of all the things sentries learned, constant vigilance was perhaps the most important.

Tamani managed to get to the beach without further

incident, and wound his way carefully around sightseers who had lingered past sundown and, more commonly, various romantic entanglements. There was something he and Laurel never did except when they were in Avalon. Salt water simply didn't have the same appeal when one was a plant.

He did his best to ignore the discomfort posed by the ocean's salty spray; this wasn't the first time he'd looked into criminal activity on the beaches, and it probably wouldn't be the last. But he stayed inland whenever he could. If it ever became necessary to drag someone from the waves, he could do it, but he'd be sluggish for days afterward as his system tried to cleanse itself. If the gruesome killings he'd come to investigate were in fact being carried out by a troll—or a band of them—sticking to the beach would certainly be one way to discourage investigation by nosy faerie sentries. But a troll squatting in San Francisco should have no particular reason to suspect a faerie sentry might be poking around—

—should they?

Tamani slunk from shadow to shadow for two hours as the moon rose higher, going back and forth along the quarter mile of shoreline where most of the bodies had been found. It had been almost ten days since the last one—the second-longest stretch since the victims started showing up in the first place.

Rowen's acceptance into her dance school had proven a

convenient excuse, but in truth Tamani decided weeks ago to look into the killings, even though it meant leaving Laurel and their growing sprout home for a time. Fortunately, the house at the land was one of the safest spots in the entire human world. His job now was to make sure the home in San Francisco to which Laurel and his sprout would eventually return was safe as well.

Three years ago, a similar flow of bodies had led Tamani to a human trafficking ring that was depending on the tide to destroy evidence of their activities. His anonymous prodding of the human police and sabotage of the perpetrators had lead not only to the safe rescue of three hundred girls and the capture of the ship being used to ferry them from war-torn countries into forced prostitution, but to the eventual breakup of an international slavery ring. Tamani was quite proud of that.

But in that case, the victims had multiple unifying characteristics—race, age, gender, cropped hair, bare feet, signs of malnourishment. None were actually drowned, and none bore signs of a violent death, beyond bruises from rough treatment. Human law enforcement had already developed a pretty good idea of what was happening by the time Tamani got involved; their investigation was simply constrained in ways Tamani was not. This new rash of mutilated bodies was something else entirely. There was a pattern of sorts, but so far no one had made much sense of it.

And neither had he.

On his fourth pass across the small cove Tamani paused, peering onto the beach. There was a lump in the darkness that hadn't been there an hour ago.

Tamani looked carefully in all directions before crouching down and skimming across the sand toward the body. He wasn't the only one prowling for predators tonight; already he'd gone out of his way to avoid two law enforcement officers out for a stroll.

No one seemed to have spotted this body yet.

And it definitely was a body. A man, Tamani saw, as he approached the long, dark lump. A few wrinkles and greys, visible in the city's dim ambience. Middle aged, a bit heavy. And minus one windpipe.

Tam gazed down numbly at the violence. The ocean had staunched the bleeding and the jagged edges of skin were blanched and preserved by the chill and salt. He took in the rope marks at the wrists and ankles—the first three victims hadn't been tied, as far as anyone could tell, but every victim afterwards had. That was the only thing anyone had tried to label an "escalation," but it was hard to say what it might mean. How much could it possibly matter whether a person was bound or not when they got their throat torn out?

"There you are."

Tamani scrambled to his feet, reaching for the supple willow rod he occasionally employed as a nightstick.

A girl stood just on the other side of the body, her empty hands raised in the universal gesture for *I want you to think I'm harmless*. A lie—no one who could sneak up on Tamani was harmless—but that didn't necessarily mean she meant to do *him* any harm. "Please don't run again. My associate has been forced to reverse time twice already and I'm really not a fan of the sensation."

Tamani froze, fighting an instinct not to flee, but to attack—immediately, violently. Not that he'd hurt an unarmed human girl—subdue and bind, perhaps. Leave her above the tide line. Surely it wouldn't come to that. So why—

She said not to run *again*. Had they met before? He had no memory of this girl, but if he was totally honest, most humans still looked pretty much the same to him until he got to know them well. And she was definitely human—the tip of her nose was reddened from the cold, balmy nighttime air. Older than Rowen; younger than Laurel.

His sense of alarm ebbed, leaving a throb of curiosity in its wake.

"Have we met?"

"Not in a way you'd remember, faerie-man."

That was as good as a threat, and not a small one. Without moving a muscle, Tamani reached out with his Enticement, extending his charms to bring the human girl under his sway.

But it was blocked. No, it was *repelled*, violently, flung back into his face so hard he staggered as if physically struck. A completely new and deeply unpleasant sensation.

"Not that," the girl said, her tone amused even as she kept her hands where he could see them. "It won't work; you may as well be a locksmith trying to break into a brick wall. No one gets in my brain. And even if you could, you wouldn't want to. Trust me."

Tamani studied the girl, scarcely daring to breathe. She knew him for a faerie and had brushed off his Enticement—she wasn't merely unaffected, like a troll, but had actually deflected the attempt. The danger such a human could pose to Avalon was beyond reckoning. He found himself wishing for Shar for an entirely different reason than usual—and not only because that unfamiliar trickle at the center of his core felt very much like fear.

"Are you ready to talk? I've been waiting for you."

"Did you do this?" Tamani snapped, pointing at the body.

"No, of course not," she said in such an even voice that he felt oddly like a child being scolded. He must have twenty years on this girl, but she had a steel rod of control within her that he hadn't seen since … well, since his mentor had died in a hail of bullets to save the lives of the faeries of Avalon. Tamani took a deep breath. This investigation had spiraled out of control in less than two minutes.

"Why are you here?" he asked, forcing himself to sound as calm as the stranger.

"To make sure you play your part. To stop this."

Tamani no longer wished to fight. Running was sounding like a better idea every second.

The girl groaned and brought her hands to her head to massage her temples. "I took a red-eye from Oklahoma last night to get here, and even with my partner playing with time, I only just made it. I'm tired and cranky and I have a flight back in three hours. All I came to tell you is that if you're waiting right in this spot, at 9:27 in the evening, in four days, you'll see who's taking them. *What's* taking them."

"You won't just tell me?" Tamani asked, and though his voice remained calm, a ribbon of anger flared in his chest. This wasn't a game!

"Can't tell you what I don't know," she said. She dug into a pocket and withdrew a folded piece of paper. "This is as close as I could come, but I'm no artist."

Tamani unfolded the paper, but it was too dim to see the grey pencil streaks.

"You can't save her."

Tamani's head jerked up. "What?"

"The girl. This is the most important part. You're going to have to let them take her. They come as a group. If you stop them, they'll know they've been caught. And when they find out it's by you, well, they'll move away. Go somewhere else. Hide better. More lives will be lost. And when they get whatever they need from these victims, they'll attack."

"Attack?"

"Let her go, Tamani."

Her use of his name stunned him into silence.

"Let her die, and you just might save the world. Save her, and everyone in the city dies, and a lot of other people, too."

Tamani was clenching his jaw so hard it shook. "Who the hell do you think you are?"

She was silent for so long that Tamani had to squelch the urge to scream. "I'll tell you this much, in hopes that it calms your mind enough for you to make the right choice. I'm an oracle. I've been making hard choices since I made the wrong one and killed my father when I was six. This choice? Letting one person die to save millions? Billions?" She shook her head. "Easy."

"And you think that's your choice to make?"

"Don't think I wanted this," she said, and there was an edge to her tone. "Or that I wouldn't give it up if I could. But as I can't, yes, it *is* my choice. And I've made it."

"And I should just trust that? Trust *you?*" Tamani stared at her, challenging her to drop her gaze, but she didn't take it up. After a few seconds of confidently meeting his stare, she turned away and headed away from the shoreline.

"Wait," Tamani said, catching up with her in a few jogging steps. "Why won't you tell me more? How can you claim to be on my side and be so cryptic?" Tamani had some personal experience with oracular wisdom, and while he eventually came to appreciate it—deeply—he had developed something of an allergy to vague advice.

She took a deep breath and glanced over at him, but didn't stop walking. "I don't know any more than that. I only get flashes. But when I know something, I *know* it. And this is what I know: It has to be you. You'll figure it out. Not immediately. But you will. And then you can do what it takes to stop them. Friday, 9:27pm." She paused and looked at him again. "You *have* to let her go. You can't be caught by them. I think—*think*, mind you—that when they toss her back, they won't come as a group. You might be able to work with that. I don't know. That's only a vague impression."

"Vague impression," Tamani muttered, hardly believing he was even having this conversation.

"This is the last time you'll see me," she continued, as though he'd said nothing. "I'm only here to make sure you play your part. An entire world of people are depending on you."

She started to walk away and Tamani knew he couldn't let her. Not yet. "Stop!" he called out in a loud whisper. "What's your name?"

She turned, giving him her profile, and for a few moments he didn't think she would answer. "My name is Charlotte," she said softly. "Charlotte Westing." Then she turned and disappeared into the night.

TWELVE

"MAKE IT PURPOSEFUL!" MISS SYLVIA SAID WITH a musical lilt. "It's *tendu*, not *ten*-don't."

Mitchell groaned beside Rowen. After a week of listening to Miss Sylvia's "motivational" sayings she'd imagined herself inured to the awful humor, but this one was particularly egregious. Her partner clearly felt the same.

Rowen had discovered for certain that Mitchell was human. When someone teased him about Thomas, his cheeks did the color-changing thing, and she'd seen him eating a human food called "hamburger" than would have laid her up for a week. It had taken her a few days to be certain though, and her feelings on the matter were a thorny tangle.

Still, Mitchell was good—really good. It was a joy to dance with him every afternoon. Unlike most of the other dancers, who kept their distance and sneaked shy glances but didn't talk to her, Mitchell was a bubbling spring of conversation. Praise, jokes, and a litany of daily details he couldn't have known she would find so interesting poured forth from his mouth as though he needed to speak the way most humans needed to breathe. And when they danced together, it was as though he could read her mind, anticipate her moves, even her occasional wobbles. He was amazing.

But everyone here was good. Better than Rowen had expected. She had to work just as hard as when she'd been in Avalon but, unlike there, the other students also put extra time in at the studio. She was rarely alone in the open classroom.

These human dancers seemed to be, if possible, even more driven than Rowen. Which didn't make sense. They had infinitely more choices; they could still play some role in their community if they got cut. But there they were, after class, a decent handful of them at all hours, fine-tuning turns, pounding complex combinations into their brains, rarely chatting idly.

Instead of making her feel less alone, the discovery of this commonality somehow made her feel even more isolated.

Miss Sylvia clapped her hands after warm-ups—which was what the humans called "stretch and limbers"—and said, "*Nutcracker Grand Pas de Deux.*"

Rowen looked around as everyone around her groaned, a few voices asking, "Already?" What was so disappointing about this announcement?

"Take some time to refresh your memories and work out your moves with your new partners," Miss Sylvia said. "We'll come back together at the top of the hour." Rowen scrunched her eyebrows, waiting for some kind of further instruction, but no one else seemed confused. They were simply turning to their partners and starting to pick through steps.

She barely felt Mitchell's fingertips take hers until he pulled on her and she stumbled, falling against his chest.

"Oh, sorry, Love. First turn. I thought you'd be ready."

"First turn?"

"Well, not turn, exactly." He put a hand on her waist, nudged her up *en pointe*, and guided her leg with his hands. "*Devant développé*." He pushed her quite ungracefully under his arm in a spin. "*Pirouette. Attitude derrière.* Look, watch Meghan."

Meghan and Thomas were moving slowly but confidently through the motions Mitchell had just helped Rowen stagger through, then continuing on, working together seamlessly. "They've danced this before," Rowen said, knowing somehow that she was helplessly behind and still not exactly comprehending why.

"Not together. Obvs Meghan danced it with *me* last year," he said with a wide grin. "Thomas' old partner graduated. Dances with Boston now. It's not San Francisco, but it's a job."

"You dance it every year?" With so many ways to dance,

why would they do the same *pas de duex* over and over?

"For auditions. For *The Nutcracker*."

"*The Nutcracker?*"

"I know. Done to death, but it's tradition." He nodded toward Meghan again. "She wants Clara this year. Violently. Not that I blame her. It would be a coup."

Rowen's head was spinning and she had the discouraging sensation of having been thrown into deep and frigid water without the ability to swim. "What's *The Nutcracker?*"

Mitchell finally shut up at that. But the way he stared at her with wide, horrified eyes didn't exactly improve the atmosphere. Then his features cleared and he laughed. "Oh, you must call it something else where you're from. Scotland, yes? What language do they speak there?"

"Er, Gaelic," she answered automatically, though she remembered Tamani saying that wasn't exactly true.

"Figure out what the Gaelic word is for it, and that'll clear everything up." He paused. "Though you'd think the character names would be the same. Similar, at least. Clara? Fritz? The Sugarplum Fairy?"

Rowen shook her head at the first two names then froze at the F-word before shaking her head once more.

"You've got to know it." He paused, pursed his lips, and then started wordlessly singing an intricate tune that didn't sound like anything Rowen had *ever* heard before.

"Oh, forget it," he said after a while. "I can barely carry a tune with a bucket in my hands. It's just the language barrier; I'm sure of it. Every dancer knows *The Nutcracker.* In the meantime, let's go work with Meghan and Thomas."

"Mitchell, I don't think—"

"Come now, Darling, bark worse than her bite and all that."

Bite? Surely humans wouldn't actually bite each other! Not in the middle of ballet class at any rate. But she didn't resist too hard when her partner pulled her over to the other pair.

"Hey Lovelies," Mitchell said, still holding her wrist. "Work with us—Row doesn't know this one."

Meghan raised a perfectly arched eyebrow. "New girl doesn't know the *Nutcracker Grand Pas de Deux*? Are you kidding me?"

"Don't mock," Mitchell said, and Rowen was surprised to hear a hard edge in his voice. And even more surprised when Meghan responded by closing her mouth and shrugging a vague acquiescence.

Neither Meghan nor Rowen said a word as they went through the movements, though the boys murmured and chuckled easily. They spent the next fifteen minutes walking through the first several bars of the dance before Miss Sylvia called for their attention and began going through each step in careful detail, working on form and positioning.

The cheerful but picky instructor returned again and again to Meghan and Thomas, praising Meghan's lines, her balance, her light fingers on Thomas'. For the first time since classes started, there wasn't a single word of praise for Rowen, who spent as much time watching the other dancers as she did focusing on her own steps. Meghan mostly hid her smug grin, but Rowen had been in the theatre too long to miss that tiny tilt at the edges of her mouth.

The two hours of *pas de deux* felt more like two days, but finally Miss Sylvia released them.

"Row, come here," Mitchell said, beckoning to where his duffel sat on the floor. He riffled through it and found a large, fat pen, which he clasped in both hands in supplication. "Darling, I love you to pieces and I think you're extraordinarily skilled, but you've got to get up to speed on this dance. Casting for the winter show is based on this *pas de deux* and—even though they claim otherwise—casting for the spring audition is heavily-influenced by your performance in *The Nutcracker*." He took a deep breath and then continued, still so very serious. Especially for him. "The spring concert is your audition for every major company in the world and if you fail, you don't get a job. Ever. My career is resting on this and I need you to be one hundred and seven percent. I swear on a stack of Bibles and one copy of Luna that I'll give you nothing less in return."

Rowen nodded, but didn't trust herself to speak without

tearing up. She hadn't fully understood everything he'd said, but she knew that tone of voice. It was the one her fellow Sparklers had used the audition after a Ticer pushed one of them out. "Tell me what to do," she said.

He grabbed her arm and started writing on it with the pen—thick black letters that looked like they'd never wash off. "YouTube," he said, concentrating on the letters. "Nutcracker. *Grand Pas de Deux*. Find the one with Anna Tsygankova and Matthew Golding. They're the best." He added those names to the scrawl on her skin and Rowen was pretty sure she'd be sporting them for the rest of her life. "Our choreography is very slightly different, but that's the closest version, and I can totally show you the changes." He looked up at her as he put the lid back on the pen with a little snap. "Come on Monday with the moves basically down and we can work from there. Be ready to stay after every day this week." He stepped forward and held both her hands in his. "I can't teach you the whole dance from scratch and still expect to be where we need to be in six weeks for auditions. It's too much. We've got to be fine tuning within a week."

"I'll learn it," she said, needing to interrupt this frenetic current of desperate words. "I promise. I—I'm sorry I don't know it already."

"No, no. It's okay." He grinned, but there was a nervousness there that kept the smile from shining in his eyes.

"You'll probably get two minutes into the clip and realize you totally *do* know it. I mean, Scotland isn't Mars—surely they have *The Nutcracker*."

Rowen gave him her best fake smile and hoped it reassured him somewhat. "I'll work hard," she promised. And hoped Tamani wasn't planning on going home to Orick this weekend. Or, if he was, that he wouldn't mind leaving her in San Francisco.

With another brittle smile at Mitchell, she shouldered her rucksack and headed out the door. Tamani had requested she not stay late tonight—said he had an appointment of some kind—and besides, it was Friday. People rarely stayed late on Friday; they came back on Saturday instead. Rowen had come in herself last Saturday, for some extra studio hours, but this weekend she wouldn't be ready. She apparently was going to have to go home and watch videos of this ballet that everyone knew except her. It was more than a little humiliating. Ducking her head, she made for the door where she'd be able to see Tamani when he pulled up to the curb.

Standing right in front of that door was a tall male she didn't recognize. She slowed as she approached and something skittered inside her chest as she took him in from shoes to hair. He was tall—taller than most of the danseurs at the school—and though he wasn't one of them, he had that lithe, supple build that suggested he could have been. He was wearing tiny soundmakers in his ears and was staring down at a device—what had Tamani called it? An intelligent phone?—but even though he wasn't looking at her, she had the sensation of being prey in the presence of a hunter.

"Hey, Shawn," Mitchell called from behind her, and edged past to do a sort of complex hand-shaking greeting that Rowen had observed only happened between males of the species.

Rowen stopped walking. There was no point; this Shawn creature was blocking the doors and, in Mitchell's chatty company, she doubted either of them would be moving along any time soon. Besides, still trying to push human friendships on her, Tamani continued to show up a little late every day, hoping Rowen would use the time to strike up conversations with her classmates. Which she might be willing to do if only she knew how to start. Instead, she was utterly baffled and fairly certain the other dancers interpreted that as snobbish. The few times she had attempted to start a conversation, the girls had kept asking her to repeat herself until she grew so rattled she started stammering, which only made the problem worse. So she'd given up with everyone except Mitchell.

And she was on the verge of failing him.

"Oh hey," Mitchell said, his hand snaking out so quickly Rowen couldn't dodge. He dragged her close and slung an arm around her shoulders. "My new partner."

"You don't have Meghan anymore?" Shawn asked.

"We get a new partner every year." He leaned over and kissed her temple, making Rowen feel a little better. "She's good though. A worthy replacement, and I don't say that lightly."

"Big compliment, then," Shawn said, grinning.

Rowen dropped her eyelids. That smile. It sent a vibration of something pleasant radiating out of her core and into her stems. Her breath felt short and her knees were wobbly, as though she'd put in far more time in the studio today than she actually had.

"She's modest," Mitchell said, the humor heavy in his voice when he squeezed her shoulders. "But you should watch her through the windows one of these days. She's amazing. Even if she doesn't know what *The Nutcracker* is."

Rowen elbowed Mitchell, but he only laughed and stepped out of reach. "I'm off. Get into some trouble while I'm gone," he said in a sing-song voice and waggled his eyebrows at them suggestively.

Rowen waited for the disgust at his insinuation to well up within her, but instead it felt as though fireworks were going off in her belly and she felt irrationally shy. She ducked her head and stared at Shawn's shoes, even as she wished she had the courage to look at his face.

"Mitchell's really good," Shawn said. His voice was quite low and rumbled like gentle thunder. "Even though he's super friendly, he's actually picky as hell. He must really be impressed with you. How long have you been dancing?"

"Since I could walk," Rowen muttered, kicking herself for this paralyzing bout of panic that barely let her stammer out her words.

"Ah, same as Meghan, then."

Meghan? This was the second time he'd mentioned her. "Meghan is … your girlfriend?" She forced the words out, not understanding why it seemed so very critical that she know this answer.

But Shawn only barked out a loud laugh. "No, no, no. My sister."

"Oh." Rowen straightened, feeling nearly jovial at that. But, of course, she should have seen. Shawn had the same dark skin and hair as Meghan, and she'd already noted his height and supple build. She just hadn't made the connection that he was a masculine version of Meghan. "Of course you are." Why did she feel suddenly cheerful?

Rowen forced herself to raise her eyelids, trying to figure out what was so different about this human. He wore the bulky footwear Tamani referred to as "tennis shoes," and his legs were bare up to a pair of shorts that just covered his knees. They weren't quite the denim Rowen often saw males wearing in films, though never on Tamani, but they weren't the soft shorts the other danseurs wore either. They were a bit poofy and had a number of pockets down each side of his thighs. She imagined them quite useful. But what yanked at her attention was they way they hung, low slung, just beneath his hipbones. And even though she couldn't see any actual skin at his waist, his shirt was fitted such that she could see the curves and shadows of ridges and ripples just above the waistband. She was holding her breath and didn't bother to let it out as her eyes traveled higher, noting his slender torso and corded arms.

Then she was peering at his face.

And he was looking right back.

His features were statuesque, as fine and sleek as any faerie could wish, with eyes dark as moist soil, the kind delicate seedlings were planted in. Completely against her will, she found the corners of her mouth rising upward.

He smiled back and for a moment the world stopped and a cloud of perfection settled around them.

"Hey Shawn."

Two words broke the spell. While the other girls seemed put off by Rowen's shyness, Meghan had no problem tossing Rowen nasty looks, whispering comments in her direction, or snickering if Miss Sylvia had cause to correct her. What Rowen had said about the scholarship—the compliment she'd so carefully tried to give—had backfired in a massive way. Meghan's front row seat at today's *pas de deux* disaster hadn't helped.

The human girl stepped right up beside Shawn, tucked herself under his arm, and tried to push him toward the door.

"Simmer," Shawn said with a grin. "I'm making friends." And then he looked at Rowen and there was an invitation in his gaze that made Rowen's mouth feel dry and glued her feet to the floor. What in the name of the Goddess was wrong with her?

Meghan gave a brittle laugh and said, "Her? That's Rowen." She tipped her head nearer to Shawn and said, meaningfully, "The new one."

"Ah," Shawn replied, and his eyes shuttered, all invitation vanished in an instant.

It felt like a slap across her face. Her thoughts reeled, speech fled, fiery darts of indignity pinned her to inaction.

Shawn smirked, his expression taunting. "Nothing left to say?"

Rowen only pursed her lips and remained silent. She'd never been one to beat against walls of stone.

"Oh, Rowen doesn't talk," Meghan said. "She's better than the rest of us."

The insult left Rowen feeling hot and cold at once—in part, somehow, because Meghan had said it in front of her brother. Meghan's brother, who was looking at Rowen like she deserved such treatment. Something about him, about his brown eyes, darker than any faerie could ever have, finally helped melt the ice that was holding her in place. With a flip of her head she tossed her hair and let her not-of-this-world brogue roll out *extra* heavy.

"I doon talk 'cause people laugh at my accent. 'Tis nae aboot being better. Doon need to spake to dance. But, aye, there ye're right. As far as dancin' goes, I am better'n the rest of ye."

Straight and tall, with that natural grace Miss Sylvia frequently praised in front of everyone, she shoved past the both of them, knowing without looking that *his* eyes followed her all the way down the hall.

THIRTEEN

TAMANI STUDIED THE ROUGH SKETCH AGAIN, though he'd had it all but memorized for days. Whatever the girl's talents, she wasn't much of an artist. The figure she'd drawn appeared to be an asexual humanoid of indeterminate age, with hair falling past its waist. Her waist? Maybe. It was draped in something that might have been a dress or a long tunic, but also had some kind of ribbons hanging off of its arms.

Something about its face was … inhuman. Not bestial, like a troll, but wrong, somehow. Of course that could just be the Oracle's artistic failing. Still, whoever—or whatever—this was, they didn't look like the sort of person human law enforcement would handle well. If it *did* turn out to be some kind of deranged cultist cosplay, Tamani could pacify the perpetrator without resorting to violence. And if it was something *else*, well, all the more reason for Tamani to be the one to deal with it.

So it was that at 9:25 on Friday night, he was waiting exactly where he'd been told to wait by a human girl who somehow managed to know far too much and far too little at the same time. He had dressed in his usual blacks and was tucked deep into the shadows of the rocky cove, where he could see a vast expanse of the shoreline while remaining essentially invisible to others.

And he was pretty sure he'd identified the victim already. Between the darkness and distance, he couldn't see very many details, but there was a human down by the shore, wandering around alone. She was definitely a woman, on the younger end of her twenties, stomping back and forth with her head down while kicking up arcs of sand. Probably out looking for solitude to vent some sort of frustration.

A decision she was going to pay for with her life, if Charlotte was to be believed. It was a devilish trap—if the Oracle was some kind of fraud, then there was no reason to pester the woman. But if she was right, Tamani's urge to interfere, to run out and Entice the woman away from the beach, could cost the lives of everyone in San Francisco.

And of course there was always the slim possibility that this was a trap of some kind, though he couldn't imagine how anyone would even know enough to set a trap for him. Was that why the human authorities sometimes ignored his anonymous tips until he'd called them in a few times—or Enticed others to do so? Fear of being manipulated by others with an information advantage? Because, Tamani realized, if he had any other leads to follow, likely he wouldn't have bothered, in spite of how certain the Oracle has seemed.

But of course he had no other leads.

A soft sound caught his ear and he jerked to attention—as did the woman. But it was just a snippet of song, an *a capella* number likely carried on the breeze from a nearby beach party, or passing traffic. It was kind of relaxing, actually. Beautiful, if a bit haunting, and Tamani had never heard anything quite like it. It suited his mood and, thinking Laurel might enjoy it as well, he made a mental note to look for it online.

The human woman, meanwhile, was gazing out into the ocean, her sand-kicking utterly forgotten. Did she see something, out there in the waves? Something Tamani couldn't? That seemed unlikely, but it wasn't impossible, so Tamani crept a few feet toward shoreline.

As he did, he realized that the singing was getting louder—and wasn't coming from anywhere on land. It was coming from the ocean. As the waves withdrew, they revealed the source. There were shadows emerging from the waves at a slow glide, and they were *singing*.

Tamani worked his way around the large rocks scattered along the cove, his feet soundless on the slick surface. But the closest rock big enough to conceal him was still a hundred feet from the shoreline, and it was dark. Tamani shoved a hand under his hoodie and grabbed a dropper bottle from his belt. "Thank you, Laurel," he whispered, and tilted back his head, putting a drop of the dark solution into each eye. Two blinks, three, and the darkness receded; to Tamani's eyes, the beach appeared much as it might just after dawn.

As he looked back toward the singing shadows, he realized that he'd actually been kind of hoping that somehow, this string of grisly murders was the work of trolls. An enemy he knew—a creature he'd faced before. But the pale green faces of the figures emerging from the water were mesmerizingly lovely and perfectly symmetrical. There was no way they were trolls.

The creatures emerged from the water, revealing thin swaths of fabric that hung from one shoulder and wrapped around their torsos and hips, not unlike a Greek toga. Even so, with his vision enhanced, Tamani could easily make out indications of gender tracking, those of humans, fae, and trolls alike.

These creatures, however, were plainly none of those things. These *people*, Tamani realized. At least probably. Some of them were singing; their arms were outstretched, swaying back and forth, and long strands of what looked like lacy seaweed hung down into the lapping water—the ribbons in

Charlotte's drawing, presumably. They all wore their hair long and unbound. It exhibited an odd texture that made it hang in thick, swirly tresses down their back or in front of their shoulders, instead of being flat and lank like his own hair was when wet.

He almost fell off the rock when a piece of one of the creatures' hair *moved*, wriggling like a tentacle—or a snake. Combined with their togas, the animated hair reminded Tamani of nothing so much as the Greek Medusa—but this hair definitely wasn't snakes. In fact, the longer he watched, the less he was convinced that the creatures had any control over the slight motion of their hair at all. It writhed gently, sometimes lifting tentatively from their body, as though searching for something in the air. Almost like the fronds of a sea anemone.

A rock dug into Tamani's knee, making him realize he'd been bending closer, trying to get a better look. Whatever these things were, they were fascinating! Which would be great if they weren't also likely hostile intruders bent on murdering a human woman. His eyes snapped back to the woman on the shore. She was stumbling awkwardly forward, as if dragged by unseen hands—but not unwillingly. Her shoulder bag had fallen from her hands and laid on the sand a few steps away, and her shoes, which had been dangling from her fingers, were also lost.

The lead creature—one of the few *not* singing—was only a few yards away, knee-deep in the waves. As Tamani watched, the creature's form began to shift. Not suddenly, like the appearance of a Sparkler's illusion; instead, it warped like unfired clay being molded by a master sculptor's hands. The creature stretched a few inches taller and his shoulder widened; his roiling hair gentled and shortened until he looked more like a regular human with dreads than a sea creature with hair that had a mind of its own. His face lost its green pallor and the bits hanging off of his arms curled upward to join to his skin, taking on the appearance of a decoration—a three dimensional tattoo—rather than an appendage.

He looked *human*. Mostly. Not quite, but the differences had become subtle enough that anyone walking by in the darkness would see only an attractive human man, reaching out one hand to a woman.

While a cadre of undersea nightmares serenaded them both.

Abruptly Tamani realized that, in his shock, he'd let the woman get close enough for the creatures to drag her beneath the waves—but they didn't. Instead, the human-looking one stepped closer and smiled. Started to speak. Tamani couldn't make out what was said, but it didn't seem to matter as the woman started shaking her head. She didn't understand him, either.

The man made slow gestures, as one might when trying to communicate with a frightened child, pointing at the sea, then himself, and her. The woman looked confused, but didn't back away, or try to run. She started making gestures back, but it was clear to Tamani that the effort was fruitless. Still the woman didn't take so much as a single step backward.

Was it possible that she wasn't in danger at all? Perhaps these creatures were merely *connected* with the murders, and the Oracle had misunderstood? Or perhaps they would murder the woman in a blind panic, but only if Tamani surprised them? Just the idea the someone could *actually see the future* had apparently twisted his brain into knots. He was going to have to get over that. He could almost hear Shar reminding him, *caution will save you a thousand times, but hesitation only has to kill you once.* The trouble was knowing the difference.

The creature seemed to give up its attempts to communicate and went back to smiling and charming the woman. He gestured to the other creatures something that needed no translation; *come, join me.*

They all walked out of the water and the singing started up again, louder than ever. Tamani expected them to start changing shape, as their leader had done, but they didn't. Nor did the woman appear at all afraid of the odd-looking creatures. They smiled, showing sharp, triangular teeth, but they were still singing, and the woman seemed completely at ease. There were half a dozen of the singing creatures along with the human-looking one and, having mentally labeled them, Tamani realized they seemed to have two different roles: singers, and the one that changed. Was the singing a lure of sorts? Whatever the process, the woman was helpless against it.

Tamani wanted to go to her. Save her! But the Oracle had at least been right about the time and place, so he had to assume she was right about the peril San Francisco faced. It had been many long years since Tamani was forced to weigh the needs of the many against the needs of the few, but some lessons could never be forgotten. He clamped his teeth so hard he was a little afraid he was going to break a tooth. Standing by went against everything within him—it made him warm with anger. *Hot* with anger.

No.

He *literally* felt warm. Tamani narrowed his eyes and watched as the other creatures joined the transformed one on the beach and made a circle around the girl, continuing to sing. They weren't attacking, but there was a very distinct warm feeling in Tamani's chest as they moved in a slow, undulating circle around her that looked almost like the choreography Rowen lived to study and perform. Now that they were nearer, the warmth in his chest was stronger—and undeniable.

"Earth and sky," Tamani breathed as he watched the girl join the creatures and walk toward the ocean entirely under her own power, her hand in the handsome male's. He knew what he was feeling; he'd felt it a thousand times. This was Enticement. Those weren't trolls out there, leading a human girl to her death in the sea—they were, somehow, impossibly, *fae.*

The woman was up to her knees in the surf, her jeans soaked, probably shivering, but she didn't protest.

"Screw this," Tamani grumbled, and started to step out from behind the rock.

But one look out to sea stopped him in his tracks. He wouldn't have seen them without Laurel's night vision potion, but there were dark mounds out in the ocean that he had thought were choppy waves, beyond the breakers.

They weren't waves at all. They were the strange sea fae, their heads poked up just above the water. Dozens. Maybe a hundred. His eyes darted desperately between the woman and the hordes of sea faeries awaiting her.

The woman was up to her neck, her progress utterly peaceful, and Tamani fought the urge to close his eyes. To turn away. Charlotte was right. Saving this one human tonight would cost them everything. At best, all of those creatures would swarm Tamani, kill him—kill the woman anyway—and go right on abducting humans.

At *best.*

At worst, they'd run away, regroup, and go to another

shoreline city. Maybe Tamani would find them before they attacked *en masse*, but hundreds of lives could be lost before he even knew it was happening. Thousands. More, if Charlotte were to be believed. And after what he'd just seen, Tamani was *very* inclined to believe the cryptic Oracle.

But if there was one standard Tamani stood by, had had pounded into him by Shar, it was facing the consequences of one's actions. So with his fists clenched, and one sugary tear tracing its way down his cheek, he watched as the water closed over the woman's head, and the creatures dragged her out to sea.

FOURTEEN

"AND TURN AND RIGHT ARM, AND, YES, THERE WE are!" Mitchell's frenetic coaching had finally turned positive. Victorious. It took a full weekend of dancing in front of Tamani's computer screen, and four days of working through the steps for hours after class, but finally, the *pas de deux* was coming together.

Mitchell laughed his contagious laugh as they struck the final pose. He left her, briefly, to turn off the sound-making devices Rowen couldn't have even begun to figure out, then ran back to kiss her on both cheeks. Walking was never good enough for Mitchell, who was eternally swaying, sashaying, or skipping to beats both real and imagined. "You're saving my career."

"Please, you're so good—I'm practically an ornament." She grinned up at him. She'd come to the realization that his overblown flattery really did make her feel more confident, even though she knew it was just that. Praise, much less exaggerated praise, didn't come easily Rowen, but she liked attempting to return the favor. He certainly beamed when she managed to do it without sounding sarcastic.

In fact he was beaming now, his eyes sparkling and with a brightness in his face that still made her shake her head in wonder that he wasn't actually fae. He lifted her hands to his mouth and kissed them enthusiastically. "We're both exquisite, but it does help to know the choreography." He sobered and squeezed her fingers. "Row, it took a lot of extra effort on your part and you need to know that I really, *really* appreciate it. It matters so much."

"Anything for you," Rowen replied, letting his compliment roll off her.

"I," Mitchell said with a dash of melodrama, "am going to let you off early tonight."

"Early?" she said, an eyebrow raised.

"Only two hours of extra practice *is* early!"

And Rowen had to confess he was right—this week, anyway. All week long, neither had left the studio until the sky was dark. And once Rowen got home—to an empty apartment, as Tamani had gone back to Orick for a bit—she'd put in another hour with the computer and her barely-functional new knowledge of YouTube, mirroring the dancer on the screen, over and over. But the smile on his face when she'd managed to complete the dance without a single misstep had been worth it.

She and Mitchell hugged and made their farewells—with a gaiety that had been sadly absent since his discovery that she didn't know the dance—and Mitchell headed out of the studio ahead of her, already dialing his phone. Rowen moved more slowly. It had been an odd, lonely week. The plan had always been for Tamani to only come down to San Francisco occasionally; he and Laurel had a sprout to nurture, after all. But his departure had seemed … abrupt, somehow. And while his absence wasn't terrifying, as it might have been scant weeks ago, it was a *little* scary to be surrounded by humans without a Spring faerie nearby to control them, if necessary.

Furthermore, his departure meant that she'd ridden the train in to the dance school every day. That by itself was almost as much an education as her hours exploring this *Nutcracker*. Humans in dizzying variety rode the train—old and young, large and small, every color of skin and hair and clothing imaginable. They were a mixed flowerbed to rival any in Avalon. And so many! Hundreds upon hundreds, everywhere you looked, like there was a festival going on at every place the train stopped. The humans talked, ate, read books, listened to music, or—like Rowen—simply sat in silence, hunched down in their seats. The children looked much more like fae children than the *baby* Rowen had seen at Cheslea's—still alarmingly slow-witted for their size, but Rowen had to keep reminding herself that in their minds, *she* was physically behind for her own age.

Different species, different species, she often chanted to herself as she watched those young humans on the train. But she'd gotten used to them, for the most part. They knew how to follow rules and create some semblance of order. They weren't the completely mindless animal herd she'd imagined as a sprout. They weren't fae, they weren't even proper *plants*, but she was starting to see what Tamani enjoyed about them. Why he felt that odd kinship. They were cute—amusing. Like Mitchell.

Rowen stood and shouldered her rucksack, anxious to get back into the sunlight. Going without sunlight most of the day was proving her most difficult adjustment, and in that regard the extra hours after class weren't helping. Laurel had provided her with some energy potions—though Rowen hadn't really understood why, at the time—and while they helped some, Rowen had learned to take advantage of sunlight when she could. She'd adjusted her sleeping schedule to rise with the sun and take a book or her new *lap top* out to the apartment's balcony to soak in the sun for a couple hours before it was time to leave for the studio. Then she would spend as much of her lunch break as possible on the rooftop courtyard of the dance school in order to make it through her afternoon.

Between that, and more food than she'd ever eaten in her life, it was working, but with the addition of the long hours this week, it was a near thing.

As Rowen left the studio, she pulled her hoodie up around her face, not wanting anyone to stop her for a chat on the way out. She hadn't felt the long, sharp rays of sunset on her face for days and she craved them—could almost feel them calling to her through the hallways as they bent through windows: reds and oranges and purples washed out by the humming white tubes that accounted for most of the indoor lighting here. Closer, closer. And then she was at the door, bursting through, her face tilting toward the sky.

If she'd have just kept her eyes on the ground, maybe she wouldn't have missed him. Instead, she bounced right off of Shawn and almost fell—would have, if large hands hadn't closed around her arms, righting her.

"Careful there. If you injure your feet Mitchell will kill me." A pause as Rowen tried to catch her breath, not looking up; as if not seeing him would keep him from being there. "Possibly literally," he added with a chuckle.

Rowen groaned in her head. Meghan's brother. *Shawn*, her traitorous mind filled in. *Meghan's brother*, she argued back.

She regained her footing and pulled away from him as quickly as possible. Their eyes met for an instant, before Rowen scrunched up her nose and looked at the ground beside her shoes. "Excuse me," she mumbled. She stepped to the side searching with lowered eyes for the nearest patch of sunlit concrete.

"So you're mad at me now," he said, falling into step beside her, to her great annoyance.

"Wouldn't you be?" She halted, not wanting to talk to him, but also not wanting him to follow her. She pushed her hood back, turning her face away from him and to the waning sunlight again. At least *that* was working out as planned.

"Because I didn't defend you, a stranger, to my twin sister? My very best friend in the whole world?"

His words were true—Rowen couldn't have had any expectation that he would do such a thing—but it wasn't that. Or perhaps it was more than that. But she didn't let that paralyzing sensation get it's hooks into her. She spoke, because if she didn't, she'd never be able to get the courage up to do it again, and somehow she knew she would always resent that. "No. Because as soon as you found out who I was, you looked at me like I was something disgusting. A weed you wanted to pluck out and cast into the burn pile." Rowen forced herself to snap her mouth closed—Tamani had warned her that fae idioms would put people off. She leaned against the warm, grey wall, suppressing another flicker of annoyance when Shawn joined her.

He was quiet for a long time, but Rowen wasn't going to

slink away. She'd been here first; if he didn't want to talk to her, *he* could leave.

"I thought about you a lot over the weekend," he said at last. "Realized a couple of things. Everything went sour after Meghan came. In the hallway, I mean. But even though you didn't talk much, things happened before that. We were friendly, weren't we?"

He paused and Rowen realized he actually expected her to answer that. "Aye," she said tentatively.

"You'd seen me by that point, and it's pretty obvious that I'm black, so you're not a racist, which some ballet people are. And you'd heard that I was Meghan's brother from Mitchell, so whatever Meghan says, I'm inclined to believe you're also not a classist."

Rowen didn't even know what a classist was, but she'd learned to keep her mouth shut when she didn't know what a human word meant.

"But most importantly, Mitchell totally vouched for you." Shawn crossed his arms over his chest and turned his own face to the sunshine. "I like Mitchell. And despite his happy demeanor, that boy's been through things in life. He's a good judge. That he likes you means something to me. So now I'm left with Meghan, who definitely despises you."

Rowen let out a snort and turned away from him.

"She says you're as big a snob as everyone else in her class, but that you mock her to her face. That you go out of your way to make her feel small, and downplay her effort and skills."

Rowen's mouth dropped open and indignation burned within her at hearing such false accusations. It was completely unfair to be judged so harshly without ever getting a chance to defend herself. But pride burned just as fiercely and, even as Shawn turned and caught her with her mouth open, she slammed it shut and gritted her teeth.

"So you tell me, *Rowen*," he said, drawling her name. "Why does Meghan hate you when Mitchell doesn't?"

Anger warred with her need to defend herself and even as she spoke, she wasn't sure which one would win. "I'd said not twenty words to your sister before last Friday, and half of them were that she was very good. If that's mockery, I wish people would mock *me* more." She pushed away from the wall and started to walk away, but Shawn lifted an arm and blocked her path.

"This is your chance, Rowen," he said softly. "I'm listening."

"Listening for justification I shouldn't have to give you."

"My sister is my closest friend. Has been my whole life. If she knew I was even talking you she'd feel betrayed. I don't do this lightly."

"I did nothing. Maybe if she gave anyone a chance instead of assuming they all hate her!" she shouted, then felt silly and folded her arms across her chest, retreating inward again. "Doesn't she understand it's become a self-fulfilling prophecy?"

"Has it?"

What did he want her to say? Did he expect her to apologize even though she'd done nothing wrong? That would be totally unreasonable, but he didn't *seem* unreasonable. After a long look he lowered his arm, giving her the option of walking away. In that moment Rowen decided to talk to him. She wasn't trapped—a human was just trying to *communicate* with her, as no human had. Even Mitchell, who was a fantastic partner, had a tendency to talk more *at* her than *with* her. After sneaking a couple of glances at Shawn's face, Rown finally said, "I didn't know what a scholarship was."

"You what?"

She closed her eyes and counted to five. "I thought a scholarship was a person. A skilled person who earned a special label at auditions. That's what I thought the teachers meant. When I asked her the first day of class if she was the scholarship I thought it was a badge of honor. She had to be better than everyone to get to come here as a—no, *with* a scholarship. I didn't know the other dancers thought it was bad." She stared back down at her shoes.

After long seconds a low laugh rumbled out of him. "Really?"

"Where I come from, no one pays tuition," she muttered defensively to the ground. "They just try out. You make it, or you don't."

"Where are you from, Russia?"

"A little town in Scotland," she recited by rote. "I tried to make nice with Meghan—I told her she was really good. But that only made her angrier."

"Makes sense," Shawn said with another low laugh.

Rowen didn't think it made sense at all.

A car horn gave a series of short honks and she looked up as Tamani's convertible pulled to the curb.

"That's my uncle," she said, hiding her surprise. He had to have just gotten back into town. She hedged past Shawn, speed-walking for Tamani's car. She didn't know what brought Tam back but was in no mood to question her luck.

Her hand was on the door handle and Tamani was opening his mouth to greet her when Shawn said, "Now that you know, you've got to understand how she must have felt. Surely you can see that."

Anger boiled inside her and, ignoring Tamani's questioning look, she pivoted and was back in front of Shawn in three long steps. "Know this, Mr. Make-Peace," she said in a hissing whisper. "I would never, ever, form such a negative, hurtful opinion about someone—not to mention spread it around to others—on such a flimsy foundation. Never."

She tossed her bag into the back seat of the convertible and slid into the passenger seat, refusing to look at Shawn again, much as she wanted to.

Thankfully, Tamani only raised his eyebrows and pulled away from the studio—but as he did, Rowen realized, with a deep pit in her stomach, that she had just told an enormous lie. Wasn't that *exactly* what she'd done, when she first came to the human world? Laurel's dad, Chelsea's baby, the humans in her dance class—looking over at Tamani, her eyes wide, she finally understood what her uncle had been trying to teach her for weeks. No, for years.

And she started to cry. Wrenching, core-deep sobs that hurt her stomach as she gasped and doubled over, scarcely hearing Tamani's words of concern. She barely felt it when he brought the car to a stop, reaching out to hold her against his chest, both arms tight around her, not saying a word. For a long time she sobbed in his arms, oblivious to the world around her, remembering only how deeply it hurt to be so dismissed and discarded through no fault of her own. To be looked at as so undeserving of even minimal esteem.

She'd done the same thing as she hated Meghan for doing—she'd done it to humans who didn't even know it, and worse, a handful who *did*. When she finally regained control she looked up at Tamani, who said nothing—didn't press—but his eyes were full of questions.

Rowen stared down at her hands as fear overwhelmed her anger, but she knew it was time, and that she wouldn't be able to live with herself if she didn't do what she knew needed to be done. As soon as possible. *You'll be sorrier*, Tamani had said. *That's when I'll take you back to apologize.*

How right he'd been.

"Tam," Rowen said, her voice shaky, "can we go to Chelsea's house?"

FIFTEEN

"I'M PROUD OF YOU," TAMANI SAID—AND HE WAS. It took strong fibers to admit you'd done something wrong. Even more to admit it without offering any justification or excuse. And if Rowen wasn't entirely anxious to hold the little one afterward, well, human babies were quite messy; even Tamani had to admit that.

Rowen stepped out of the elevator, still jumping over that tiny crack as if afraid she might slip through the half-centimeter opening, and they made their way into the apartment.

Tamani was exhausted; though the sun was barely setting, the evening rays casting a pinkish glow across the furniture, all he wanted to do was fall into bed, or even the couch, and sleep.

"I'm going to Orick tomorrow," he said, tossing his car keys into a dish by the door.

"Orick? But—you just got back."

Tamani hesitated. He knew he needed to tell her, but his impulse as an uncle was to protect his niece. His niece who, in his eyes, would always be the frightened five-year-old he and Laurel had rescued a decade ago in Avalon. The day she became an orphan. "Um," he said, caught in minor indecision, "Technically I never left."

"What do you mean, you never left? You certainly weren't here."

"No, but I didn't leave town. I've been at the shore."

She blinked. "Staying there? *Living* there?"

He could practically see what he was imagining; one of the *urban campers* that were as much a fixture of California's beaches as the sand and the palm trees. But "living" was hardly what he's been doing. He'd spent every waking moment looking for signs of the sea fae. He'd ranged as far north and south as the abductions—and bodies—had appeared, entirely without success. That woman they took hadn't even washed ashore yet. The human news media was still talking about her as a missing person rather than a murder. Tamani knew better.

His impulse was to continue searching, but the salted air had seeped into Tamani's skin and worn down his stamina so badly he simply couldn't stay another day. Especially not when he hadn't seen Laurel in ten days. Not when he hadn't talked to their sprout in just as long. It felt almost like when he'd been serving as sentry to Laurel during high school and could only observe her from afar on an irregular basis. He thought he'd left those days behind forever. Being separated from her was a dagger in his chest; a wound only she could close.

"Sort of," he said when he realized Rowen was waiting in silence for an answer. "Investigating." He straightened. "Point is, I'm going back to Orick tomorrow, back to Avalon, and I think you should come with me."

"I can't," she said casually, dropping her rucksack. "I have practice tomorrow with my partner. But maybe next time. Send Grandmother my love."

Rowen started to turn, but Tamani stopped her with a hand on her shoulder. "I didn't mean for a visit."

She studied him with glittering eyes. Hard eyes. An expression she'd never used with him before. "You want me to leave permanently?"

"Permanent sounds so … permanent," Tamani said lamely, feeling his weariness catching up with him.

"It does, fancy that."

"I'm … dealing with something dangerous," Tamani confessed. "And I would feel better if you were farther away from it."

"So dangerous that this is the first I've heard of it?"

"Threats like this aren't the kind to give a lot of warning." Tam remembered what the Oracle had said, that the entire city, and after them, the entire world, was in jeopardy. "If Laurel were here, I'd be sending her to Orick. And I'm going to have to increase the guard, there, anyway."

"I can't."

"I know, practice. But call someone or something. Beg off."

"No," Rowen retorted, "I seriously mean that I *can't*. Mitchell needs me."

"Mitchell?" Tamani sifted through his memories for references to the name. "Is that the boy you were talking to when I pulled up to the school?"

"What? No," Rowen said, but her eyes darted away from him. "That's just a—a guy," she said, waving her hand as though she could distract him with it.

Tamani was having none of that. "What kind of guy?"

Rowen spread her arms in a wide shrug like he was speaking gibberish. "A human guy. The only kind they grow around here."

If only. "You seemed to be having a pretty intense conversation with him."

"Fight. Not conversation. Fight. He was being a jerk, and I called him on it."

"He made you cry." Tamani's words hung in the air.

"I don't need you to kill him to defend my honor," Rowen said dryly.

Tamani closed his eyes and groaned. "That is *not* what I meant." He was too exhausted to hold his temper but, sadly, it was probably time to have this conversation. "I meant that he obviously inspired strong feeling in you. Typically that means you care what his thinks."

"I don't know what you're getting at," Rowen said, turning and walking to the fridge for a can of Sprite.

But her easy dismissal told Tamani that she knew precisely what he was getting at, *and* that he was right. "You like him."

She looked up and met his eyes, her cheeks round with the gulp she'd just taken. For a fraction of a second he though she was going to sputter and spit it on him. But she managed to get it down with minimal coughing. "You're kidding, right?"

"That's not a no."

"No! Absolutely not! Don't be ridiculous."

"Is it?"

"Yes!" After a moment, she added, "Ew," but it was half-hearted.

"Well, if things ever change, you should be careful."

"Change? Yeah, because what I really need in my life right now is someone to twine with who I have to lie to, hide from, and never—ever—take home to meet my friends. That sounds splendid."

"It wouldn't be the first time, you know."

"Yes, I know the story of Guinevere and Arthur. I

probably know it better than you do," Rowen grumbled.

"I *lived* it—with Laurel. And David."

She raised her eyebrows at him, but the expression softened and then turned sheepish when Tamani's serious face didn't budge.

"If things ever do go that direction, you need to be careful … about kissing."

She let out an agonized wail and covered her face with her hands. "Uncle Tam! Really?"

"Hey, there's no one else here to tell you these things." He spread his hands in compromise. "Let's make this about humans, not you. Human tears and sweat and … such … aren't sweet; they're salty."

She peeked out from between her fingers. "What?"

"Ours are sugary. Like flower nectar." He paused, fiddling with a piece of junk mail on the counter. "That also applies to your … spit."

"So? Oh!" He saw the understanding dawn on her face and if it was possible for faeries to blush, he knew she'd be as red as a poppy.

"So, Laurel and David—um—oh."

Rowen stopped before actually forming a question, much to Tamani's relief. Coming out the victor had blunted his jealousy, but the physical aspects of his partner's first love really wasn't a subject on which he wanted to converse in detail. "So," he said, too-loudly, "I really think it would be better for everyone if you came back to Avalon with me. Or Orick, if you prefer. Just until things die down."

"I can't ditch Mitchell," Rowen said slowly, deliberately, as though she were speaking to a young sprout.

Goddess, but he was tired. "Who is Mitchell again?"

"Mitchell's my *pas de deux* partner. The guy I dance with."

Tamani stared at her silently. She seemed to think that was all the explanation required, and Tamani still didn't understand.

"We've been working for hours upon hours on this dance that we're auditioning for next week. I can't drop out; he'd never be able to get someone else ready in time. He's depending on me, Tam."

Tamani studied her. "What's so important about him?"

She leaned over the counter on her elbows. "When he found out I didn't even know this dance that everyone else in, apparently, the whole world knows, he didn't give up on me. He showed me how to catch up, and we've worked so hard just to be as good as everyone else was to begin with. We have a super long week ahead of us if we're going to be ready for auditions by Friday."

"It's one audition."

"It's not one audition; it's *the* audition. The one that will determine his entire career." She straightened and folded her arms over her chest. "You can't teach me to see humans as equals and then expect me to be fine sloughing off this one just because *you* don't know him."

Tamani grimaced. She was right about that, of course. But— "Is it worth risking your life?"

"I've seen you risk worse to keep your word."

He pursed his lips but couldn't argue.

"I don't know what's going on, Tam. And you clearly don't feel like telling me. But I can't leave him. I can't leave *them*. I know I haven't been here very long, but there are people in this school counting on me. A dance *corps* is like … I don't know."

"A family?" Tamani whispered, his chest aching all over again at his longing for his own.

Rowen shook her head. "Different. More like your sentry teams. They work together, compete with one another, even, but it's for the good of the whole. They need everyone. They need *me*, Tam. I haven't felt needed in so long."

It was the tiny wobble in her voice that made the decision for Tamani. The decision that he should let *her* make the decision. He slid off the barstool with a sigh. "Okay. You can stay. *I* still have to go, but you can stay."

She bounced around the counter and threw her arms around him. "Thank you, thank you, thank you!"

But when he put his hands on her shoulders and pushed her back enough to see his face, he was deathly serious. "While

I'm gone—no, all the time—stay away from the beach."

"Why would I want to go to the beach? I don't know why *you* wanted to go to the beach. Salt and sand? No, thank you."

"Human kids like to. You might get invited along. I want you to promise me."

"That I won't go to the beach?"

"Yes."

She finally registered his intensely serious tone and she nodded and said, "I promise."

He hesitated and then added, "And if something should happen on the beach—attacks, people going missing, people … people coming out of the water—I want you to get on the BART and go east. Go as far east as it'll take you and then keep walking."

"Walking east?" she asked, confusion clear on her face. "You're kind of scaring me."

"Good. Because I haven't figured out what's happening yet, but some humans have died already. It's not trolls—" he added, noting the panic creeping into Rowen's expression, "—but I have reason to believe it could get just as bad if I don't find a way to stop it. If something happens, you use that phone to call me, or call Laurel if I don't answer." He looked out at the pink horizon. "And you get as far from the ocean as you can."

SIXTEEN

IT REALLY WAS TAMANI'S FAULT. ROWEN WAS SO focused on his nebulous warning that she wasn't really watching where she was going. Someone gripped her by the arm and pulled her into a closet, closing the door and plunging them into darkness. Panic fluttered in Rowen's stems until something illuminated Shawn's face.

Just Shawn. Not trolls, not a mysterious monster on the beach, just the human boy who refused to like her. Rowen closed her eyes and sighed, her whole body threatening to crumple in relief. But the blue-tinted light reflecting from Shawn's eyes was coming from his phone—and seeing it made Rowen realize she'd accidentally left her own phone on the kitchen counter, in spite of the promise Tamani had extracted that she'd keep it with her at all times. If he tried to call and she didn't answer, what would he do?

Rowen grimaced.

"Sorry," Shawn said with a grin that might have been appealing in regular lighting, but the phone shining beneath his chin just made him look spooky. "I dropped Meghan off outside her studio, but who knows when she'll pop back out and …" He shrugged. "No need to make her upset."

"So, instead you're chatting with me in a dark closet," Rowen deadpanned.

"Only for a *moment*," he said in leaning toward her in mock offense. "You were right, and I should form my own opinion of you."

"Gracious," she said, raising one eyebrow.

"I'd really like to go back to the opinion we were forming of each other the day we met."

His face was close to Rowen's and when his warm breath curled around her she remembered what Tamani said about salty tears—wondered if his mouth would taste of salt, too. The scent that traveled on his breath wasn't salty at all—it was a rich, bitter smell that she recognized from the steaming concoctions Mitchell was always drinking. She tried to respond, but her throat seemed to close around her words, locking them in.

"We were off to a good start, don't you think?"

And then she felt his hands slide onto her hips. Not hard, not to pull her forward, just lightly sitting on her hips. She could easily have pulled away—but she didn't. It was the same place Mitchell had set his hand a thousand times in preparation for a lift; why did it feel different when Shawn did it? Why did she want to cover Shawn's hands with her own and pull *herself* closer? Closer to this *human* boy? It felt so terribly wrong and right all at once.

She found herself uncomfortably aware of the way her arms were folded across her chest—she didn't want to seem aloof—but when she loosened them, there was nowhere for them to go except onto Shawn's thick forearms.

Her fingers were like skittish butterflies, alighting on his skin, flinching away, settling again. She was breathing in fast, erratic puffs, and couldn't seem to stop as her fingers slid up his arms, almost of their own accord, up to his shoulders. Then her fingertips were tugging, gently, tugging him toward her.

Or were his fingertips pulling on her hips?

His forehead touched hers and his breathing was as ragged as her own, puffs of air that breezed by her chin. The tips of their noses touched, slid to the side, and when his mouth was just a whisper away, she heard Tamani's words. *It wouldn't be the first time.* Her conscience pricked, but like a roaring river, there was no halting what was about to happen.

Warm lips brushed hers. Almost a question.

May I?

Her fingers tightened on his shoulders and she pushed her mouth against his, tasting just a hint of the bitter scent she'd caught before. It was short. A brief, firm touching of mouths before she turned her head and looked away, feeling … ashamed? Confused?

But still happy?

She'd made up her mind to treat humans with greater respect, and this particular human was especially interesting to her, but she was working against a lifetime of mental inertia. Things seemed to change so *fast* on this side of the gate!

To Rowen's surprise, Shawn was grinning.

"So we can start from scratch?" he whispered.

"Is this scratch?" she asked, forgetting that she shouldn't question humans on their saying and idioms.

He chuckled, as though she'd said something clever. "Maybe a step above scratch." He pushed back her bangs and cupped her face with one hand. "I'll let you get through auditions—I know how important they are," he said solemnly. "Then let's get together. Away from here." He leaned forward, his cheek against hers, mouth close to her ear. "This place makes people a little crazy."

She laughed. He wasn't wrong; it had been much the same in the *corps* in Avalon.

"You sneak out first," he said, reaching for the doorknob. "I'll wait a couple minutes. We'll talk later."

Rowen nodded and reached for the knob, her hand over his, then paused. "Will you tell Meghan?"

He sucked in a loud breath and held it for several long seconds. "I think," he finally said, "that depends on how auditions go."

***

"I don't understand how they can be fae," Yasmine said, her face crumpled with concern as she joined Tamani and Laurel on one of the Gate Garden's many stone benches.

Tamani held Laurel's hand in his lap, fingers clasped tightly in his own. He hated that he was, for the second time in little more than a decade, bearing ominous tidings to Avalon. Of course, Klea's attack wasn't the last time Avalon found itself torn by conflict; though Yasmine's coup had been relatively peaceful by comparison. But Laurel—and, by extension, Tamani—had been safe in San Francisco, in the student housing at Berkeley. About as surrounded by humans as possible.

Tamani hadn't grown complacent, exactly, but there had definitely been a settling in—a feeling of safety that had become his new baseline. His new *normal.* He couldn't remember a time in his life when he didn't love Laurel, so the risk of personal loss had been with him during the years he faced constant danger on her behalf, but in the last dozen years their love had grown like an oak, becoming a stronger and more deeply-rooted version of the sapling it had once been.

The concept of loss felt far more tragic now. And with a seedling on the way? Tamani couldn't put into words the degree of fear that washed over him at the thought of that round, green pod coming to harm.

Which was why he'd struggled with the decicion of whether to send Laurel to Avalon with his questions, while he remained in Orick—or to go to Avalon on his own, leaving Laurel to protect their home. Much as she hated fighting, Laurel was an extremely gifted Mixer; in her home, surrounded by her gardens, she would make an extremely dangerous foe. But in the end, he'd had to trust Laurel's parents and the Gate sentries to mind things for a while. Tamani needed to be here because he was the one who saw the sea-fae, and he needed Laurel here to lend her wisdom.

"I don't understand it, either, and I've had more than a week to think about it. They didn't look a thing like us. I mean, they looked like … plants. And they came up out of the *salt*water like they belonged there. All I know for certain is what I felt, and what I felt was Enticement. It's unmistakable—any half-trained sentry would be able to confirm it." He was actually a little chagrinned it had taken him as long as he did to identify the sensation. But he couldn't have expected anything of the sort!

Yasmine rose and slowly paced the verdant clearing, her long, sparkling train spreading out behind her. She was stunning regardless, but in her regal attire and the sparking noon light, she looked exactly like what she was: the stately monarch of this and every forest—the center of Avalon's magic and might.

"Here is my dilemma," Yasmine said softly, turning to face him. "This simply is not my problem."

Tamani's brow furrowed. He wasn't sure just what he'd expected from the faerie queen, but this wasn't it. But she met his eyes resolutely, and he found himself wanting to look away.

"My first and most sacred responsibility is the safety and welfare of Avalon and its occupants. With the help of a traitor, our land was ravaged by our ancient enemies, and in the wake of that upheaval we took it upon ourselves to cast off much of our culture as well. I'm doing my best to hold our world together, but I'm only barely succeeding." She swallowed hard and finally dropped her gaze. "Especially since Jamison left me."

"I think you're doing admirably," Tamani said, but stopped when Yasmine held up a hand.

"I wasn't troweling for compliments," she said. "If there was one thing Jamison taught me, it was to never make any decision lightly. *Quickly* is sometimes necessary, but never without grave regard for the consequences. The choice he made to grant David and Chelsea passage into Avalon all those years ago was one he agonized over, and he wasn't fully certain until the very, very end that he'd made the right decision."

"Even after the sword?"

"Even after the sword," she said steadily. "The second thing he taught me is that a ruler's responsibility is to her people first, and her ideals second." Yasmine returned to the bench to sit beside Tamani. "The idealist in me wants to defend the humans against this threat. But my people?" She shook her head. "They're not equipped. Not physically or emotionally. Not even with the appropriate knowledge to predict whether or not we could defeat such a foe. Am I wrong?"

Tamani realized he'd been grimacing. He forced the disgruntled expression from his face and conceded, "You're not wrong."

"If I were to go to the Spring Square right this moment and ask who would be willing to risk their lives for the humans, for an unknown length of time, against a completely unknown foe, how many do you think would volunteer?"

Tamani flexed his jaw, but all three of them knew the answer.

"I could order them," Yasmine said. "And they would obey. But who would that benefit? The faeries? No."

"So you won't help me?"

"It's not clear to me that I *can*," she said. "If I sent you back today with soldiers, potions, weapons—what would you do with them? How would you prepare them against an unknown enemy? It will be many years more before the Spring guard is fully replenished, far longer for the population of Fall faeries, and what weapons and potions we have already seems too little. I can't endanger my subjects to protect a group of people exponentially more numerous than us, who don't even know of our existence." She hesitated. "And I fear that if I did, the result would be an immediate need to protect ourselves from *them*."

Tamani couldn't fault her logic, but he also couldn't deny his core-deep disappointment.

"A queen can never be selfish for herself," Yasmine said. "But she must *always* be selfish for her people. I know you straddle both worlds—both of you," she added, looking at Laurel. "And it is an important role—a *crucial* role. But when forced to choose between my faeries and your humans, I will choose my faeries every time."

Tamani knew she was right, even as he struggled to hold his temper.

"What about my task?" Laurel said, gently. "Protecting the gate could get a lot more complicated if a magical disaster happens in San Francisco. If the U.S. government decides that human-shaped plant life poses a threat to national security, they'll start looking for ways to tell humans and fae apart. And if history is any guide, they'll be inclined to treat us *all* as the enemy."

"Which is why I hope a solution can be found," Yasmine said calmly. "Avalon's resources are, as always, at our scion's disposal—so long as they remain in Avalon. Books, histories, the Academy. You might even check at the Manor, though you'll want to tread carefully there." She leaned forward. "Find me a reason Avalon should participate in your fight, and we will. For now, I can only wish you the goddess' blessing."

Tamani nodded, watching silently as Yasmine and Laurel made their farewells. Then Yasmine's *Am Faire-fear* escorted her back toward the gate that opened into the rest of Avalon.

"What now?" Laurel asked, watching the procession vanish into the forest.

Tamani felt nearly hopeless, but Laurel's very presence kept him from that edge. He always had her. "Resources. Like she said. We find the wisest faerie in Avalon."

She twined her fingers through his. "Yeardley it is."

SEVENTEEN

"WE HAVE A VAST LIBRARY HERE AT THE Academy, of course," Yeardley intoned in the low, gravelly voice that always made him sound older than Tamani knew him to actually be. "But this is only where we keep the texts having to do with biology and chemistry—those directly applicable to our work. I'm not certain that's the sort of research you need."

"Perhaps a potion that would allow a faerie to be submersed for long stretches of time in salt water?" Laurel suggested. "It's possible they come out of the water only to snatch their victims, then they retreat to a more plant-friendly environment."

"Saltwater can be a plant-friendly environment, of course," Yeardley said. "We keep half a dozen large aquariums here."

"Ocean flora," Laurel said softly, and Tamani could almost see a list of potential ingredients racing through her mind. "Sea grasses, kelp, thousands of species of algae."

"But not faeries," Tamani said stubbornly. The idea of submerging oneself in salt water was so counter-intuitive as to simply not be a realistic possibility.

"Still," Laurel said, "salt water plants could potentially be used to protect a faerie against the salt. Like a … vaccine," Laurel said, and Tamani knew she was remembering Klea's work inoculating trolls against Fall faerie magic.

A wrinkle appeared on Yeardley's brow, but he didn't question Laurel's comparison or speak the renegade's name. "It's a start. I can certainly work with Laurel here, but might I suggest you also consult the library at the Manor? You'll find all the historical texts there."

Tamani considered this. History? Could there be records of a faerie species like what he'd seen come out of the ocean? "You … think they once lived in Avalon?"

"I think nothing," Yeardley said. "I'm as mystified as you. But I believe that researching as many hypotheses as possible is in our best interest. Besides, if I remember correctly, you're already well-known at the Manor."

Tamani nodded but didn't speak. The Manor, the fae stronghold built to hide the gate to Avalon in Scotland, was where Shar had taken him to learn how to pass as human. He hadn't been back since Shar died and, even now, it was those memories that made him reticent. But he cleared his throat, forcing his melancholy away. "That's a very good idea, Yeardley, thank you." He turned to Laurel. "Potion research first? Then we can go to the Manor together."

Laurel pursed her lips and peered silently up at him for several long seconds before speaking. He loved that about her; how she considered every word she said. *Before* speaking. But today that considering look made him uneasy. "It really would be more efficient if we split up. We could focus on our own tasks."

Going to Scotland alone—being half a world away from Laurel and their sprout—did not appeal to Tamani. With the magic of the gate it would be little more than a stroll down a path, but he could hardly bear the thought of being separated from her again so soon.

As always, Laurel knew him so well it was as if she could read his thoughts. "I know you want to stand at my back and protect me," she said, softly enough that Yeardley could hear them, but certainly no one else milling around the Academy foyer. "But the best way to protect both me and our seedling is to neutralize this threat as soon as possible." She stroked his arm, softening her words. "I vote for haste."

He gritted his teeth, but she was right. The impulse to remain near wasn't actually helping either of them. He nodded, even though he hated it. "Alright," he said, "you two work here." He grinned, trying to disperse some of the tension. "Looks like I'm walking to Scotland."

***

The Manor never seemed to change. It wasn't just the enormous grey stone building, a craggy mountain of turrets and angles against a bright skyline. The plants looked the same too: acres of gorse, vines hugging the walls, the soft green grass inside the moat, always just a little too long for true elegance. It was a mossy haven that had once welcomed Tamani when he'd felt hopeless, with nothing left to live for. Now it welcomed him again, but he was overwhelmed by the equally devastating state of having everything to live for. Everything to lose.

The front desk was manned by the same ancient faerie who'd been there fourteen years ago, and briefly Tamani wondered if she ever left the desk, or simply slept behind it, waiting for someone to arrive. The wizened fae checked the records mechanically before allowing him entrance. He gave her a long look before entering the cavernous front atrium—even with the natural longevity of fae, the woman was *old.* He recognized the handful of staff and librarians who minced quietly about the halls and a few even smiled at him, apparently recognizing him in turn. He remembered the brash, hot-headed youth he'd been so long ago, going back and forth between sulking darkly in his assigned room and throwing himself into his human lessons with a mania.

The emotions he felt today were no less turbulent; he'd simply learned to hide them better.

After consulting with several librarians who then whispered amongst themselves, they finally decided to take him to the oldest archives. The Manor's stone foundations dated back to the tenth century; the contents of the Manor were even more ancient.

Tamani stood in the doorway of one of the many cavernous rooms, packed with books and scrolls, wondering where he could possibly start. Laurel was the one who enjoyed reading and studying. Tamani was quite fond of fiction—especially human fantasy and science fiction, which he often considered quite humorous in ways he had no doubt the authors didn't intend. But poring over technical material, sieving for information, had always been wearying to Tamani.

And now here he was alone, with thousands upon thousands of ancient texts at his disposal, not to mention an archives assistant waiting to help him with carefully preserved documents, and he had no idea where to even start. He'd hardly known what to even tell them he was looking for. He'd simply asked for written records from before King Arthur. From that point on, Avalon had mostly been closed. Tamani knew nothing like what he'd seen on the beach had existed in Avalon at least that far back.

What he hadn't counted on was how much the language had changed in the last millennium. The librarian assigned to help him had gleefully set out some of their oldest texts and—with an admonition not to touch—left him to study.

He couldn't read them. Gaelic was an ancient language for certain, but this was something else. He had documents that dated back over two thousand years, but he couldn't make out more than a word here or there. He'd finally started peering at the pictures instead, but there was nothing portrayed on the crumbling papyrus that looked anything like the strange sea fae.

Someone cleared their throat behind him and Tamani whirled to find a somewhat diminutive woman with carefully coifed auburn hair, wearing a sleekly-tailored pantsuit and staring at him critically.

"Marion," he said stiffly, inclining his head in greeting, but not in respect. A cast down faerie queen in Chanel—how bizarre. Every cell of training within him urged him to bow, but he refused to do such a thing before the former Avalonian queen ever again. Not as a subject, not as a sentry, and certainly not as a lowly Spring faerie.

"Tamani de Rhoslyn," she said, and part of him felt complimented that she remembered his name. Even as an underling, his impertinence had made enough of an impact on her that she'd remembered his name. He liked to think of himself as the catalyst in the chain reaction that eventually cost Marion her throne—that act of rebellion twelve years ago had forced Marion to show her true colors. Her selfish, bloodthirsty true colors. Her willingness to harm her own subjects merely to get her way. It had truly been the beginning of the end: one brilliantly bright spot in a sea of tragedy, a lighthouse on the shores of the future.

She looked small now. Though Yasmine had been little more than a child the last time Tamani saw the two queens standing side by side, the new queen had grown taller while Marion, stripped of her crown and authority, looked small. Small, and ordinary. He suspected that her expensive human garb made her unique here in the Manor, but in Laurel's world—and, by extension, Tamani's—women with sleek hair and custom-tailored business suits were commonplace. He remembered how Yasmine looked that morning—the way she sparkled in the sun. There could be no doubt, seeing the two of them, who was the true ruler of Avalon.

It occurred to Tamani that if he had come to Marion on behalf of the humans, she'd have refused out of spite. Yasmine hadn't said yes, but she hadn't cut him off completely, either. She's given him a mission.

Marion hesitated a moment longer, as though hoping Tamani might change his mind and genuflect, then she waved at the documents laid out on the table and asked, "What is it you're trying to find here?"

Tamani was silent for a long time, trying to decide how much he could trust her. No, it wasn't even that—he wondered how *helpful* she could possibly be. That she hadn't internalized it didn't change the fact that she'd spent over a century listening to Jamison's wisdom. What other information was the secretive circle of Winter faeries privy to?

"Faeries who can abide salt water?" he finally said.

Both of her eyebrows rose before she could stop them, but an instant later her expression was neutral again. "Drinking it?"

"Swimming in it."

"There isn't such a thing."

He just chuckled and turned his back on her.

"Don't turn your back in my presence."

"You have no authority over me," he said, keeping his back straight to her, peering down at a smudgy drawing. Not because he'd spotted anything in the picture; just because he could.

"And don't you love that," she said sardonically.

He paused, straightened and faced her again. "What are you waiting for?"

"I'm leaving now, don't worry."

"Not me. The Manor. What are you waiting here for? The faeries in Avalon are never going to want you back. You're never going to be queen again."

She laughed softly. Almost sadly. "I know that. I always knew that."

Tamani stilled. "You left. You abdicated your throne to Yasmine and declared to everyone that you would come back when she failed. And you're telling me now that you knew she wouldn't fail?"

"I'd be an idiot if I didn't."

He shook his head. "I don't understand you—I never have."

"They were going to overthrow me." She said it as one would pronounce the sky to be blue, or water to be wet. "They were going to kick me out. So I left before they could. There's a dignity in it."

"Why are you telling me this?"

"You of all fae can understand. Empathize."

"Empathize?" Tamani scoffed. "You're insane."

"Am I?" Her sharp green eyes were anything but. "You're telling me that if Laurel had chosen her human boy, you'd have continued being her *Fear-gleidhidh* for the next hundred and fifty years? You wouldn't have abandoned your post rather than play second best?"

Tamani was stunned into silence, remembering his determination to do just that when he was certain Laurel was going to choose David. He had intended to go to Jamison and beg to be released from his Life Oath.

"The reason we don't get along, Tamani de Rhoslyn, isn't because we're so different, but because we're so very much the same. Brash, determined, unable to handle defeat on any level. That's why you're here, isn't it?"

"I'm here to research a threat to the human world," Tamani said between clenched teeth.

"Because you want to be the hero. The savior." She leaned forward with a sympathetic smile. "You want to be the one everyone looks to in admiration. Just like me."

Tamani wanted to snap back that his intentions weren't so self-serving, but she'd planted a seed of doubt. Was he doing this for himself? Was he casting his motivation on Laurel and their sprout when in reality he had aspirations of grandeur?

"The reason Winter faeries continue to rule Avalon, in spite of the … *egalitarianism* you've imported from human culture," she said, mocking, "is that a only the Winter fae can maintain the barrier around the island that prevents its discovery by the humans, and purifies the ocean around it. There are, of course, other reasons you want us around—you've seen more of what we can do than most. But the threat of salt is the ability most directly associated with faerie survival."

"So because you can't personally imagine something, it must not exist," Tamani said, his words cutting. "Tucking your head under a cabbage leaf and ignoring the existence of anything you don't personally approve of is your specialty." He glared at her. "And your downfall."

"I've learned my lesson, you know."

"Have you?" he asked. "My apologies if I fail to see any evidence of such a thing."

She laughed. "Now who fails to accept what he cannot imagine? Nonetheless, you are right. I didn't want to believe inconvenient truths, like a Fall faerie gone rogue. Or any faerie who would join forces with a horde of trolls, even if she ultimately had their deaths in mind. Or the destructive strength of her potions. There were many mistakes made that day, and not just mine. But what I'm telling you now is that salt is inimical to our lives and our magic both. In all my years, I've never heard of a fae who could abide it for long."

"Which is why I'm here," Tamani snapped with growing impatience. "To read about faeries you *haven't* heard of."

"There's an easier way."

He turned again, and Marion was leaning against the doorway, examining her fingernails. "I'm listening. With great skepticism," he drawled.

"There's one place in the world that has always protected secrets and mysteries nigh unfathomable to any other fae."

Tamani forced himself not to shout at her, but it took three deep breaths. "That, Marion, is why I am here."

Her laugh was pleasant this time, almost musical but for

the harsh edge that seemed to flay him from the inside out. "I don't mean the Manor, you ridiculous Ticer. You want facts, histories, legends, even, you come here. Read the dusty tomes and take your copious notes, and even if you stayed for weeks, I wager you'd find nothing." Marion took a few steps toward him. "You want to learn about the impossible? The forbidden? The stories so dangerous no one would dare utter them louder than a whisper, much less write them down?"

They were almost toe to toe, and the deposed queen seemed taller, somehow, than she'd been when she entered the room. Tamani forced himself to hold very still as she sidled up to him, bringing her mouth close to his ear.

"For that, you go to the same place Callista went. You go to the Unseelie. Your departed mentor, Shar de Mischa, taught me that—weren't you listening?"

EIGHTEEN

THE TENSION IN THE AIR AT SCAZIO CRACKLED like a popping fire and burned just as hot. Rowen walked around the crowded studio in her toe shoes, keeping her stems limber, staying in motion. Mitchell, who seemed to cope with nervousness by spouting nothing but uselessly obvious advice, had chased her down and *stopped* her to suggest she keep moving—as if she didn't already know, wasn't already doing that, hadn't in fact *stopped* doing that to speak to him. Unable to get a word in edgewise, she'd finally flashed him a glare, prompting a stuttering apology—and a quick recitation of his confidence in her, which would have been more convincing if he hadn't gone on to remind her to spot during her turns, as if she'd started doing ballet *yesterday.*

She and Mitchell were scheduled for about halfway through the audition lineup. Rowen had tried to read some sort of meaning into it, but Mitchell insisted it was always random.

"In all my years here I've been first and I've been last, and it doesn't seem to make any difference at all. You're trying to read tea leaves."

Tea leaves? Rowen didn't ask.

The stage door opened to the sound of applause as two of Rowen's classmates burst through, grinning and breathing hard. Other students weren't permitted to watch the auditions, but family and friends had been invited to make the auditions feel more like true performances. Of course, there was no one out there to watch Rowen. She swallowed hard against the sudden disappointment that realization brought. She'd been so busy this week, going over every tiny move with Mitchell, that her personal issues had been crowded aside. Mostly, anyway. And in those rare moments she stole for herself, she'd ruminated on her kiss with Shawn—and tried *not* to think about the dire cautions given by her absent uncle.

Tamani had been gone since Monday morning and even though she'd sent a few texts throughout the week, he hadn't responded. Wherever he was, he wasn't getting very good cell service.

"You okay?"

Rowen glanced over at Mitchell. "What? Yes, of course."

"You stopped moving. I don't think I've ever seen someone stand so … *still*."

"Sorry," she mumbled, springing back into motion. She

couldn't afford to let her limbs grow stiff because she was thinking about warm lips brushing hers. "Distracted."

"I'll say." He hesitated, trotting after her, then asked quietly, "You're not going to freeze up on me, are you?"

"Please. I just … need something to drink," she said, pivoting as though that was what had made her pause. It was true though. They'd had classes today, though their teachers hadn't pushed them too hard in light of the evening's auditions. But it was still evening, after a full day of class, and Rowen's body yearned to sleep until the sun was up again. In her bag she had a can of Sprite and one last energy potion from Laurel that she'd saved for tonight. Hopefully Tamani remembered to bring her more when he returned from wherever he was.

Rowen drank the potion first, stretching up and down on her toes as the concoction went through her with a magically invigorating chill, then started on the Sprite. Though the carbonation meant she shouldn't drink *too* much of the latter; how humiliating it would be to let out a belch in the middle of an audition.

After what felt like hours—an impressive feat for what had in actuality been precisely twenty-eight minutes—the time arrived. Good wishes were whispered as they slipped through the door, and Rowen took several deep breaths and stretched her arms back and forth as she rosined up her pointes in the shallow box just offstage.

"You're going to be incredible," Mitchell whispered, smacking her cheek with a loud kiss.

"You too," she said, though without the same gusto. It struck her that, despite years of experience in Avalon, this was a first—the first time she was going to dance before a human audience, in the human world. She was surprised to discover that fact did make her a little nervous.

But then her name was called and Mitchell was escorting her to the middle of the stage. They bowed to the judges, then held very still in their opening pose, and Rowen was surprised to feel the warm sensation of sunlight on her arms. It took her no time at all to realize that it must be the electric stage lights—but even so, it grounded her. Performances in Avalon were usually held during the daylight hours, and in an amphitheatre that opened to the sky. She'd braced herself for this performance to feel much more like dancing in the stifled, enclosed studios, and the refreshing illusion of being back in Avalon bolstered her confidence.

When the music began, hours of practice took over. For now, there was only the dance. She almost could have performed the entire piece with her eyes closed; part of her wanted to do it. Ten seconds later, most of her wished she had. As she came under Mitchell's arm near the end of the *pas de deux*, her eyelids rose and she was bent at just the right angle to see one face, even in the dim auditorium.

Shawn's.

He was smiling—beaming, really—with a smoldering appreciation in his eyes for more than just her dancing. It struck her that this was a boy who could appreciate her on many levels. That she *wanted* him to appreciate her on many, many levels.

It was only when Mitchell pushed her into a turn she should have spun herself into that she realized she'd frozen at the sight of him. How long had it been? It couldn't have been even a full second—they were right back in synch with the music. Rowen smiled at the judges and lifted high on her toes for her next pirouette, wondering if they'd even noticed.

Regardless, Mitchell had—and good thing, too, as he'd managed to cover for her. She knew he'd never mention it, never evoke the guilt she was already feeling, but he knew. He'd had to *push* her back into action and she was furious with herself.

She refused to let her eyes wander in Shawn's direction again for the final minute of the dance, determined to make it up to her partner, drawing on years of experience pushing herself past her limits to reach farther, spin faster, smile wider. When she stepped into their final lift, she knew she'd done well.

But only when the bows were finished and the applause from their test audience rolled in did she let her eyes stray back to Shawn. He was sitting beside a man and a woman who looked remarkably like Meghan, clapping enthusiastically—though the man and woman weren't clapping at all. A strange twist squeezed Rowen's middle, but there was no time to consider it. Mitchell took her hand and they ran off the stage.

On their way out they passed Meghan and Thomas; Mitchell paused to give his boyfriend a good luck kiss, releasing Rowen.

She drifted away from him like a boat untethered from a dock. It had been *years* since she'd frozen in a performance. She glanced back as Meghan and Thomas disappeared behind the curtains, a terrible doubt curling within her as she forced herself to relive that awful, wonderful moment of meeting Shawn's eyes. That smile. No, not a smile, a grin. Perhaps even a smirk.

Had he done it on purpose? She thought back on those blissful moments in the darkened closet, hidden even from Mitchell—who was, she knew, Shawn's friend. Would Shawn risk sabotaging Mitchell if it meant helping Meghan? Had Shawn been trying to sabotage her all along?

No—that was ... paranoid. Rowen was making excuses for herself.

Surely.

Probably.

Without meeting anyone's eyes, Rowen wrapped a skirt over her leotard and tights, then swapped her laced toe shoes for comfy flats. She shouldered her rucksack and was halfway across the studio before Mitchell caught her.

"Where are you going?"

"We're finished," Rowen said, not meeting his eyes, tugging her arm out of his grasp. "I'm going home."

"You can't go home."

She looked up at him. "Why not?"

He squirmed. "Well, I mean you *can*, but it's just not done, Row. We all stay for the whole audition—support, you know. We'll go to Shari's after."

Rowen stifled a groan. Human food at the nearest all-night restaurant. Staying up even later, and expending more energy on illusions to hide what she *wasn't* eating. *So* not what she needed. "That just doesn't sound fun to me, Mitchell," she said, edging toward the door.

He blocked her again, bodily this time. "Rowen, you're the one who wants to be accepted. Part of that means joining us in our traditions. Even if you don't love them. We're a team here and this is a big deal."

She looked around at the other dancers, several of whom were sneaking glances at her and Mitchell.

"Okay," she said, already regretting her choice. "I'll come."

***

Those regrets grew heavier when she realized that Shawn was among a handful of teenagers everyone treated as honorary members of the class; then heavier still on the way across the parking lot, where Rowen found herself choking on a cloud of the toxic smoke some of the other dancers apparently breathed to calm their nerves. She'd coughed the burn out of her throat, but still felt ill.

Rowen knew she couldn't be making a great impression on anyone, but it was almost midnight when she curled her knees up to her chest and burrowed against Mitchell while her sundae melted in front of her. She simply didn't have the energy for illusions right now. Besides, she wasn't the only one not eating the ice cream—several in the group looked like they were there just for the company, including Shawn, who was sitting across the crowded line of tables the server had shoved together to accommodate their group.

Rowen ignored his attempts to catch her eyes.

When even Mitchell's familiar body heat became too oppressive, Rowen excused herself for a breath of fresh air, forcing herself not to run for the door. She lifted her nose toward the clear sky as soon as she got through the door, breathing deeply. The fall air was crisp and humid, and Rowen stood there for several seconds, enjoying the cool stillness; she always preferred being cool and couldn't understand the animal insistence on warmth. Not that it was bad. Just different. So different.

The door to the restaurant squeaked open behind her. "Rowen?"

His voice was a soft whisper, but she heard it as though he'd shouted.

"Shawn." His name fell from her lips without conscious thought.

"You okay?" he asked, coming to stand close to her.

"Yeah," she said, turning away and gesturing vaguely. "You know, air. Stuffy."

He rolled his eyes. "Yeah, it's not my favorite tradition, but Meghan loves it."

The name was like a bolt of lightning between them, making them both stiffen and still.

"Come here," Shawn said, taking her elbow lightly and leading her around the corner. "I just … I just want to see how things go for a while before I get her involved." He gave her a crooked grin. "You don't have to deal with her for the rest of your life, like I do."

She glared. If he thought she was mad that he hadn't told Meghan, it seemed unlikely that he'd distracted her intentionally. But she was emboldened by exhaustion and embarrassment and an insistent need to *know.* "Did you do it on purpose?"

The smile dropped from his face. "Do what?"

"Distract me. Was it all a plan?"

"Whoa, whoa, what?"

She felt her chin tremble, her weary fury melting away, leaving her only with disappointment in herself. "I froze. I met your eyes and you … you *smirked* at me, and I froze. Did you and Meghan plan that?"

"I didn't see you freeze."

She shrugged, looking away from him. "Mitchell pushed me into the next turn. I guess we covered well."

He stepped close and she felt the warmth of his breath against her skin. "All I saw was the best dancer I've ever seen since Meghan got so good."

Rowen's lashes rose and she gave him a hard stare, daring him to patronize her.

"No, really. You were *gorgeous.* I was smiling because I couldn't … not." He grinned, and it had a distinctly sappy quality to it. "You were amazing."

"You didn't try to make me mess up?"

"I would never do that."

"Not even for Meghan?"

He laughed. "No one would be more mad than Meghan if I had done such a thing. The only thing she values more than winning, is winning fair."

Rowen looked for any sign of dishonestly in him, but she found none.

"I tried my best not to distract you. That's why I didn't talk to you all week, like I promised." He groaned. "Oh, I wanted to. Every time I saw you I wished I could talk to you." He tentatively put his hands at her waist. "Hold you." He leaned forward, tipping his head. "Kiss you."

She didn't remember putting her hands on the front of his hoodie. Didn't mean to clench her fists around the fabric and pull him toward her. But then his mouth was on hers and everything—the weariness, the anger and frustration—melted away and nothing existed but the two of them. She kissed him so hard her bottom lip ached, but he didn't pull back and neither did she. His hot breath filled her mouth—such a contrast to the cold air around her—and suddenly she understood the appeal of heat.

He was softness and warm flesh and gasping air and she felt like she couldn't get enough of him. Her shoulders were pinned against the building, Shawn's hand at the back of her thigh pressing her to him, hips together like he was about to stretch her backward in their own intimate *pas de deux*, but this was choreography far older than ballet, these were the steps from which all other dances descended.

This time, Rowen didn't freeze.

NINETEEN

TAMANI PAUSED BEFORE THE GOLDEN SQUARE OF gates that led to the four corners of the wide world. After Marion's departure, he'd spent the rest of the day searching through every faded document the librarians brought him, but she was right. There was nothing there about a secret race of faeries, not so much as a rumor. Only reminders of the rules Tamani already knew. Rules under which it was more likely that Tamani had simply lost his mind than that he'd seen what he thought he saw.

You want to know about broken rules, you go to the people who break them.

He hated that Marion was right. He wasn't willing to risk the lives of millions of humans to soothe his pride, but that didn't mean it was easy to lift his key from the chain he always wore hidden beneath his shirt. A keyhole appeared in the center of the gate leading to Japan and Tamani hesitated—

risking exposure of his secret, his fingers gripping his forbidden key—before forcing himself to insert it, to push open the golden door and feel the chill of the noticeably colder air on his face.

The sentries on the human world side—twice as many as were ever posted at the other three gates—turned as one, their sparkling diamond blades leveled at his chest. They relaxed when they saw him, recognized him, but stayed at attention until the gate closed and disappeared with a flash, resuming its usual shape as a massive cherry tree.

It was, Tamani knew, covered with fragrant pink blossoms all year round, which made for poor camouflage three seasons in four. Fortunately, the land surrounding *this* gate had been secure and under Avalon's exclusive control for centuries; different cultures varied less than some humans liked to imagine, but the people of Japan did seem to have an unusually healthy relationship with the supernatural.

The captain of the company stepped forward and gave a shallow bow. "Tamani de Rhoslyn. It's an honor to receive you. What's your purpose here?"

Honored or no, suspicion colored the captain's tone—likely owing to the fact that no one had caught sight of Queen Yasmine, nor received word from her in advance. Fortunately, suspicion could be ignored, at least temporarily, and Tamani didn't plan to be here very long.

"I need to speak with the Unseelie."

A discontented murmur spread through the group, which seemed odd. It wasn't an ordinary request, especially coming from someone in Tamani's position, but it was hardly unprecedented. Family members occasionally received permission to visit; Shar had made sojourns to speak with his mother almost annually.

He'd always come back unhappy.

"Something wrong?"

"Nothing to worry about," the captain said brusquely. "Some of the green spears just lost a bet they shouldn't have taken in the first place. Before you go inside you'll want to stow your weapons, potions, any ingredients that might go into a mixing. Maybe strip off any outer layers of clothing the prisoners might take advantage of. Not that I expect you to have any problems with them, but … things happen."

Tamani nodded curtly. "Which way?"

The captain pointed Tamani down a path that veered sharply to his left.

"Is it far?" Tamani asked, his words vanishing into the forest that surrounded them.

"Half a mile. It's a delicate balance, keeping them close enough to manage easily but far enough to minimize any threat they might pose to the gate itself."

The captain seemed tense, and Tamani wondered if it was

because he'd arrived unannounced, or because he'd become something of a celebrity among gate sentries, or if it was something else entirely. He'd only been to Japan once before, many years ago, and guarding the Unseelie wasn't a job that had ever interested him, so it was hard to gauge likely points of concern. After a moment's hesitation, he decided to just ask. "Anything I ought to be prepared for?"

"Other than how normal they seem?"

"Do they?"

"In most ways. Listen too closely and you're sure to hear something that'll give you six season's worth of nightmares, but otherwise they're mostly harmless. And their enclosure is quite homey, all things considered."

Homey? That seemed … unlikely. The word "enclosure" made Tamani think of zoos and animals—and of the broken-spirited Winter fae he'd once chained to a chair in his apartment.

But now was not the time for regretful ruminations on the creator of Tamani's remarkable key.

The captain accompanied Tamani down the neatly-manicured path, through mighty conifers and towering broadleaf trees far more reminiscent of Avalon than the forests of America's Pacific Northwest. Nestled between roots or shaded under berry-laden bushes he occasionally spotted tiny decorative houses or neatly-piled stones; signs of a human presence surprisingly near the gate—albeit not *recent* signs. How many of Japan's legends and folk tales had originated, he wondered, in this very forest?

And how many had come from the sea, instead?

"Wow," Tamani said when they came at last to the place of Unseelie exile. He didn't know what else to say. The prison was set in a small, steep depression in the earth, with rune-carved monoliths ringing the enclosure. No guard towers were in evidence, though Tamani saw signs of habitation in the trees on the upper embankments of what observation automatically labeled the "pit." Trees grew from the center of the prison, though none of their branches crossed the ring of monoliths. From above, human technology might pick out a vaguely-circular stone feature peeking through the canopy, but nothing worthy of comment.

So this was where Avalon sent its malcontents—the disenchanted, the deluded, the deranged. It wasn't a crowded prison, especially by human standards, as even under Marion's stern rule it had been rare for fae to be exiled. Those in Avalon who still dared to practice the ancient rites of the Unseelie mostly knew better than to get caught. In fact Klea had given Tamani reason to suspect that at least some of the fae imprisoned here were not Unseelie at all—just criminals who'd rejected all other avenues to justice.

But one—at least one—was Unseelie for sure.

As they drew closer to the ring, Tamani realized that they weren't the only etched stones surrounding the prison. The ground itself was alive with meandering script, unrecognizable as any human tongue Tamani had even encountered, some of it glittering—

A suspicion clicked into place, and, licking his index finger, Tamani knelt to swipe at a crystalline cluster nestled among the weather-worn engravings. He popped his finger into his mouth as the captain stopped to eye him with a puzzled frown.

Salt stung his tounge and he spat it out on the ground. Strange, how such a mundane substance should so often appear at the heart of Tamani's puzzles.

"These runes—they contain the Unseelie's magic?"

The captain nodded. "Ours too, unfortunately—not that it matters much for the likes of you or me. It's possible to do some things inside, Mixings especially, but the range and power is so limited you'd do better with a sharp stick. And no magic can pass by the sentinel stones, in or out. But it's nice enough on the inside; they don't try to escape very often. Certainly not more than once a decade, and our guards have the high ground in any event."

Tamani wondered if the runes scrawled across every stone surface actually did anything at all. If the basin's geology was shot through with crystalline salt, it could very well function as an enormous, natural version of the small salt circle he'd used to interfere with Yuki's magic, all those years ago. It had never occurred to him that Winter magic might not be the only magic that could be contained in this way. Even if the only power possessed by the eldritch runes was to conceal the secret of salt, he could understand why someone had gone to the effort.

Following the captain's quiet instructions, Tamani unlaced his boots and pulled his long-sleeved shirt over his head. Every time he'd shed his shirt in the last several years it had been in Laurel's presence, and no one else's, so he forgot about the key on the chain until he saw his escort studying it.

Oh.

Tamani gripped the small bit of metal and tried to decide the best course of action. This was the most dangerous artifact in the entire world, as far as Avalon was concerned. Which was better: to leave it here unguarded, or to take it with him into a cage of Avalon's most devious criminals?

Sadly, he'd always trusted himself more than anyone but Laurel—and Shar.

"Is Mischa de Lila still in there?" he asked quietly.

"Indeed," the captain replied, placing Tamani's clothing in a cupboard built into a thick tree-trunk. "She's a model prisoner. Which is why we keep such a sharp eye on her. She informed us this morning that you'd be coming to speak to her—some of my more enterprising sentries took advantage of the new recruits and started a betting pool. The veterans knew better than to bet against that one."

Tamani studied the captain for a hint of humor, but there was none. "Hecate's eye," he swore.

The captain laughed, bitterly. "Careful whose name you invoke in there."

The key clenched in Tamani's hand started to pierce his skin and he loosened his grip. Mischa had a habit of being dangerous in ways that should have been impossible. He worked off the chain that only just fit over his head and, without showing the captain what was in his hand, shoved it into the pocket of his cargoes. "This stays with me."

The captain shook his head and Tamani felt panic rise within him. "*Fear-gliedhidh* work for Avalon's scion. I can't be without it."

"In there?"

"It never leaves my person. Ever." He inclined his head toward the enclosure. "I'll keep it in my hand, and my hand in my pocket."

"What is it?"

Tamani shook his head wordlessly.

The captain gave Tamani a hard stare, doubtless trying to recall what he'd seen in the brief moment after Tamani removed his shirt. It was hardly camouflaged and if the captain had gotten any sort of a good look at it, and he was as intelligent as Tamani suspected, it was possible he could piece certain events together.

After a long silence the captain merely raised one eyebrow and said, "On your head be it."

"As ever," Tamani replied.

"I don't want to hinder a royal errand—" here the captain paused, as if waiting for Tamani to correct him. When Tamani held his peace, the captain continued. "But it would help me a lot if I had some explanation for my men. Mischa's little … *predictions* … rarely bode well for us."

Tamani sighed. "Captain, if I were to honestly divulge the nature of my errand, you wouldn't believe me."

"I'd be willing to try."

The camaraderie Tamani had long enjoyed with his own sentries in Orick was eating at him, a little. Yasmine hadn't exactly sworn him to secrecy. But he didn't want to start rumors, or worse, a panic—Yasmine wouldn't appreciate having her hand forced in that way, and Tamani well knew the benefits of being in her good graces. After some thought, he said simply, "I'm here because the Unseelie might know something that can help me stop merely unusual events from sprouting into serious problems."

The captain pondered this, then nodded. Two of his sentries lowered a hemp ladder into the depression and Tamani placed one foot on the highest rung, then found something within him balking. There was nothing even remotely fear-inducing about the ladder or the height—yet his instincts were screaming at him to turn back.

Ignoring his intuition in a way he'd spent years training himself not to, Tamani descended the ladder.

He almost fell off the bottom rung.

He felt it! Felt the moment that his magic was stripped away. As a Spring faerie, whose only power was to entice animals that weren't trolls into following him and perhaps doing his bidding, Tamani rarely thought about his magic. Most Ticers didn't. Even the sentries who worked on the human side of the gates rarely employed their abilities. The cowherd and beeherds did, certainly, but in Avalon there simply wasn't much reason to exert control over members of the animal kingdom.

Still, Tamani felt the moment when he no longer *could*, and it terrified him. Never mind that his power was already useless here, surrounded by fae, and they similarly handicapped—Tamani still felt vulnerable. He shoved his hand back into his pocket and clenched it around the key. It was tricky, bearing the persistent burden of something to protect.

As soon as Tamani and the captain were on level ground, the ladder was raised and stowed. Tamani looked back at the drop—it was steeply sloped rather than perfectly vertical, dotted with shrubs and outcroppings such that a climb might have been difficult, but far from impossible. He noted a likely escape route, should such a thing become necessary, then forced himself to follow the captain, who registered no emotional upset whatsoever.

There were two lines of fences and gates to pass through before one could reach the actual prisoners. Tamani stood very still while the Captain opened the final padlock. "I'll be right here," the captain said, leaning in close to Tamani's ear. "And I've got sentries at the ready. You shout, we'll come."

Tamani nodded, but as he entered the vine-laden enclosure, he could hardly imagine what physical danger he could encounter here. It was oddly peaceful, for a cage filled with criminals. The central clearing was the size of the coliseum in Avalon, with lush grass springing from the soil, snaking earthen paths connecting houses of bubbled sugar-glass, like those of the Summer quarters in Avalon. Every home had its own garden space, and crawling vegetable and fruit vines covered the enclosure so fully you had to look carefully to see the bars. *Idyllic* was an understatement—though Tamani also noticed that there was little variety in the things that grew. Food sources almost exclusively. A Mixer would be hard-pressed for diverse ingredients such as those Laurel tended back home.

No wonder Klea had resorted to using her own petals.

Faeries were emerging from their bubbles as they noticed

his arrival, silently approaching. None of them were young—the youngest must be closing in on a century—and there were only perhaps a dozen. Fifteen? Not very many. Avalon was not heavily populated, and exile was an extreme case.

The Unseelie stood in a ragged circle around him, but none spoke. Likely no one recognized him—he had no family or friends here—and they stared with suspicion.

Desperately uncomfortable, Tamani cleared his throat. "Anyone want to tell me about a kind of faerie who can live in saltwater?"

"You jest in poor taste."

A woman whose strawberry-blonde hair was streaked with gray, marking her as well into her second century, stepped toward him; the others were regarding him with a mixture of anger and distaste, as if he'd said something sufficiently impolite to border on offensive. Though if they knew the secret of their prison—and at least one of them knew enough to have shared it with Shar—Tamani supposed he could understand their annoyance. The woman pursed her lips and crossed her arms over her chest—and Tamani knew who she was. He'd seen that tight expression, that rigid body language, a thousand times. More.

"Mischa," he said, and her knowing smirk told him he was right, and that she knew who he was—that she might even suspect why he was here. "I hear you've been expecting me."

TWENTY

TAMANI DIDN'T LIKE THE SLIGHT RISE AT THE corner of her lips; anything that made Mischa de Lila happy was worth worrying about.

"I have indeed," she said, not expounding on the foretelling. "Please, come inside."

Tamani glanced around the circle of older fae, feeling much like an insect invited to dine on the leaves of a flytrap. "Can't we talk here?"

She waved her hand as if the other faeries didn't matter at all. "We'll have a meeting later. You come with me now." She started up a dark earthen path and paused when Tamani didn't follow. "Scared?"

"Absolutely."

She held his gaze for a long moment, lips pursed in a disconcertingly mothering fashion. "I suspect you can help me as much as I can help you. So I wouldn't want you harmed in any way. Come, now."

It wasn't Mischa's words that goaded him into following his old friend's exiled mother into her home, but the way the other Unseelie were regarding him—their expressions unmistakably communicating that he'd have to be a half-wit to miss the chance in front of him. They were probably right. He grumbled under his breath, but he followed.

Mischa's house was bright and spartan, clean with a few colorful decorations to draw the eye. She gestured him to a wicker chair, and the soil beneath his feet was rich and fragrant. It was odd to feel so comfortable in this traitor's presence. But when she offered him a carved wooden cup of Goddess-knew-what, he held up a hand and shook his head.

"I believe there's an old human rule about being trapped in a faerie ream if you eat or drink the food. It doesn't apply to Avalon and the Seelie court, but I don't trust your magic. And this," he gestured at the enclosure, visible through the ceiling of Mischa's house, "is not a realm in which I have any interest in remaining."

"We have that in common," Mischa said, taking the offered cup as her own and sipping before setting it on a low table.

"The saltwater fae?" Tamani asked.

That enigmatic smile again. "I hear talk. What do you hear?"

"I hear nothing." He tilted his head, leaning forward. "But I've seen things."

Her eyes brightened. "Have you, now?"

Tamani shook his head. He'd given the first morsel; it was Mischa's turn to reciprocate.

"There are whispers, that when Avalon was created—and isn't *that* a trick we're sorry to have lost!—some were left behind. For what reason, I doubt we'll ever know. A feud? A mistake? No room on the ark?" She chuckled. "Some stories say it happened before the Glamour came upon us, others think it was later, but either way, we changed, and they changed. We adapted. They … fled."

"Fled? From what?"

"Our enemies, of course! Silly sapling. From what else does one flee—sunsets? Of course it was our enemies. We've been shaped by them since they learned to walk upright."

"Trolls."

Mischa fixed Tamani with a contemptuous scowl. "Those grasping, misbegotten lumps? Don't make me laugh. Trolls we kept as *pets*, leashed to our purposes. Pets they would still be but for their unstable breeding. Thank you for culling that herd, by the by—arranging their extermination from here was an enjoyable challenge, kept me busy for years, and I was afraid it would all come to naught when they took my son. A shame they got the seedling, too. I had such plans for her! But I suppose the might of the Benders isn't what it used to be."

The way she flitted from past to present, then spoke of Yuki and Shar—her son!—as if they were pawns on a gameboard left anger and confusion warring for control of Tamani's tongue. Best, perhaps, to focus on the task at hand; no sense getting drawn too far into the tangled root bed of Mischa's mind. "So the enemies—"

"The humans, of course. Never has a human population encountered the fae but that they try to kill us."

"I have human friends."

"As a *whole*, Tamani de Rhoslyn. Do keep up."

After further charged silence Tamani said, "So the fae left behind fled to the sea? That makes no sense."

"Plants do live in the sea."

Tamani cringed, remembering almost those exact words coming from Laurel's lips. "The faeries I saw were—they weren't like us."

"Oh, they wouldn't be. No Glamour, child, now I *know* Shar taught you these things. When someone teaches you an arcane mystery, you must take care that it doesn't fall right back out of your head!"

"They were *nothing* like us," Tamani pressed, failing to keep the frustration out of his voice.

But Mischa was as placid as a lagoon, sitting very still and sipping occasionally from her cup. "Weren't they?"

"Well for starters they were … green."

"Because skin color has ever mattered in Avalon?"

"They had …" He raised his arms and gestured vaguely. "Things hanging off of them. I'm quite certain they were attached."

"Fronds? I see. And are they so different from our own stems, all things considered?"

Tamani snapped his mouth shut. Was it really so difficult to imagine that sea fae would resemble other ocean flora? "They're taking humans," he said, forcing himself to pursue the most salient point. "Killing them."

Mischa didn't so much as twitch. "Are they?"

"Yes. They come out of the sea, snatch humans, and throw them back later, their throats torn out." He realized he was nearly shouting, his left hand gripping the key in his pocket painfully tight. He forced himself to draw a deep breath.

"How do they take them?"

"What do you mean?"

She shrugged like she didn't care, but there was a crackle of anticipation in the air. "I don't imagine them walking out of the ocean and taking them at gunpoint."

Tamani opened his mouth to ask how she even knew about guns, then realized he didn't actually know when humans invented the things. "They sing."

Mischa smiled. "Do they?"

"It's Enticement, somehow. I felt it."

She simply raised an eyebrow. "Anything else?"

He tried to figure out how in the world she could find this information useful, then finally just said, "There was one that … changed. He became more humanoid, and handsome. Tall and attractive. He's the one the woman went for. He took her hand, the others sang, and she walked into the sea of her own accord."

"Hmm, sounds like Illusion to me. Enticement and Illusion, tell me again how vastly different these faeries are from us?"

Tamani frowned. She was right. Songs that Enticed, illusions that took time to shape but had physical heft, rather than being only visual. "I wonder if they have Mixers, too. And what in the cradle of Gaia could a Bender of the sea do?"

"What indeed?" Mischa said, eyes gazing into her cup as if it held fathomless depth.

Then she chuckled, reminding him that Mischa never did anything without a reason. Usually, two or three.

"How does this help you?" Tamani asked.

She blinked rapidly. "Nothing can help me, Tamani. Not in here."

Right. "Then why are you so pleased?"

"You've brought me welcome news, child. How many

centuries has it been since a faerie last killed a human? Surely that sort of chaos and destruction is reason enough for rejoicing."

"No, it's not. That's a shallow sentiment. And whatever else you may be, you're not shallow."

"That almost sounded like a compliment."

"It wasn't."

"I was always proud of my son, you know."

Tamani clenched his teeth. He didn't want to talk about Shar. He definitely didn't want *Mischa* to talk about Shar.

"He was so very talented. Most parents think their child is exceptional, and most parents are wrong. But not me. Shar's Enticement, well, if Avalon wasn't sequestered from the humans, he'd have been a military hero."

"He *was* a hero."

She lifted one shoulder, dismissing Shar's sacrifice for the second time in their brief conversation, and Tamani found himself wanting to strike an old woman for the first time in his life. He gripped the edge of his chair instead, but it was a close thing.

"It's a family trait, you know."

"What?"

"High-level Enticement. Being able to control so many animals at such great distances. Why do you think they sent me away so fast?" She bent forward, her glittering eyes just inches from his. He wanted to pull back, but refused to show weakness. "The things I could do, Tamani de Rhoslyn. The things I had *planned*."

Tamani's fingers were shaking by the time she pulled her face away and settled back in her chair, a demure smile curling her lips.

"What do you want with these new sea faeries—to protect them, or to annihilate them?" she asked.

Tamani hadn't thought in terms of the faeries—he'd been thinking of the humans. That realization made him feel guilty. Especially now that he was pretty sure they were the same species, simply altered by centuries of divergent evolution. "I'm not certain," he hedged.

"It doesn't matter which outcome you want, actually. When you have two races who can weaponize human beings, the winner will be whoever can do it better."

"We're not going to weaponize humans."

"You will if you want to win, sprout, make no mistake. After all, *they* will. You already said so."

"I said they kidnap them—not turn them into weapons."

"Why else would one lure humans into the sea but to discover the best way to use them?"

Tamani closed his eyes. Of course, of *course* that was why they were abducting people! Predicting villainy was much easier if you could think like a villain—something Tamani had never been very good at doing. Apparently Mischa was happy to do it for him, and her explanation seemed to fit the puzzle. The sea faeries took the humans one at a time and, after the first few, tossed them back with their throats ripped open. A creature living in the ocean might not understand that humans need to breathe air, and a drowning human trying to communicate their distress might very well clutch at their throat. Tamani had simply never considered that tearing open their necks might not be to kill them, but a sad attempt to keep them *alive.* The sea fae were studying humans, and with no apparent concern for their lives.

Mischa was right.

Charlotte had been right.

Tamani just hadn't seen it.

How in the hell had Mischa? Tamani leaned forward, scrutinizing her. "How did you know I was coming?"

Mischa said nothing. He didn't really think she would, but it was worth a try. He shook his head at her stubbornness and started to rise. He had work to do.

"Has my granddaughter inherited the gift?" Mischa asked, stopping him.

"The gift?"

"You have the most deplorable listening comprehension, sprout. High-level Enticement. Like her father. Like me. Does she have it?"

Like her father. It took a moment before Tamani realized what such a thing could mean for him. For the humans. For Lenore. For the sea fae.

And he knew it showed on his face because Mischa let out a low chuckle. "I think your work here is done. Off with you."

Tamani rose wordlessly; he'd seen the trap too late. This was what Mischa wanted him to know—that her granddaughter might be of great use to him, securing her family legacy of carnage and death. Tamani hated the thought of doing anything that made Mischa happy, but given the stakes, how could he not use the weapon she'd just put in his hand? He cursed under his breath as he ducked through her doorway.

Behind him, Mischa laughed and spoke once more, scarcely loud enough to hear. "Well, well, well, what has it got in its pockets?"

Terror sliced through Tamani and he squeezed the key in his left pocket, assuring himself that it was still there. Still safe. Just Mischa playing her games. But how had she known? And what might she one day do with that knowledge? Tamani hadn't run away from an encounter in years, but he fled from this Unseelie faerie who always knew too much and cared too little.

With his hand still clenched around the key, Tamani jogged back down the path toward the base of the steep incline that would let him leave this awful place, feeling even more naked than he was.

"Sir?"

A soft voice stopped him, but when he turned, he didn't see anyone.

"Over here." He spotted the old woman sitting on a stool outside the nearest bubble house, beckoning him near.

Indecision churned within him, but finally, with a muttered curse, he walked over and stooped down so he could hear her.

"Can you tell me of Avalon?" she asked.

Tamani shifted his weight from foot to foot. He wanted so badly to leave—to get away from Mischa—but this faerie asked intently and her eyes had a softness around them that was conspicuously absent from Mischa's. So after a quick glance toward Mischa's house he said, "What do you want to know?"

The wrinkles on her cheeks grew deeper as she smiled. "I hear there's a new queen and that she has destroyed the boundaries between the seasons. That everyone is considered equal. Tell me it's true."

"It's true," he said warily.

She sighed contentedly, puzzling Tamani all the more. "Then it is as I always hoped. That was my crime, you know."

"How so?" Tamani found himself drawing near, resting one knee on the soft ground to crouch close to her.

She lifted her chin and met his eyes. Hers, though wrinkled at the edges, their light green irises a touch cloudy, were nonetheless earnest—bold, even. "I fought for a revolution. I tried to rally the Ticers to demand more rights. I knew of our worth far better than they did. I wanted them to fight for it."

"Violently?" Tamani asked.

"If we'd gotten that far, I suppose. Do you not think it would be worth it?"

"We did it peacefully."

"Easy to say now, little spring blossom. But you made the rest of us wait. You were able to pick up peacefully what I wanted at any price. Does that make me wrong?"

Tamani weighed her words, the urgency of his errand temporarily forgotten. Fifteen years ago he'd brought Laurel to her first Avalonian festival. He remembered the way she watched him bow and trail along behind her. He thought nothing of it. She'd been appalled. Change hadn't come quickly, and it hadn't come easily, but it had come for him as surely as it had come for all of Avalon.

"Would you … talk to that new queen? The pretty young one?" The old faerie's hand was on his arm, as wrinkled as her face. He couldn't imagine she was long for the Earth. "I should like to see Avalon once more before I die. Inciting rebellion was my only crime. I was fierce, and I refused to cease or to recant. But I was never accused of anything else. Tell me, now that the revolution is over, what is my crime except that I did not win?"

He met her eyes, a devastating spark of injustice flaring to life within him. He couldn't know yet if she was being entirely truthful, but if she was …

"What's your name?" he asked in a whisper.

"Tera. Tera de Salina. Yours?"

"Tamani de Rhoslyn."

"Tamani," she repeated. "I've been here a long time, Tamani. And I wasn't young when I arrived. Seventy years trying to exist peacefully and on my own, not letting myself be poisoned by the lot they send in here. I've done it as best I can. But I'm tired. I just want to go home."

Tamani swallowed hard. "I'll talk to her. I swear it." He stood and looked down at her. "Perhaps some good can come out of my visit today."

"Thank you," she said, and she took his hand in hers and pressed it to her dry lips. "The only thing that could please me more than ending my days in Avalon would be ending them in the Avalon of my dreams."

TWENTY-ONE

SO "TEXTING" TURNED OUT TO BE A LOT MORE fun than it sounded—though learning how to tap out messages would have been easier if her phone worked better with non-human fingers. Tamani had warned her about that, but it was still annoying. She and Shawn had texted all weekend; it was the first really compelling reason Rowen had found for carrying a phone at all.

Conversation had quickly taken on the feel of an intricate dance—and an improvised one, at that. She knew some of the steps, but there was no choreography, and the stage was littered with unseen edges. What could she say about herself? How could she steer him away from subjects she *couldn't* discuss? It might have been frustrating, had it been less exhilarating, and he was doing his own careful stepping, as he still wasn't ready to say anything to his twin sister. *Yet*, he said.

So there were two sources for the anxiety zipping through

her stems when she pulled open the doors to Scazio on Monday morning—only to flinch back from the wave of sound that broke over her. The crowd loitering in the foyer was much larger than usual. Her eyes darted about, looking for Mitchell and Shawn at the same time.

She found Mitchell first. Rather than coming to her, Mitchell waved her over to where he and Thomas were standing, hands clasped so hard both their knuckles were stripes of white and red. Thomas was bouncing on the balls of his feet, trying to peer over the crowd.

"Morning, love," Mitchell said, half-distractedly dropping a kiss on the top of her head. "Few more minutes. I swear to you they make us wait on purpose. They've had those paper printed since Saturday. Sunday at the latest."

"Where's … Meghan?" Rowen asked, hesitating and then directing her question to Thomas.

Thomas tilted his head. "Oh, she staked out her spot fifteen minutes ago."

There she was, back braced against the wall, arms crossed over her chest, wearing a stormy expression and an aura of gloom. She looked angry rather than nervous, but Rowen was beginning to suspect that this was simply Meghan's default cover-emotion.

And that was all the attention Rowen spared the brooding human, as she locked eyes with the boy who'd already been staring at her. Shawn lifted one corner of his mouth and gave her a wink. Rowen dropped her gaze to the floor, unable to hide the grin that instantly stretched her mouth.

This might be harder than she thought. Her stage face always disappeared around him.

The buzz of the crowd built from the far end of the room as Mitchell practically squeaked, "Oh, oh, here they come!"

The head instructors of each of the three age divisions within the Academy emerged in a shoulder-to-shoulder triangle, looking more like they were preparing for battle than posting audition results. Armed with pieces of white paper and scotch tape, they elbowed their way through the frantic crowd, hung the papers, and retreated.

Rowen had never been one for shoving, and was especially disinclined by all these warm bodies. Perhaps it was their short lifespans that always had humans in such a rush? Rowen hung back and observed—mostly, observing Shawn.

Meghan, who'd somehow managed to position herself *exactly* where she needed to stand to be the first person to see the lists, was now sobbing into her brother's shoulder while he grinned. That seemed … needlessly cold, but before Rowen could catch Shawn's eye or wrap her head around what she was seeing, a whooping, cheering Mitchell came bounding out of the crowd and swept her off her feet, high into the air, spinning her around crazily over his head. *Pas de deux* partners were like that.

"What, what?" she asked as she tilted lopsidedly, momentarily concerned that Mitchell might actually drop her. Only the trust she'd developed in her dance partner kept her from flailing—and sure enough, strong hands were righting her torso an instant later.

"Sugar Plum Fairy!" he gasped. "And Cavelier! We did it! We did it, love!" He set her on her feet and hugged her tight.

"Mitchell," Rowen said, pushing back so she could see his face. "What about Meghan? She's so sad."

"Sad?"

He looked so confused that Rowen turned his face toward her and pointed.

"Oh. Happy tears; she got Clara."

Rowen blinked. "You said Sugar Plum Fairy was the harder part."

"Yes, but smaller. Less stage time. Clara's the lead." He grinned, glancing back at Meghan and Shawn. "She's the first scholarship student *and* the first black dancer at Scazio to land the role."

"First black dancer? Is that a big deal?" No one took such things into consideration in Avalon. Of course, they didn't have scholarships, either.

"Yes," Mitchell said, as though he were speaking to a very slow child. "Ballet is so white; it's a *huge* deal. Don't they have black people where you're from?"

"Of course," Rowen said distractedly, watching Meghan laugh up at Shawn while wiping tears from her cheeks. "Our queen, for one."

When Rowen glanced back at Mitchell he was peering at her oddly. "Queen … Elizabeth?" he asked, drawing out the name slowly.

Oops. Scotland apparently did have a queen. And judging from Mitchell's reaction, her skin wasn't the deep mahogany hue of Yasmine's. Rowen opened her mouth to say something, then realized there really was nothing she could say to correct the sheer nonsense of her reply. "So Meghan is happy?"

"Damn straight," Mitchell said with a smirk.

"Good," she said, trying to catch Shawn's eye again. "Excellent."

For almost ten minute the foyer was a cacophony of shrieks and cheers and a fair number of disappointed sobs. Rowen tried to keep her smile wide on her face as her classmates traipsed past, offering their congratulations. This was what she wanted, wasn't it? Dancing success in the human world? So why did she feel so torn?

Her eyes kept drifting to Shawn, standing by Meghan and beaming as though it were his accomplishment, too. It was odd to watch them. Rowen had never had a brother, let alone a twin. She scarcely remembered her parents, and though she loved her grandmother, she'd never truly had this sort of relationship with anyone. Even her best friend, Lenore, was naturally solitary; it was something they had in common.

The bond between Shawn and Meghan was so strong you could *see* it, and Rowen found herself wrangling an awkward jealousy. She certainly didn't want to take Shawn away from Meghan—or even come between them—but she wished that she could have that kind of bond. With Shawn, perhaps, but really with anyone. She stood in a room filled with people, and felt utterly alone.

Was that what it took, to be special?

Finally the instructors began herding all the dancers to the hallway that led to the studios. Rowen watched Meghan throw her arms around Shawn, then they waved at one another as Meghan picked up her duffel and headed off in the flow of students.

Rowen didn't have to try to meet his eyes this time; his gaze went straight to her. He smiled. Rowen couldn't keep an answering grin from her own lips. He tilted his head toward the front doors and started walking in that direction. Rowen looked back, trying to figure out how she was going to shake Mitchell, but he was already gone. She'd be late to class, but it looked like half the studio was going to be late anyway, so Rowen figured she could indulge herself. Ducking her head so her hair fell on each side of her face, she followed just behind

Shawn as he pushed through the double doors and veered off to the left, where he'd be out of sight of the occupants of the foyer.

As soon as Rowen was within arm's length Shawn grabbed her hand and pulled her against him. "I missed you all weekend," he murmured, his face close to hers.

"Mmm," Rowen hummed back, lifting her face for a kiss. It was incredible, the urge she had to be with him. To touch and kiss him and have his warm arms wrapped around her. It was the only desire she'd ever had that even remotely compared to her desire to dance.

"I can't stay long," Shawn said, sounding miserable about his own words. "I'm already late for school because I came to see the postings."

"We're both late then," Rowen said playfully. "What a shame."

Shawn kissed her long and hard, then pulled back. "Well, congratulations. I knew you'd get one of the leads."

Rowen grinned and dropped a little curtsy.

"I even brought you a present."

"Really?"

He pulled a small bag out of his pocket. There was a note taped to it reading *Congrats soloist!* With a small flourish he placed it in her hands, cupped together in front of her. She caught the word *Kisses*, and a jolt of excitement shot through her. "Thank you," she said, trying to hide how touched she really was, her eyes falling to the crinkly bag instead. "Oh." The disappointed syllable was out of her mouth before she could stop it.

"What?"

She almost didn't tell him, but they must be poor for Meghan to need a scholarship and surely gifts like this cost money—Tamani had been quite clear that money was an important thing in the human world, all the more for people who didn't have much. She didn't want Shawn to keep buying her a gift she couldn't use. She held up the bag of candies and smiled apologetically. "It's chocolate. I can't eat chocolate. Allergic," she added, remembering the word Tamani had told her to use in any situation involving food she couldn't eat.

"Oh." He seemed surprised, but then grinned. "Then spill. You're always eating *some* kind of candy. What is it?"

"I'm … what?"

"Something. And it's not mints or gum." He leaned close and smiled in a way that made her stems feel weak. "You always taste so sweet."

Her mouth dropped open and she said … nothing. Twice in less than ten minutes she'd been caught bare-branched in the sun—was she having a bad morning, or was she really just this bad under pressure?

Shawn's arms were around her waist, his nose so close it

was brushing hers, and Rowen was scrambling for something to say when she heard a funny squeak.

"Oh, there is this bright little shining sun of happiness inside me right now."

They both whirled to find Mitchell standing with a huge grin on his face, one hand over his heart and the other still holding the door open. He approached, throwing one arm around each of them and kissed first Shawn's cheek, then Rowen's. Then his face snapped into a flat, serious expression. "The Godfather approves, young ones. You," he added, pointing at Rowen. "We're wanted inside. Shawn, you're already late for school. Meghan told me. So," he swirled his finger in the air between them, "to be continued." He grabbed her hand and started pulling her away.

Rowen looked back at Shawn with a sappy grin and, at the last second, tossed him the bag of Kisses. "You eat them."

He brandished them at her melodramatically. "I'm going to find out."

I certainly hope not. Not that he could ever guess. But it was problem. He'd noticed already—she'd have to say something. Mostly she hated that her uncle had been right. And she hadn't listened.

As soon as they were in the foyer Mitchell turned and clasped Rowen's face in both hands, placing a loud kiss on her forehead. "Oh, sugar, I am so thrilled! I felt the chemistry the first day you two met. I knew it. I told Thomas within the hour."

"No, no, no," Rowen said, hands out in front of her in supplication. "You can't make a big deal out of this. Not yet." She lowered her voice. "Meghan doesn't know."

Mitchell's face was immediately serious. "He has to tell her."

"I know."

"No, I'm not sure you do. If Meghan finds out another way she'll hate you forever."

"She already hates me," Rowen muttered.

"No, she misunderstands you, and eventually she'll come around. But not if she find you sneaking around with her twin brother behind her back."

Rowen shushed him, even though he was already whispering. "Shawn wanted to wait until auditions were over."

At that Mitchell snorted and raised an eyebrow. "Smart. I'll give him that. But now Meghan's nabbed the part she always wanted. If there was ever a perfect time to tell her, it's now." He stepped back and pointed at her sternly. "Make it happen."

TWENTY-TWO

TAMANI HAD NEVER BEEN SO HAPPY TO SEE Avalon as he was coming back through the gate to Japan. After spending time with the Mischa, he wanted nothing so much as a cleansing shower—but simply breathing the air of his verdant homeland was a close second. Avalon was a place of life and connection, in stark contrast to the way the Unseelie witch gloried in death and detachment. What sort of rot would have to take hold of your core to poison your entire being that way? Had it ever even occurred to her, at any point along the way, that she might be doing wrong?

Once the gate was closed, his mind went immediately to Laurel. Finding her, touching her, simply reminding himself that she was alive. They'd been apart just two days, but it felt longer. Much longer. She would be staying at her quarters at the Academy, which was a good distance uphill, but Tamani barely noticed the slope as he counted the steps to reunion.

"I'm afraid you've come all this way for nothing," Yeardley called out as Tamani approached the gate to the Academy grounds. He was clipping leaves off a currant bush with a small set of silver pruning shears, gathering the greens into a stone bowl while a group of young Mixers watched. As Tamani closed the distance between them, the Fall faeries under Yeardley's tutelage turned away from their lesson to gawk. They looked too young to have been at the Academy during the trollish invasion, but they would have heard stories from their older classmates. Inaccurate stories, doubtless, as stories were wont to grow in their retellings. Rather like weeds.

"Laurel isn't here?"

Yeardley shook his head, handing his tools to one of his students and shooing them back toward the Academy. "She said she had something to attend to at home."

Tamani frowned. "Was she able to make much progress with—"

"I suggest you catch the Queen before she's too much farther from the gate," Yeardley interrupted, a strange gleam in his eye. "Laurel wanted you to follow as soon as possible."

"Then I guess I'd better do that," Tamani said, bowing slightly before catching himself and giving a polite nod instead. Moments like that were fewer, ten years on, but there was no particular reason to *not* bow to Yeardley—Laurel's tutor had proven his worth and worthiness time and again. Snubbing people who *demanded* obeisance, people like Marion, was easy. The overthrow of the old social order had not yet resulted, however, in any new ways to communicate respect to the people who deserved it.

A puzzle for another day. By the time Tamani got back down to the Gate Garden he was more than a little irritated. He'd considered trying to find Yasmine so she could pretend—as she had so many times—to open the gate, but between his failure at the Manor, the creepy advice from the Unseelie, and the looming threat of the sea fae, Tamani was having a hard time worrying about secrecy. If someone saw something and decided he was a secret Winter faerie, well, it wouldn't be the most outrageous thing whispered about his heroic feats.

Probably.

His phone started pinging the instant he returned to California. Twenty-eight texts in three days—not many if he'd been one of the humans attending school with Rowen, he imagined, but there were only a handful of people who even possessed Tamani's number, and most of them lived in the same house. By his standards, it was an avalanche.

He glanced down, ignoring six messages from Rowen—if something serious *had* happened there, he wasn't in any position to act on it now. Laurel, meanwhile, had sent him twenty messages over the course of the last twenty hours—updates on where she was going, but nothing about why. Had she discovered a new way for him to deal with the sea fae? Some ingredients were difficult to get in Avalon; she may have come back to gather materials from her personal garden.

Tamani ran along pathways as familiar to him as Laurel's face, exulting in the scent of the crisp autumn breeze and the feel of once more being fleet in a way that would have been impossible anywhere else in the world. Here, every rock and tree and streamlet was known to him, and it felt good to run, to leap, to move as fast as he possibly could on his way to the place he most wanted to be. Avalon was his homeland, but this? This was his *home.*

Rather than go around to the front of the house, he burst through the back doors. Laurel's name was on his lips when he froze at the sight of her blossom. His knees felt weak as his eyes drank in the long petals, colored every shade of blue from navy to powder, that curved up from her back and hovered just over her shoulders.

Fall was Tamani's very favorite time of year.

He'd known it was coming—the bud on Laurel's back had been quite large when he left for the Manor—but it simply hadn't occurred to him since. In fairness, he'd been a touch preoccupied. Now she turned toward him and smiled. His fingers trembled as he reached for her.

She opened her mouth to say something, but he took advantage and covered it with his own, holding her tight against him and kissing her; parched for her kiss like a sapling in the Sahara. Her arms twined around his neck and all he could think was that they'd spent far too much of the last two months apart. More than the rest of the years they'd been handfasted all added together.

"Goddess, but you're gorgeous," he rasped, before feasting on her lips again, his fingers tentatively stroking the curve where her blossom blended seamlessly into her skin. He started to guide her backward, steering her toward their bed.

"Tamani," Laurel said, scold in her voice.

"I've missed you," he said. "I always miss you, but to come back and have you in full bloom?" He groaned. "You know what that does to me."

He sprinkled her face with kisses, then pulled down the strap of her camisole and tasted the skin at her shoulder as he laid her back on the comforter. "Your mother is here," she hissed.

"So I'll lock the door," he said into the skin at her neck.

"You don't understand," she said, breathlessly.

"*Your* parents are *always* here," Tam said with a grin. "Never stopped us before."

"This is different!" She placed a palm in the middle of Tamani's chest and pushed him away, sounding both firm and serious. Tamani froze.

"What?"

Laurel smiled sweetly. "Your mother's here because our sprout has decided it's time."

***

It took three more days, but each morning when Tamani woke he would run to the garden box, thrilled at each new sign of progress. A sprout could spend as many as four seasons in its penultimate maturation phase, unchanged from month to month, so the final week before blossoming felt like a mad rush forward.

"It'll be today," Rhoslyn finally pronounced after examining the sprout the third morning.

Laurel's hand was wrapped around Tamani's, but when his mother's words sank in she squeezed so tightly he flinched. "Today!" Laurel said, turning to him with sparks flashing in her eyes. "A Fall faerie!"

She laughed, the sound lifting the corners of Tamani's mouth. He was … stunned. The moment was here, and this child—*his* child, his son or daughter—would be one of the powerful, one of the rare. Once, it would have meant something very close to nobility in Avalon. In some ways it still did.

"What are the chances?" Tamani asked, pulling Laurel close.

Oddly, she sobered. "Possibly high, actually."

"Really?"

She nodded. "There's something called a non-Fisherian sex ratio, where a species makes up for a drop in one sex, by producing more of that sex, to balance the population. I wondered if something similar might apply to us here."

"Oh?" Tamani said, failing utterly to understand. Mixers did that, sometimes—and Laurel was a professor at a human university, besides. It was usually endearing, when it wasn't completely maddening.

"It's not common, but it's the only hypothesis I have to explain season distribution." She never referred to them as *castes*, though that was what Tamani understood her to be talking about. "If the fae are non-Fisherian organisms with regard to seasons rather than sex, it would explain a lot."

Tamani thought about this for a few seconds, then gave up. "I have no idea what you're talking about."

Laurel looked over at Rhoslyn, who just smiled and shook her head. Clearly this was a topic the two women had already discussed. "In non-Fisherian organisms, if, for example, half of the female population was wiped out, the remaining organisms would suddenly start giving birth to significantly more females than before."

"To replenish the population," Tamani said. "It makes sense."

"Except it doesn't," Laurel countered. "There's no logical

reason for these species' reproductive systems to somehow *sense* that the population ratios have changed, and to stimulate them to make up for it. But it happens."

"Glad we got you that advanced anthropology degree," Tamani said with a grin.

"You're missing the connection."

"I absolutely am."

Laurel paused, seeming to need a few seconds to collect herself. When she spoke again, her voice was shaky. "No population in Avalon was decreased as drastically as the Fall faeries."

Oh. Tamani reached out and stroked her hand. Even a decade later, Laurel mourned the huge number of Mixers Klea had decimated in one day during her attack on the Academy. If they hadn't been smart—and had David to assist them—it would have been an almost complete annihilation. "So you think evolution is helping to make up for that?"

"It's the only answer that fits. And *I* wasn't the one to notice. It was your mother."

They turned to Rhoslyn, whose eyes remained fixed on the sprout. "I'm retired, but I still help the Gardeners when they need an experienced hand. Since the war, more than one seedling in ten have opened in the fall. It used to be more like one in fifty."

Tamani's eyes widened. "That's actually fascinating."

"And so," Laurel said with a smile and gestured toward the garden box, "our little Mixer." She hesitated, then said more quietly, "Do you mind?"

Tamani didn't hide his grin as he leaned over and kissed Laurel's forehead. "I couldn't care less."

The pod gave a distinct wriggle and Rhoslyn sucked in a breath. "Here we go," she said softly.

Tamani's mother had already warned them that watching a faerie pod open was much like watching a bird hatch; one could cheer the little one on, but helping them from their gestational prison would only result in a weakened baby—one that might not survive. Still, Tamani was surprised by how hard it was to keep his hands at his sides and not to wrench open the pod so they could see their new child.

Judging by the bruises Laurel was surely leaving on his arm, she felt the same.

But after a long, tense silence, the seal around the end of the pod gave way and a blanket of lavender petals unfurled. Laurel let out a loud, *oooh*! but they still couldn't quite see inside the protective petals. They held their breaths as one and, slowly, a nest of black curls pushed its way through the purple petals. Rhoslyn wordlessly reached for Laurel's hands, and even though Laurel looked both confused and afraid, she let Rhoslyn cradle both her hands over her own and help extend them toward the end of the pod. And with Rhoslyn's fingers showing hers what to do, Laurel reached out and caught the tiny sprout as it slid from the pod.

With her fingers curved protectively around the small, naked sprout, Laurel held the little body up where both she and Tamani could see it. A tiny, perfect face turned toward them, eyes squinting in the sunlight. Laurel and Tamani held utterly still as the sprout's eyes went back and forth between them, finally settling on Laurel. "Mama?"

Laurel gathered the little baby girl to her chest and burst into tears as Tamani wrapped his arms around them both.

TWENTY-THREE

TONIGHT, SHAWN PROMISED.

After that—nothing. No texts, no call. Rowen had managed to fall asleep anyway, and this morning—still nothing. She approached Scazio Dance Academy on light feet, afraid she might be sneaking onto a battlefield. She pulled open the front doors with a tiny cringe—

But everything appeared to be normal.

Rowen walked tentatively through the foyer, twitching each time a dancer—never the one she was avoiding—called out a greeting. Her innards clenched and writhed like she'd caught some sort of violent rot, so she judged it best not to actually open her mouth and just gave fluttery waves in reply.

In the hallway that led to the studios she remained unambushed, and when she poked her head into her first class there was no sign of Meghan. Rowen wasn't entirely sure if that was a good sign or a bad one. But it was the beginning of another day of rehearsal, so Rowen did what every dancer does at the start of a new day; she laced on her pointe shoes.

This consumed her focus sufficiently that she nearly jumped out of her tights when the studio door burst open, slamming into the wall as Meghan stormed through. She stopped in front of Rowen, towering above her, duffel swinging crazily from the strap on her shoulder. "What the hell do you think you're doing?"

Rowen looked up with wide eyes. She sensed that the question was rhetorical, so rather than state the obvious—that she was lacing up—she held her tongue.

"Is this some kind of revenge? Going after my brother—my *twin* brother—to get back at me?"

Rowen suspected this was still not the time to actually respond.

Meghan flung her bag to the floor, clearly disgusted. "Well, it worked, okay! I hate that he likes you. I hate that you were able to entrance him with your wiles or whatever. And it hurts that he's decided to stay with you even though I asked him not to. So I hope you're happy."

"I am not happy," Rowen whispered.

"What?" Meghan said, quietly.

Rowen had never known a single syllable to sound so *threatening*, and she found herself shrinking away, abruptly recalling all the most terrifying bits of the human tales Len used to tell her when they were small. It crossed Rowen's mind that she could simply disappear—but of course, *that* would be disastrous. Taking her terror firmly in hand, she managed to repeat herself, and was pleased at the strength and volume of her words. "I'm not happy! Why would I be happy?"

"Is this because I got the lead?" Meghan demanded, standing so close the tip of her shoe caught the edge of Rowen's skirt, pinning her in place. "I worked hard for that part. I sweat and bled for that part. Did you think you could just *jeté* in here and steal everything I've spent years working toward?"

A whispering crowd had formed around them and Rowen's fear was subsiding as her temper bubbled hot. "Do you honestly believe you're the only one who works? Who spends hours upon hours perfecting her art?"

"That's not what this is about."

"No? Then let me tell you what I think this is about."

"By all means," Meghan said, crossing her arms over her chest and rolling her eyes. "Enlighten me."

"I think you're the best damned dancer in this whole school," Rowen yelled.

Meghan recoiled, a marionette on retreating strings, freeing Rowen's skirt as the circle of girls around them hushed.

"*I* think the reason you're the best dancer is because you work harder and want it more than anyone else here. And the fact that some people resent you for that makes *them* worse dancers." Rowen's eyes flashed as she met the gaze of every one of her classmates who dared look back. "If they really wanted to be better, they'd watch you and try to learn from you, instead of whining and whispering and pretending you're not worth their time."

Rowen rose and stepped forward, straightening—though she still had to look up to meet Meghan's eyes. How did humans get so *tall*?

"And yes, I do like your brother," she said, more quietly. "I didn't entrance him, or trick him. And I certainly didn't do *anything* for your sake. But he did take *some* convincing. " Megan's mouth dropped open, but Rowen hurried on. "I had to convince him to trust himself instead of blindly depending on his twin sister's biased judgment. He wanted to trust you, but he couldn't when you were being so stubborn."

Meghan's mouth snapped closed.

"You are your own worst enemy. Yes, some people are ignorant, and jealous." The gathered crowd rewarded *that* with more than a few angry mutters. "But if you'd give anyone—*anyone*—a chance to be your friend, maybe you'd find out that some people *want* to be."

Meghan stepped back as if Rowen had bodily shoved her—and then, as if suddenly realizing they were surrounded by a score of other people, she straightened herself to full height. Loftily, she spoke. "You're invited for dinner tonight."

With that, Meghan turned and stomped out of the studio with a grace that wouldn't have complimented an elephant.

***

Rowen had no idea what to expect when she arrived at the neat, pastel-colored house that reminded her a bit of Chelsea's. She had a little flowerpot in her hands, planted with a cutting from a flowering vine Laurel had imported from Avalon. A gift was appropriate, yes? Surely human etiquette wasn't so exceptionally different than fae.

Though, on second thought, humans seemed to have a complicated relationship with plants sometimes. Would they find her gift in poor taste?

"This is ridiculous," Rowen muttered, shaking her head to banish her gnawing doubts. She located and pressed the doorbell—such strange devices humans built!—and was immediately rewarded with sounds of a scuffle from within the abode. Several very loud thumps sounded against the door, and then Shawn's voice, muffled but unmistakably sharp. A few more seconds of quiet were followed by the door opening to reveal Shawn himself, looking sheepish. Rowen's eyes were wide, but at the last second she caught sight of Meghan's back just over Shawn's shoulder.

Oh.

Rowen couldn't focus on her nemesis for long—her eyes were riveted on Shawn's height and breadth, filling the doorway. Her stems seemed barely able to hold her weight.

"Aww, did you bring me flowers?" he said with a grin.

Her hands were shaking as she held out the earthenware pot and she struggled to still them. "For your mother."

He brought his face close to hers. "She'll love it," he whispered, stroking her cheek with his thumb. Before Rowen could get her breathing back under control, he'd straightened and placed a hand on her shoulder and pulled her inside. "Mom!" he called. "She's here."

So Rowen was simply *she.* Already discussed and monickered. "What was the problem at the door?" Rowen whispered.

Shawn rolled his eyes. "Meghan wanted to open the door so she could glower at you."

"Ah." After extending the invitation to dinner, Meghan had essentially ignored Rowen through the rest of rehearsal—but so had all the other girls, which was how they generally treated Meghan. Mitchell assured Rowen that the cold shoulders would warm eventually—and probably more quickly than was respectable—but there was a strange solidarity in sharing Meghan's ostracism.

It didn't make Meghan friendly, but Rowen was satisfied for the moment to simply be downgraded from open hostility.

"She'll come around," Shawn murmured. "She's in a weird place."

"Oh?" Rowen said in a clipped tone. "Is she the first sister in history to completely misjudge the girl her brother is dating?"

"Not that. She's just going to have to deal with that." Shawn wrapped an arm around Rowen's waist and pulled her close. She couldn't help but feel a little bit better at that. "It's just, she thought you hated her, and she found out you actually respect her—no reason for you to say it publicly if you were faking it. That's got to feel good. But you still called her out in front of everyone—again, not your fault—but nobody's pride survives a beating like that. So … she's got some mixed feelings. That's all I'm saying."

Rowen hadn't really thought of it that way, and realized she'd probably feel conflicted, too. But if Meghan could nurture a grudge against Rowen, then Rowen could nurture a grudge against Meghan, so she did.

Just a *little* one.

And when Meghan clomped downstairs for dinner, at least she didn't say anything catty.

As the five of them sat around a wooden table, Shawn planting himself beside her, Rowen glanced nervously at the food. Some kind of meat, bread, something white that didn't smell quite right, and a bowl of green peas. Rowen *might* be able to eat the peas—humans were strangely inconsistent about flavoring their vegetables with animal fat or vegetable oil—but inedible food was something she'd learned to handle. She'd faked her way through dozens of lunches at Scazio; illusion was a fantastic power for a faerie trying to blend into the human world. She could take illusory mouthfuls with an empty fork and make the food on her plate slowly disappear.

"And are your parents still in Scotland?" Shawn's mom asked after everyone had started eating.

Rowen hated lying to Shawn's family, but she could hardly tell the truth. Tamani was always right; it was incredibly annoying. "No. I lived there with my grandmother. My parents are dead."

Both adults made the expected sound of sympathy that Rowen could only ever hear as pity. "Such a tragedy to lose them both. How did they pass?"

"Mother!" Shawn burst out.

His mother waved away his protest. "Shawn, it's a reasonable question. She's probably been asked a million times."

But she hadn't, and Rowen wasn't prepared. "I—they—our town was … attacked. They were killed."

Shawn's mother froze with her napkin an inch from her lips. "Oh dear," she said. "I'm so sorry. Maybe I should have taken my son's advice."

Rowen smiled wanly. "It's okay. It was a long time ago."

"So you live with your aunt and uncle?" Shawn's dad said, his tone chipper, clearly trying to bump the conversation to a new track.

"Just my uncle," Rowen corrected, not understanding the sudden look that passed between the human adults. Maybe they thought her aunt was also dead? "My aunt Laurel is staying at her other house. She lives there with her parents."

"Her parents. Is she … young?"

Rowen blinked a few times. "I don't know. What's young?"

Meghan started to cough, drawing concerned glances from her parents. Had she … choked on something?

"Laurel's in her thirties," Rowen said when everyone's attention returned to her. then suddenly she realized what they were all thinking. "Oh, her parents are quite old. That's why they live together.

A round of *ahh*s circled the table and everyone was nodding.

"She's expecting a … baby," Rowen added, hoping they hadn't noticed the pause as she took a moment to remember the human word for sprout.

"Oh, that's lovely," Shawn's mother said, her face beaming while Meghan rolled her eyes and hitched lower over her plate. "When?"

"It's too soon to tell."

Another look and Rowen knew she'd said the wrong thing again. Why hadn't Tamani answered her texts! This was way harder than she expected. No one asked a bunch of questions like this in dance class and Rowen had no idea why her answers were wrong—just that they clearly were.

"What do they do?" Shawn's mother asked before the silence grew too awkward.

Finally! A question she'd been coached to answer. "Laurel is a professor at Berkeley. My uncle Tamani is in security."

"One of those civil contracting gigs?" asked Shawn's father, and Rowen just smiled. She hadn't been expecting a follow-up question. "I hear those pay pretty well." Shawn's mother made a clacking sound and the man stopped talking, though it was with visible effort. Rowen decided she'd been wrong; human etiquette was a complete mystery.

At that moment she felt Shawn's hand slip onto her thigh. Rather than settle her, it made her even more jumpy and she wished her meal were actually disappearing as quickly as her illusion suggested. Sadly, in the end she couldn't even eat the peas—they'd been prepared in vegetable oil, but also salted. Thank the goddess she'd filled up on mangoes and Sprite before leaving her apartment.

Fortunately, conversation turned to ballet, and at the mention of upcoming performances Meghan perked up considerably, filling the silence while Rowen basked in the feel of Shawn's warm hand on her thigh, occasionally jostling when he laughed, or caressing her skin with his fingertips.

Still, it seemed like hours before the dinner wound down and Shawn's mom rose and reached for Rowen's plate.

"Oh, please, I'll clear my own," Rowen said desperately.

"Not a chance," the human woman said with a grin, and all Rowen could do was hope she wouldn't notice how heavy the seemingly-empty plate was. She'd hoped she could find a way to scrape it into the garbage without anyone noticing, but Shawn's mother had the plate in the sink before Rowen could say another word.

"Come on," Shawn said, pulling her to her feet. "We've got an hour before you have to catch the BART. Let's go to the beach. Meghan's going to come too," he added, more to Meghan than to Rowen.

"Oh, I can't go to the beach."

Shawn blinked. "Why not?"

Because my faerie sentry uncle told me not to, didn't seem like an appropriate response. But Rowen knew better than to ignore Tamani's warnings. Even—no, maybe particularly—cryptic ones. "It's nighttime," she finally said.

"We're not *swimming*," Meghan said, patronizingly. "The Pacific in the fall? At night? We're not that crazy. We're just going to go walk the boardwalk."

"Oh." That seemed moderately better. But Tamani's words filled her mind: *If something happens, you use that phone to call me, or call Laurel if I don't answer. And you get as far from the ocean as you can.* She shivered, remembering the intensity in his eyes as he said it. Of course, that had been weeks ago. If it were such a dire situation, surely he would have updated her. Or answered a single text in the last week.

Besides, the boardwalk wasn't *exactly* the beach.

TWENTY-FOUR

ROWEN TRIED NOT TO LOOK PARANOID AS SHE peered around every corner and jumped at every noise—and on the boardwalk, there was a *lot* of noise. Shawn actually commented on how quiet it was, now that summer was over and all the tourists had gone home, but if this was quiet Rowen was quite sure she didn't want to come back when it was loud. But her fingers were twined through Shawn's and that helped her feel secure. Safer. Illusions aside, Shawn was about a foot taller than her and his shoulders nearly twice as broad. Realistically, between his bulk and her magic, there wasn't much that could threaten them.

"Sorry about my dad," Shawn said as they traversed the space between two attractions.

Rowen had no idea what Shawn was talking about. She tried to puzzle it out for a moment but finally just asked. "What do you mean?"

"You know, prying about your uncle's job."

"Oh." Seriously, human etiquette. Defied logic.

"Dad's an engineer, so, you know. Kind of awkward, just says whatever comes to mind. He knows what tuition costs at Scazio—"

"—and tights, and pointe shoes—" Meghan added in a grumble.

"—and that." Shawn grinned and made a half-hearted shrug. "He's always curious how people pay. Almost everyone there is old money, or Silicon Valley big shots."

Rowen was getting the idea that humans had an incredibly unhealthy relationship with money. Not quite like trolls, who hoarded gems and metals the way ravens hoarded buttons and sugar-glass—instead humans seemed to separate themselves into castes, the way Avalon used to be. Only instead of grouping people by their abilities, they were separated by a secret money number at which others had to guess through clues, like who got scholarships and who lived in the sand valley. (The sand valley sounded like a terrible place to Rowen, but judging by how much humans liked the beach, presumably they would enjoy a sand valley, too.)

Apparently Shawn's dad had been trying to figure out what Tamani's secret money number was. And even though humans thought it was a very important thing to know about each other, they also thought it was impolite to ask about it, so

Shawn had apologized.

Every time Rowen thought she was getting a handle on this new life of hers, the world seemed to open up to new complexities. She decided it might be best to go with the truth. Just this once. “Honestly, I really don’t understand money. I tell Tam what I need and he makes sure I have it.”

In perfect synchrony, Shawn and Meghan stopped walking and gave Rowen the same look she got from Mitchell whenever she tried to answer his questions.

“I guess that explains that,” Shawn said, raising his eyebrows.

Meghan muttered something that sounded suspiciously like *rich witch*, but—though Rowen had never met any witches, and maybe humans had different ideas about them—Rowen was pretty sure she’d misheard.

Shawn chuckled and took her hand. “Don’t take this the wrong way, but I’m gonna say it because I think maybe nobody ever said it to you before. You’re one of the privileged elite, Rowen. I bet most people have problems you’ve never even *heard* of, because your family has so much money that you don’t even know what money is.”

“I do—” Rowen began to protest, but realized that if she pressed the issue she might wind up exposing just how ignorant she really was—and not just about money. “I mean, that is—”

"It's okay, really," Shawn said lightly, in spite of his sister's glower. "Don't worry about it. We're pretty comfortable ourselves—but you have to be a lot more than *comfortable* to afford Scazio, unless you're super-human like Meghan. Honestly my parents would probably have just financed her senior year, if that's what it took." And then, practically shouting straight at Meghan, he finished, "They're very proud of her!"

Meghan turned her face away, but Rowen thought she was smiling a little.

An odd buzz rose from further down the boardwalk. Shawn slowed down, pulling Rowen closer, and reaching out for the sleeve of Meghan's jacket.

"What?"

He pointed, silently.

The crowd seemed to be moving strangely—as if being drawn to someplace Rowen couldn't see. Shawn was taller; maybe he could.

But another sound, coming from the direction of the ocean, caught Rowen's ear. She turned to the inky-black waves.

Music hung eerily in the wind.

"Do you hear that?" Rowen asked.

"Hear what?" Shawn asked, an uneasy quaver in his voice.

"The music," Rowen said, tugging on his hand. "It's getting louder." She turned back to Shawn, but he was standing stock-still, his eyes unfocused. Meghan looked more graceful—her head cocked to the side, her arms in a soft first position—but she, too, wore an oddly blank expression. "Meghan?" Rowen said, quietly.

Meghan turned—not to Rowen, but to Shawn. She was glaring at him, her face twisted into a grimace of rage and hate so powerful Rowen stepped back in fear. A screech escaped Meghan's lips and she slammed a fist into Shawn's face.

Rowen leapt back with a shriek of her own as other screams sounded all around her, centering on whatever it was Shawn had noticed ahead of them on the boardwalk. Her eyes widened as she whirled, trying to look everywhere at once. All around her people were fighting, the sickening thud of flesh striking flesh playing percussion as the haunting music continued its awful crescendo.

Shawn cast his sister to the ground with a backhanded blow, then knelt over her prone form, and drew his fist back.

Without thought, Rowen grabbed Shawn's raised forearm and tugged at it, but his eyes were fixed on Meghan with a murderous glow .His free hand was reaching for her neck, gripping tightly. Tears poured down Rowen's face and she screamed his name, over and over, but he didn't hear her. He didn't seem to be hearing anything at all.

Hearing...

Rowen glanced back toward the ocean. Shawn hadn't been

able to hear the music—which had started about the same time as everyone on the boardwalk lost their minds.

Everyone *human*.

Rowen had to stop the music.

But … how?

Rowen heard a gagging sound and turned back to see Shawn had gotten both hands around Meghan's neck and was now choking the life out of her. Rowen had seen this sort of thing on Netflix and it never ended well. Desperation made her throw herself at Shawn once more, but the physical might that had made her feel so safe five minutes ago was now a fairly immediate problem. Meghan didn't have time for Rowen to figure out where the music was coming from and put a stop to it.

Could she stop *Shawn* from hearing the music?

Rowen flung herself across his back and covered his ears with her hands, but he simply reached up and slapped away one hand, then the other. It gave Meghan a chance to wheeze in a strangled breath, but that was temporary fix at best. Rowen's chest was starting to ache with her sobs and she had to gulp in air and try to *think*!

His phone. His music. He was never without his headphones.

Dodging around Shawn's flailing elbows and Meghan's kicking feet, Rowen darted quick hands into the front pocket of Shawn's hoodie and came out with a metal rectangle wrapped in white cords. Grateful that she'd spent so much time texting the last few weeks, Rowen opened the phone and went right to Shawn's music, selecting the first playlist she found and cranking the volume all the way up. Crossing her toes for luck, she jumped onto Shawn's back and jammed the earbuds into his ears.

For a few seconds she thought it wouldn't work, but then Shawn yanked his hands away from Meghan's throat and a wordless wail of dismay escaped his mouth. Rowen grabbed his ears with both hands, holding the earbuds in, and pushed her face in front of his, where he couldn't help but see her.

She's never seen Shawn terrified. It seemed wrong for someone like him to feel such fear. He raised his hands to where hers covered his ears, but she shook her head. His hands fell back to his side.

Pain radiated through Rowen's shoulder as Meghan dived into her, shoving her away from Shawn. By the time Rowen righted herself, Shawn was fending off blows from his sister, shouting wordlessly. Rowen tried to help, but Shawn had apparently had tussles with his twin sister before, because after another moment's hesitation, he spun her arms behind her back and simply restrained her.

Meghan writhed in his hold and Rowen rushed forward to check her pockets, hoping for more headphones, but even though she found Meghan's phone, there were no earbuds. Rowen held her hands over Meghan's ears instead, and that did make her stop struggling so hard, but this method clearly wasn't as effective. Finally she gestured to Shawn that they should retreat back the way they'd come, but Shawn hardly needed her encouragement. They were surrounded by noise and chaos and violence like Rowen had only seen once before, back in Avalon.

The day her parents died.

Rowen gasped as her memory assaulted her, every psychic scar she'd ever sustained splitting open anew. She grimaced against the onslaught; she wasn't in Avalon, these were not trolls, and if she lost her head now, she might lose Shawn and Meghan too.

A woman fell to the ground in front of Rowen, blood pouring from a gash on her forehead, and all Rowen saw was her mother's headless corpse, it's glassy eyes staring, and yet not staring, right into her. Rowen bit off a shriek, and it took all of her self-control to swallow her terror and step over the injured woman.

She had to get Shawn and Meghan *out.* Rowen stumbled on a loosened board, both hands slipping from Meghan's ears, and she began writhing against Shawn's hold. Rowen reached up to block Meghan's ears once more, but seconds later a man started waling on Shawn, slackening his grip and allowing

Meghan to wrench her head from Rowen's grasp. They were only perhaps a minute's walk from the parking lot and Shawn's car, but there were fifty raving humans between it and them and now *two* people were hitting Shawn. Something in his eyes told Rowen that Shawn would never let his sister go, no matter what it cost him, but a few more hard blows and it wouldn't be his choice to make.

It was after sunset and Rowen was already feeling weak, but she wasn't helpless. Gritting her teeth, she closed her eyes and felt for the river of photons rushing over her skin. It would take some effort to bend them around herself *and* her friends, but she thought she could manage it—there.

When Rowen opened her eyes again, Shawn's former assailants were beating one another bloody—and his sister's expression, though still full of rage, had taken on a hint of confusion. Rowen placed her hands over Meghan's ears and nodded her head toward the parking lot, but Shawn was looking around uneasily, his eyes unfocused. For a moment Rowen was afraid he'd fallen sway to the madness once more, but . . . no. He wasn't acting murderous.

He was acting *blind.*

Making *other people* invisible was harder than she'd realized. All Summer illusions were manipulations of light, and vanishing was especially tricky—though after the trolls invaded Avalon, many more Sparklers worked to master it than ever before. Forcing light to go *around* yourself instead of bouncing off of your skin was challenging enough, but unless you also wanted to be blind you had to keep some light flowing to your own eyes. Rowen had been able to do so for years, but she didn't think she could adjust the illusion to accommodate Shawn. And she wasn't sure how long she could maintain the illusion as it was.

Trusting Shawn's strength, Rowen let go of Meghan's ears and circled to Shawn's shoulder, where she began pulling him down the boardwalk toward the car, doing her best to ignore the mayhem around her.

When they reached Shawn's vehicle, Rowen dropped their cloak of invisibility, weak-kneed and short of breath. She'd held bigger illusions longer, even helped with Avalon's mighty fireworks shows from time to time, but that had always been in full sunlight, with plenty of sugar in her system.

Shawn held a squirming Meghan in one arm as he dug a set of keys from his pocket, but she seemed to be thrashing somewhat less violently. Or was that was wishful thinking? Blackness was closing in on Rowen's vision and her words slurred as she tried to tell Shawn to put Meghan in the back seat. It was only when she couldn't make her tongue work that she realized it didn't matter; with his music blaring Shawn couldn't hear her anyway.

Luckily, he seemed to have made a few connections and he

tossed Meghan into the back seat and slammed the door shut behind her.

"Hurry and get in!" Shawn bellowed, flinging open his own door as Rowen stumbled around the back of the vehicle.

"*Sguirhh!*" called an impossibly high-pitched voice—and in spite of herself, Rowen turned toward the command. It had been a long time since someone had commanded her to *stop* in Gaelic, and the person issuing the command had seriously butchered the pronunciation, but it was close enough—

Rowen froze.

Running toward them from the direction of the beach were three humanoid figures, too small to be trolls, too *green* to be humans, and far too heavily armed to be friendly.

Throwing out one arm to help her aim, Rowen threw out a burst of light between herself and her assailants. They reeled back, clawing at their faces with webbed fingers, as Rowen sank to her knees.

Oh. With a sinking feeling she realized she'd officially pushed herself past her limits.

Rowen half-stumbled-half-crawled to the passenger door, pulled it open, and slid into the vehicle, barely managing to get the door closed before Shawn squealed his tires backing out.

Meghan was sobbing in the back seat, but at least she wasn't fighting anymore. Shawn slammed the car into gear and zoomed away from the boardwalk.

"What the hell just happened!" Shawn shouted. He'd removed his earbuds, but his stereo was pumping out music at near-deafening volume.

Rowen was having trouble making her mouth move, but there was one more thing. She had to do one more thing. Her fingers fumbled as she reached for her phone and held it out to Shawn. "Call … Tamani. Promise … call … Tamani."

Darkness descended.

TWENTY-FIVE

TAMANI LOUNGED ON THE BACK VERANDA WITH tiny Sharlet curled up, asleep, on his bare chest. They'd been napping in the last of the evening rays, but even when he woke in the darkness Tamani couldn't bear to disturb his daughter. Laurel would come out and check on them eventually. He stroked Sharlet's back softly, pausing when she stirred beneath his fingertips. It was so strange to transition from not-a-father, to a father. How could one small moment change so much?

Despite how peacefully she was sleeping now, his tiny fae was quite the chatterbox when she was awake, rattling on in frenetic Gaelic—which was emerging as her language of choice, much to Laurel's dismay. But Sharlet spoke English just as well and her preference wouldn't hinder actual communication with her mother. Probably.

Tamani heard the swish of the sliding door opening behind him, but rather than treading softly to avoid waking

Sharlet, Laurel's footsteps came in a clattering rush. Tamani looked up at her, brows scrunched together.

"It's a boy," Laurel said. "Calling on Rowen's phone. He won't tell me anything. He said Rowen made him promise to talk to you."

As quickly but carefully as possible, Tamani shifted their sleeping daughter to Laurel's arms and took the phone. "Hello?"

"Is this Tamani?"

"Yes," he snapped. He glanced at Laurel, who was carrying Sharlet inside, but his intuition was crackling. Something was terribly wrong.

"There was a … riot," the boy said, sounding panicked. "Weird things happened. Rowen *did things*. I don't know how to explain. But she fainted."

"Fainted? Is she still unconscious?"

"Yeah. But she told me to call you right before she went out."

Tamani rubbed at the bridge of his nose. "What's your name?"

"Shawn."

"Listen, Shawn, this is *very* important. Was Rowen injured? Is she unconscious because someone hit her, for example."

"No. I mean, she got pretty jostled, but nothing that would knock her out. She—I know this sounds crazy, but she was …

I think she did something so we could get way. I don't think anyone else got away, the lights went out and then there was a huge flash and … and she fainted. I don't know how else to describe it. I've got her in my front seat; I'm taking her to the hospital."

"No! Don't you dare!"

"It's okay. My mom works there. The staff knows me. I can get her in fast."

"Shawn," Tamani hissed in a voice he rarely used, even with brand-new sentry trainees. "If you care for this girl at all do *not* take her to a hospital. If you do, you will never see her again; I promise you that."

Either he'd stunned the human into silence, or the call had dropped. Tamani looked up and saw Laurel standing in the doorway, her eyes wide and frightened. He twisted the phone away from his mouth. "Can you turn on the news?" he whispered, following her into the house before turning his attention back to Rowen's friend. "Are you still there?"

"I don't understand," the voice said.

"I know. But that's why Rowen told you to call me. She needs help a hospital can't give her. She needs you to go back to her apartment. Can you do that? I'll text you the address as soon as I hang up. There's a keycard in her purse. Once there, you need to turn on every light in the house." He hesitated in front of the TV as Laurel flipped through the channels. "Yes,

Shawn. Every light in the house. Then get the Sprite out of the fridge and try to get her to drink as much of it as possible."

Laurel straightened and turned to him, pointing at the screen. She'd found a newscast with live footage of a police helicopter shining lights down at a riot on the boardwalk at Torpedo Wharf.

"No, don't bother with water; that won't help her at all." He wished the reporters would show more of the ocean in the shot, but obviously that wasn't the humans' focus. They had no idea it *ought* to be their focus. And even if they had, it was pretty hard to make out details on the jumpy, grainy video. Were there sea fae in the waves? It was too dark to be sure. "What? Yes, I know this all sounds weird to you, but I promise, it's what she needs. No, don't cover her with a blanket. In fact, if you can take her jacket off, all the better."

Good, now he was telling a boy to undress his niece. This was just fabulous.

"Just take her there and stay with her, okay? I'm almost five hours away, but I'll drive as fast as I can." Luckily, there was no cop in the world who could give a Ticer a ticket. With luck he could make the drive in half the usual time.

Ending the call, Tamani shoved his phone into his pocket and reached for Laurel, pulling her close. "I want you and Sharlet in Avalon."

"Tonight?"

"Right now. I want you two safe before I leave for San Francisco."

"Rowen—"

"Didn't follow directions. And now she's paying for it." He tilted his head at the TV. "The sea fae did this. I've had an amazing week with you and Sharlet, but it looks like vacation time is over. Probably should have been over sooner," he added in a mutter.

Laurel nodded stoically as Tamani grabbed a shirt and pulled it over his head.

"I'll go to Avalon while you pack. I'll let you through on my way back out."

"Why?"

Tamani gritted his teeth; he hated the feeling of being a puppet on Mischa's strings. "I need Lenore."

He turned to Laurel, and her eyes reflected his. Reluctant acceptance. "There's really no other way, is there?"

"If there is, I haven't got time to figure it out." He touched the key at his chest, feeling more like Klea than Yuki—planning to use someone else's power to advance his own agenda. His intentions were better than the rebel Mixer's ever had been, but the line felt thin tonight. "When you come to the gate, please bring me anything you think might help Rowen recover from burning herself out. And …" he hesitated. This was a touchy subject, but there was no getting around it. "I'm going to need a couple of memory elixirs."

"Oh, Tam." He couldn't tell if she was sad or disappointed. And he didn't want to think about it too hard.

"Rowen has left me with no choice. She was warned," he added, but his tone lacked heat.

Laurel touched his shoulder. "The elixir Yeardley and I were putting together still isn't strong enough to protect you from immersion in seawater, but it should help with the sand and the spray."

He pulled her close and kissed her hard. "Every little bit helps." One more squeeze of her hand and Tamani was off to Avalon.

***

"It's the middle of the night," Ariana said, her voice raspy. "I wouldn't open the door to anyone but you."

"I'm afraid I counted on that," Tamani whispered, though it hardly mattered; he was here to wake the only person still sleeping in the house. "I need to speak to Lenore."

"Len?" Ariana asked, wide-eyed—but her expression betrayed a flash of knowing as instinct kicked in; prescience honed through decades handfasted to one of Avalon's most battle-hardened sentries.

"I need her. If she's willing," Tamani whispered, not speaking his regret. Ariana would hear it anyway.

"Willing?" Ariana said, with more than a touch of bitterness. "If only that were an issue. She is her father's daughter."

"Ari." Tamani rested his hands on the slight woman's shoulders, faced her in the dim glow of the phosphorescing blossom she held in one hand. "It shouldn't be dangerous. Not to her. I'll do my very best to keep her safe."

"You did you best to keep Shar safe, too." It wasn't an accusation.

But Tamani shook his head anyway. "No. Shar did his best to keep *me* safe."

Ariana looked away, her lips pressed tightly together. She knew the difference—knew that the reason Tamani hadn't died was that Shar had.

Agony filled Tamani's chest, but he forced the words out anyway. "You've sacrificed more than enough for the good of others. If things get bad, Len's safety will be my first priority. I promise."

Ariana swallowed visibly, then nodded. On silent feet she padded out of the room and returned a few minutes later with a surprisingly alert Lenore. She was taller than both Rowen and Laurel, but Tamani had known her since she was a brand-new sprout; in his eyes she would always be small. *Too* small. Self-doubt rippled through him. She'd never even been out of Avalon. She might have no idea how powerful she was.

For that matter—maybe she wasn't.

Tamani's mouth went dry and for a few moments he couldn't speak.

Lenore sat on the edge of a settee and stared at him, wordlessly, her appearance and manner both an aching echo of Avalon's unsung savior.

"Lenore, did your father ever take you outside of Avalon to test your Enticement abilities on humans? Through the Manor, maybe?"

She rolled her eyes up to him. "What do you think?"

The answer came to him instantly—even in death, it would seem, Shar was one step ahead of Tamani. What other contingencies had he prepared, during those years when Tamani had found it impossible to plan his own life past his next encounter with Laurel? "Of course he did. Was he impressed?"

Lenore was silent for a long time. Then she simply said, "Very."

Tamani closed his eyes against the hope this kindled in him. Hope—and concern. He really was Mischa's pawn, now. But perhaps it had always been so; did knowing it actually make anything worse? He was gaining a new appreciation for Shar's legendary grumpiness. "Will you help me?" he asked softly.

"Every year," Lenore said, looking pointedly away from

her mother, "on my birthday, my father would take me on a walk up to the World Tree. He would tell me about his work, and what he'd been doing all year. He told me secrets no one but he was supposed to know. And every year, underneath the canopy of the World Tree, he would ask me if I was willing."

"Willing?" Tamani asked before Ariana could find her voice. There was no way she'd known about this.

"Willing to carry on his work if anything should happen to him. Protecting Avalon by any means necessary. And every year, I swore to him that I was. My father was the greatest champion of Avalon in a generation. I had only five birthdays to hear of his work, but I remember every word." Lenore rose, seeming to grow a hand's span in an instant, her eyes boring into Tamani. "To question my willingness is an insult to his memory."

Tamani couldn't stop the grin that slid onto his face. He extended a hand to the scion of the Unseelie, the half-orphaned heir of the hidden court.

With fire in her eyes, she took it.

TWENTY-SIX

TAMANI WAS CAREFUL NOT TO LAUGH AS LENORE spent her first elevator ride gripping the handrail for dear life—and when she emerged, she braced her hands against the wall like a tree frog, looking more than a little sick. She seemed to be recovering quickly enough, and anyway she'd managed it far more stoically than Rowen.

When her pushed open the front door every light in the apartment was blazing, and Tamani found three teens draped in a haphazard snake across the entirety of the cornered sectional. A human girl was slumped face-up over Shawn's shins, his torso bent around the angle and curled alongside Rowen's back, one hand resting on her shoulder.

Tamani hadn't been expecting a second human, but no matter. He had plenty of memory elixir. Laurel hated making the stuff, so whenever he prevailed on her to do so—which wasn't often, though it was undeniably helpful in his vigilante work—she made a large batch.

He noted two cans of Sprite on the coffee table; both were open and a line of condensation indicated that one was empty, the other halfway. At least the human boy knew how to follow directions.

"Interesting," Lenore said dryly from just behind him.

The humans looked pretty beat up. Tam took a few moments to catalogue their injuries: multiple scrapes and bruises, a few pretty good gashes, but nothing too serious. He wondered if they had rifled through the medicine cabinets when they got here, looking for first aid supplies. Those that were of any use to humans they wouldn't have recognized as such—no sense stocking conventional human remedies in a Mixer's house. One more reason to make them forget the whole night.

Tamani leaned closer toward the human girl, peering at the swelling and discoloration at her neck. Anger and guilt twined within him—someone had come damn close to killing her. A sea fae? Another human, under the influence of their musical Enticement? Tamani shook his head. He couldn't be sorry he'd spent the week with his new family, but proof that his idyll had yielded serious consequences was hard to face.

The radio had reported a steady increase in injuries as he and Lenore sped down from Orick, and a few deaths had been confirmed once the human authorities quelled the riot. It was blood on his hands—far from the only blood on his hands, but blood nevertheless.

"Hey," Tamani said, nudging Rowen gently. "Let's move you to the balcony. You can get the first rays when the sun rises."

"What?" Rowen mumbled. "Ow!" She grasped her elbow, where Tamani spotted a three-inch gash, glazed over with coagulating sap.

"Lenore, my kit?"

Rowen's eyes widened as Shar's daughter offered a box to Tam. "Len! What are you doing here?"

"We can discuss it later," Tamani whispered. "We've got to get these two on their way first. He's got a car, right?"

"Yes?" Rowen's voice was rich with suspicion and Tamani knew he had to get this over with as soon as possible—rip the tree out by the roots.

"The elixir won't keep him from driving," Tamani said evenly. "I'll take them downstairs, dose them, and get them on their way. Next time you see them, just pretend last night never happened."

Rowen bolted upright before Tam could get the binding strip in place.

Tamani sighed. "Rowen, *don't.* None of this would be necessary if you had done as you were told and stayed away from the beach."

Guilt flashed across her features but she shook her head and made no effort to keep her voice low. "None of this is necessary anyway!"

"It absolutely is," Tamani hissed, glancing at the humans—who had begun to stir. "You've got to realize that."

"I won't let you," Rowen said.

"It's not your choice to make," Tamani snapped, and immediately regretted his tone. He needed sleep. And sunlight. So did she, actually.

"If you do this, I will never forgive you," she whispered.

"Would you forgive me?"

As one, Tamani and Rowen turned to Lenore.

She lifted a shoulder. "I don't need an elixir. I can just tell them to remember last night differently. It's a bit more precise than the elixirs, actually."

Tamani shook his head—whatever secrets Shar had taught her, she'd never been through sentry training, and she was making a classic rookie mistake. Basic Enticement caused members of the animal kingdom to follow wherever they were led. In humans, this was accompanied by a state of extreme suggestibility. As far as Tamani knew, Enticed humans would do their very best to follow any instructions they were capable of understanding; they would adopt beliefs they were told to adopt, or forget things they were told to forget, and adjust their speech and actions accordingly. If asked to believe contradictory claims, like "this rock is blue" and "this rock is not blue," they would express confusion and doubt, but would still do everything in their power to follow the instructions they'd been given.

As long as they were conscious—a human instructed to stop breathing would do so, but as soon as they passed out, breathing would resume. They had to be able to process and understand their actions.

The force of instructions given ended when the Enticement ended, but the memory of accepting those instructions remained. Humans could be instructed to forget things, but after the Enticement ended they would remember those things *and remember forgetting them when instructed*, which led to exactly the kind of curiosity and suspicion sentries existed to eliminate. The rule was, if a sentry ever Enticed a human to do something said human might have a hard time justifying to themselves later, memory elixir was mandatory.

Walking Lenore through all of this would take time, however, and Tamani wanted things settled before the humans woke up, so he simply said, "No. They'd remember as soon as the Enticement wore off."

"Only if you do it shallow. You can't tell them to *act like* they've forgotten; you have to tell them to change the memory entirely. That way, when the Enticement wears off, the old memory just isn't there anymore."

Between Rowen and Lenore, Tamani was beginning to understand some of the things he'd heard concerning the stubbornness of youth. "Len, it won't work. They'll do their best to obey, but only if they understand. I can't tell them what to do in Gaelic, and I can't tell them to build a rocket ship—" At the furrowing of Lenore's brow, Tamani realized his mistake. "It's a human thing they don't know how to build. They would try, but they'd fail. They don't know how to change their own memories, so just telling them to do it isn't enough."

"They do know," Lenore insisted. "They do it all the time. They just don't realize it. You have to help them remember that first, that's all."

A chill went through Tamani at the realization that Lenore might not be speaking from bravado. "Len, have you … done this before?"

She rolled her eyes. "I told you—"

"About your training, yes." Tamani shoved his hands in his pockets before Lenore could notice they were trembling. On the drive down he'd asked about her physical range and how many humans she could manage at one time, but it had never occurred to him to ask if she could also do impossible things, too—like permanently rewriting a human's memories. What were the limits on *that*? Could she use it to alter personalities? Desires? Assuming she wasn't mistaken or exaggerating, Tamani could imagine a dozen ways Len could take over the entire human world in less than a month.

And he'd brought her here. Just as Mischa hoped. *Knots-for-brains*, he berated himself. *You have less control over this than a dandelion seed in a tornado.* He had a sudden desire to smack himself in the face.

"Would you prefer I handle them, Rowen?" Lenore pressed.

"No!" Rowen said, rising from the couch, imposing herself between friends and fae—not that it would make any difference.

"Why?" Lenore's voice was so calm. She didn't even sound tired. "Their knowledge threatens Avalon. It shouldn't even be a question. At this point, you'll need to convince me not to."

Tamani's jaw dropped, never mind that he was in agreement with her.

Rowen's head was shaking back and forth spasmodically. "You don't understand. I can't just lie to him."

"There's far more at risk here than a few white lies, Row."

The nickname seemed to remind Rowen that she was talking to a friend. "Please," she whispered. "Not him."

Lenore raised one eyebrow. "So it would be okay if I did her?"

"She's his twin. You do it to her, it's essentially the same thing."

That got a flicker of hesitation from Lenore. Because they were twins? Siblings? Simply because they were family? Tamani wasn't sure. "Then are you saying you want to tell them everything?"

Rowen sucked in a breath.

"Because of you're not, you're going to have to do a lot of lying about tonight anyway. So you may as well have those lies be something that protects Avalon." Lenore raised an eyebrow. "And probably a lot more believable."

Rowen looked at the boy, then back at Lenore in panic, and Tamani knew that something very serious had happened while he was out of town.

***

It was an impossible choice. Rowen knew Lenore and Tamani were right: Avalon would be safer if Shawn and Meghan just forgot what they'd been through. What they'd seen her do. But if she allowed them to erase Shawn's memory, she'd have to lie to him tomorrow. And the next day. For the rest of … however long Rowen would know him. How long would that be? Did it matter? Would they still be together in six months? A year? How many lies added up to a genuine mistake?

But the thought of telling them the truth made her feel sick. Because then *they* would have to lie to other people for the rest of their lives—assuming they would agree to such a thing. How far could Rowen trust a human girl who had hated her less than twenty-four hours ago? Who still sort of did?

Worse, she might lose Shawn entirely if he knew the truth. It had taken her months to accept humans as anything but regrettable inferiors, and she had always known they *existed.* It would surely be even harder for Shawn, having his whole world upended.

But the thought of feeding him a memory elixir and sending him on his ignorant way just felt wrong.

The easy thing would be to let Tamani do his job. But was it the *right* thing? Rown cared about Shawn, even cared about Meghan; mostly as Shawn's sister but also as a member of her new cadre. Could she lie to the people she cared about? Could she erase their memories? Laurel had—the human boy, David, had asked to have his memories taken, and Laurel had done it—

And Rowen had her answer. It wasn't her choice to make, but maybe it wasn't Tamani's either.

"I need to talk to Shawn."

"About what?"

Rowen didn't shriek at the sleepy rumble that sounded from behind her—but she did spin to face its owner.

"About her psycho family," spat Meghan, jumping up from the couch and tugging on his arm. "Shawn, run!"

"*Stop,*" Tamani barked.

Meghan stopped. Shawn hadn't moved from the couch, though his eyes had grown wide, all traces of sleepiness gone from his face.

"How long have you been awake?" Tamani asked, directing the question to Meghan. She was clearly under his power—and while he hadn't given her a memory elixir, at least not yet, Rowen couldn't help but feel guilty about the indignity of someone as willful as Meghan being stripped of that will.

"Long enough to hear you talking about messing with my brain," Meghan said—pleasantly. Respectfully, even. "But I couldn't just leave my brother here, so I pretended to be sleeping."

"We're not going to harm you in any way," said Tamani.

"Oh. That's good."

"Would you like to sit down?"

So Meghan did sit down, and the moment her back hit the couch cushions, a mixture of confusion and rage contorted her features—Rowen was surprised to realize that Tamani must have already released his magical hold on her mind. Even more surprised when Meghan didn't immediately try to run again.

"Rowen?" asked Shawn, not taking his eyes off his sister. "What's going on?"

"I want to give you a choice," she replied, turning to Tamani. "I want you to let them choose for themselves, Tam. I can't make the choice for them, and I don't think you should, either. It should be their choice, like with that—David."

Tamani's pained expression made for a bitter victory.

"What the *hell* are you talking about?" Meghan said, making no effort to conceal her anger.

"You've had a rough night," Tamani said. "And you've seen some things you'd be better off forgetting. I came here to help you with that. But *my niece* has other ideas."

"Help us … forget? What, like *Men in Black*? You know—" Shawn made a fist and wiggled his thumb, as if pressing an imaginary button on a tiny device of some kind.

Three faeries blinked owlishly at Shawn.

"Holy—Rowen, you're an *alien?*"

"Don't be stupid," Meghan growled.

But Shawn held a hand up to her. "Meghan, something freaky happened at the dock, you know it did. Rowen got us out alive, but she did stuff! Plus, she tastes like honey."

Tamani stared at Rowen.

Lenore stared at Rowen.

Rowen stared at Shawn.

"I finally figured out the taste thing," Shawn muttered, abashed.

"*Gross*," Meghan said. "I don't even want to know. Rowen's … uncle? Whoever you are, just kill me now."

Rowen felt a little like dying, herself.

"I'm not going to kill you," Tamani said, sounding a touch strangled.

"Maybe you'd *prefer* to forget everything that happened last night," Rowen said, desperate for her love life to no longer be the center of everyone's attention. She glanced back at Lenore. "My friend can send both of you home thinking that you took me to the BART after dinner. Went to that boardwalk by yourselves. Managed to get away from the riot mostly unscathed. We can all show up to Scazio—well, not today, but in the next day or two—and everything will be … like it was before."

"Why would I choose to do that?" Shawn asked. "I mean, if he's not going to kill us …"

"No one is going to kill you!" Tamani said, shooting to his feet.

Rowen felt tears build up in her eyes and forced herself to blink them back. "Because if you know the truth it'll change everything you ever thought you knew. And you certainly won't want to be my boyfriend anymore."

This time, Tamani stared at Shawn. *Glared* at Shawn. Lenore, however, continued looking at Rowen.

Oh—right. Almost everything Rowen thought she knew about humans, she'd learned from Lenore. They'd spent many a summer's evening scaring each other with tales of the ferocious beasts on the other side of the gate. Then, after abandoning Lenore in Avalon, Rowen had spent months getting to know these strangely appealing animals a little better. Or, in Shawn's case, a lot better.

What must Lenore think of her, now?

Shawn was silent, glancing from Tamani to Lenore to Rowen and back again, as though trying to gauge their seriousness. Finally, with a glance at his fuming sister he said, "If you can really make me forget everything, then you have nothing to lose by telling me now."

That was … true, actually. It felt like cheating, somehow, but he wasn't *wrong*.

He spread his arms wide. "Tell me your secret. Tell *us* your secret. This horrible, awful thing. Then I can decide if it's so bad that I'd rather not know."

That—actually, that seemed like a pretty good idea.

"Tam?" Len asked, as if seeking permission for something.

Tamani merely nodded, looking weary. Looking, somehow, old—his mouth set in a grim line.

"I'm not from Scotland," Rowen said, starting with the easy truth. "I'm not from any country you've ever heard of. I wasn't affected by the music tonight, because I'm not human. I don't taste sweet because I always eat candy, but because I'm a highly evolved plant. And I got us off the boardwalk by making us invisible and then blinding the creatures who came after us with a flash of light. With my magic. Because …

because I'm a faerie. Not an alien, a faerie."

It was like running downhill—once she'd started, there was no stopping until she hit the bottom. Rowen held her breath, waiting for someone to say something. Anything. Meghan and Shawn were staring at her, not quite in horror, but definitely in astonishment.

Tamani stepped forward, utterly breaking the moment. "And we're about to fight a three-faerie war to save the lives of every single human in San Francisco."

TWENTY-SEVEN

AS SOON AS THE SUN ROSE, A MURKY LIGHT ON the far horizon, they all moved out to the balcony so Rowen could photosynthesize. Tamani ordered a pot of coffee up from the restaurant in the lobby and Rowen learned what that odd bitter smell—and taste—she associated with both Shawn and Mitchell actually was.

There was no way she could ever drink such a thing.

Tamani spoke in a calm, even voice, imparting knowledge Rowen had always taken for granted. He spoke briefly of the nature of the fae as the pinnacle of the plant kingdom, of seasonal birth and how it translated into different kinds of magic—but he omitted a lot, too, like the existence of Avalon and its gates.

It was a smooth, practiced explanation, a reminder to Rowen that explaining these things to Laurel, the amnesiac changeling, had been his life's purpose since before Rowen was even a seed. Meghan sat unspeaking, her hands wrapped around her steaming mug, brows scrunched together. Shawn, on the other hand, questioned everything. He interrupted, badgered, demanded proof and clarification of everything Tamani claimed.

He didn't ask Rowen anything; only Tamani. Rowen wasn't sure if she should feel rebuffed or not. He was holding her at arm's length, that was for certain. But why? Because rejecting all this meant rejecting her? Because he was simply too emotionally involved with her to accept such world-shaking information from her lips? Or did he feel more and more deeply betrayed with each new revelation, the way she'd felt increasingly guilty over her lies?

She wanted to burst in, protest that her untruths had been necessary, that she's never expected to find herself in any sort of intimate relationship with *any* human. That she hadn't expected her lies to *matter*. Several times she had opened her mouth to speak, but the only words she could come up with seemed woefully inadequate.

But finally there was no way to remain out of the conversation. "So she can change the way things look?" Shawn asked.

She. Not *you*. And addressed to Tamani, as though Rowen weren't even in the room. The pain of that stabbed her like a knife. She swallowed hard as Tamani tilted his head in her direction. "You want proof of that one too?"

Everything was still for several seconds. "Yes," Shawn finally said, his voice firm. He turned and his deep-brown eyes fixed on her. "I do."

It felt like a challenge. Rowen said nothing, only blinked slowly and, almost without thought, illusioned the empty coffeepot on the table into a tall potted iris.

Meghan gasped. Shawn's hands, which had been sitting relaxed on his knees, were now clenched into tight fists. They'd felt the compulsion of Spring magic first hand—as well as its strange musical counterpart—but flashy Sparkler magic was apparently harder to explain away. As a Summer faerie, Rowen was well-conditioned to doubt the world as it merely appeared to her eyes, but it seemed the nature of humans to be convinced by what they saw.

"Do you even know how to dance?" Meghan asked, venom in her voice.

Rowen would rather have been slapped than asked that question by *this* human; she very nearly gave a hot-tempered reply. If she hadn't felt so weary, she probably would have. Instead, she let go of her illusion and leaned back on the chaise with narrowed eyes. "No illusion. Just a lot of hard work. Illusions aren't solid; I couldn't dance with a partner if I wasn't really doing it."

Meghan pursed her lips in a way that managed to convey

both her satisfaction with that response and her basically total contempt for Rowen.

"What am I supposed to say?" Shawn asked, sounding a thousand miles away, for all he was close enough to touch. "What are *we* supposed to say?"

"Nothing, ideally. The survival of our people depends on secrecy," Tamani said. "You commit to keeping our existence a secret, or we'll take that secret away from you. And there's nothing you could possibly do to stop us."

Lenore shifted in her seat, a small movement that struck Rowen as vaguely sinister—a reminder to the humans that they continued to form memories at her pleasure. It might be funny if it weren't absolutely true.

"Tell us how you really feel, Plant Man," Meghan mumbled, and Tamani's eyes went to her.

"Humor me, Meghan; what do you love more than anything else in this world, outside of your family?"

Meghan looked startled by the sudden attention. She mumbled something unintelligible.

"So we can hear it, perhaps?"

"My ballet school," she snapped.

"And what lengths would you go to, to prevent me from destroying that school and everyone in it?"

The red flush at her neck was answer enough.

"Public knowledge of our existence very likely ends with

invasion followed by genocide or enslavement," Tamani said, slowly, choosing his words with great care. "Is that something worth being serious about?"

Meghan looked away, flicking her fingers at him in surrender.

Shawn, however, continued to wear his skepticism openly. "And if we promise to keep our mouths shut, what? You'll just … trust us?"

Tamani gave a curt nod. Rowen suspected it was far more complicated than that, and felt grateful to her uncle for his willingness to bear those complications on her behalf—but she doubted it was anywhere near enough to shrink the rift that had sprung up between herself and Shawn.

"What are you going to do about these … sea fae?" Shawn asked.

Tamani gave him a long, hard look. "I think it's best you don't know."

"I can't help if I don't know."

"Don't take this the wrong way, but I don't think you can help even if you do know."

Shawn clenched his teeth, the muscle on his cheek standing out so hard that Rowen had to suppress the urge to reach out her fingers and touch the taut skin. "Last night when Rowen stuck the headphones in my ears I—woke up? But I wasn't asleep, exactly … I don't even know what to call it.

Whatever it was, my hands were clenched around the neck of the person I love more than anyone else in the entire world, and I could remember what it had been like, for just a little while, to *hate* her." He was silent for a moment and Rowen felt tears well up in her eyes. In a raspy voice, Shawn continued. "Do you have *any* idea how that feels?"

Rowen glanced at Meghan; a single tear was trailing a shiny path down her cheek. As soon as she saw Rowen watching, she scrubbed it away with her shirtsleeve.

"The way I see it, I have two choices," Shawn said, his tone simmering with anger. "I can take the easy way out and let you erase that terrible memory. Or I can fight the bastards who made me do it in the first place and make sure that no one else ever has to feel that way."

Tamani shrugged. "You're sure?"

"You let me help beat them, and I'll keep your secret to the grave." He hesitated. "No matter what happens."

"And my niece?" Tamani pressed.

It occurred to Rowen that if the balcony were to crumble beneath her feet this very instant, she might take it as a mercy. How very like Tam, to jump right to the most humiliating subject just because it happened to be relevant.

Shawn gave her the barest of glances. "I don't know. What I do know is that you could use someone who knows the area, can help with research and supplies, and can actually swim in the ocean."

Tamani raised one eyebrow in silent acknowledgment, though Rowen couldn't help but reflect that, with Lenore around, there would be no shortage of human assistance. "At some point it'll mean turning yourself completely over to—" his eyes darted to Lenore, "—our control, and trust us to use you as we see fit."

It was the first time Shawn hesitated. But it was only for an instant. "Whatever it takes. I want them gone."

"And you?" Tamani asked, turning to Meghan.

"Me?" she squeaked. "Oh, no, you're not doing your voodoo on me."

"You don't want to get rid of them?" Shawn challenged.

Meghan stared at Shawn for a long time; there seemed to be some sort of silent conversation happening between them. Then she turned to Tamani. "You asked what I love best, and I told you. I let you take control of my body or whatever, and you so much as sprain my ankle, my dream is gone."

"I think she's right." Rowen's voice cracked as she spoke up, but she cleared her throat and continued. "There's no reason for her to fight for us. Her cost is too high."

Meghan stared at her with an intensity that made Rowen think of the word glare, except that there was no malevolence there. It was a nice change, actually. "What about you? Isn't your cost the same as mine?"

"No." Rowen lifted one shoulder as though it didn't tear her apart to say it. "I can always go to another school."

Meghan's eyes narrowed. "I think you're full of crap."

Rowen threw her hands in the air. "There's no winning with you."

Meghan looked away, holding up a hand dismissively. "I'm grateful that you saved my life. I'm even grateful you're letting Shawn help." She looked over at him and smiled sadly. "He needs to get this out of his system. And if this is how he chooses to do it, it's not my place to argue. I'll keep your crazy secret, but this isn't my fight. I have my own passion."

"Fine. The next question," Tamani said, "is what the two of you are going to tell your parents. Do they even know where you are?"

"I called them last night and told them a … version of what happened," Shawn said. "I told them I thought it was better to not be on the roads near our house while so many cops were around, and that Rowen said it was okay if we crashed here. They bought it."

"What about today?" Tamani asked. "Do they know you're hurt?"

"I may have skipped over that part," Shawn admitted.

"What's your mother going to say when you come home with bruises around your neck?" Tamani asked softly.

Both humans were quiet.

"That's what I thought." Tamani rose and stepped inside, walking to a painting on the wall and swung it out to reveal a small safe. "I'll be honest, I hate using this on something so minor, but it represents a security risk I don't feel like taking." Tamani returned to the balcony holding a small vial of blue liquid. "Open your mouth, please."

Fear crumpled Meghan's forehead, but she lifted her chin in sheer stubbornness and opened her mouth. Tamani squeezed one drop of elixir onto Meghan's tongue; Meghan closed her mouth gingerly and waited for something to happen. Several seconds passed before her eyes widened as Rowen imagined every ache and twinge in her body beginning to fade. After about a minute she started patting different parts of her body and then felt gingerly around her throat.

"Everything … everything's better," she said, breathlessly. She glanced over at Rowen, then jumped off the chair and kicked off her flats. "Look at my feet!" she squealed.

Rowen looked down at Meghan's calloused dancer's feet. It took her a moment to realize that the scabs and blisters all human dancers sported were now absent.

"My feet haven't looked this good since I started on pointe!" Meghan said—with a giggle that seemed to Rowen's ears *most* uncharacteristic of the unfailingly surly ballerina.

She turned to Shawn, but he rather than sharing in her delight, he looked serious, eyes fixed on her neck. "The bruises are gone," he said. "*Gone.* Just what does that stuff do?"

"Fixes everything. In humans, anyway," Tamani said.

"Anything?" Shawn asked.

"Anything."

"But—"

"And this is all we have left," Tamani said soberly. "Even my mate, the most skilled Mixer to blossom in decades, hasn't managed to replicate this one. Yet," he added loyally.

"But—"

"No, Shawn," Tamani said, his voice harsh. "It's better if you simply don't think too hard about it. We *can't.*"

Shawn grimaced, but didn't push; Rowen was sure he wasn't satisfied with that answer.

"Now you two can get on your way," Tamani said. "After a full burn-out Rowen *must* sleep and I imagine the both of you will crash hard when your coffee wears off. I admit, I'm not doing so great myself, and I suspect we've stretched Lenore farther than she's used to as well."

Lenore didn't nod, but looked a little offended and simply peered at Tam with one eyebrow raised over glittering eyes.

"When will you … do whatever you're going to do?" Shawn asked.

"I don't know," Tamani said.

Shawn's eyes widened.

"I have no idea when the sea fae will try something like

this again. The sea fae are almost as much a mystery to me as we were to you yesterday. I have no way to track them and no way to find them. The one person I know who ever successfully predicted their appearance disappeared without leaving me any way to contact her. We have some preparations to make, but for the most part, all we can do is wait and be ready."

He spoke calmly, but a thick tension settled over the group.

"Rowen," Tamani said, breaking the silence. "Are you well enough to escort your friends downstairs?"

He managed to make it sound more like a command than a question, and Rowen shot Tamani a look for immediately putting her and Shawn practically alone so soon after his revelations—but she stifled a sigh and rose from the chaise, still fighting the feeling that her limbs were made of iron, her feet of cement. She'd never burnt herself out before and, even as the morning sun rejuvenated her, she resolved never to do it again.

After gathering their belongings, Meghan and Shawn followed her to the elevator. They rode down in tense silence. As the humans exited the elevator, Rowen hung back, one foot in and one foot out, her back against the rubberized frame, holding the sliding panels open.

Shawn paused and Meghan took a few steps without him,

then turned and looked at him questioningly.

"Scram," he said, making a shooing motion.

She rolled her eyes in mock offense, but continued walking toward their car.

Rowen's eyes flitted to everywhere but Shawn. His hands were jammed in his pockets and his own gaze was fixed on the ground at her feet. "Thanks for, um, giving me a choice. I know you didn't have to. And I guess we never would have known if you hadn't. It would just be … gone, right?"

She nodded.

"I don't hate you," he blurted out a second later. "I just don't know how I do feel."

She nodded again, but this time she couldn't have spoken if she wanted to. Her throat felt like a vise had clamped around it and she held her breath to keep from crying.

"But I thought I owed you a thank you, okay?"

Rowen just kept nodding. Nodding and nodding, like columbine blossoms in a summer breeze. When Shawn turned toward where Meghan was waiting, he didn't say goodbye. He didn't touch her hand, or hug her, and he certainly didn't bend down for a coffee-scented kiss.

He just walked away.

Rowen watched their car all the way out of the underground lot before she took a step backward and let the doors close. She leaned her back against the wall as the elevator carried her way, tears pouring like raindrops down her face. She'd known it would happen, but this feeling inside her? There was no preparation for the savage emptiness.

If she didn't have a heart then what was it that had broken into pieces within her?

TWENTY-EIGHT

THEY PEERED OVER THE RAILING OF THE BOAT, into the blue-black depths of the ocean. "You ready?" Tamani asked.

"As ready as it's possible to be, I think," Shawn replied, voice echoing from behind his facemask.

Tamani looked to Lenore and, not one to waste words, she simply nodded.

"You'll remember everything," Tamani said, meeting Shawn's eyes. "The whole thing will actually be gentler on you for the willing surrender. But you'll remember."

Shawn gave a sharp nod, then jumped into the water.

Tamani watched Shawn sink until he was out of sight.

"You have this human magic all set up?" Lenore asked skeptically.

Tamani pushed a few keys on his computer and the feed from Shawn's camera filled the screen.

Lenore stepped backward with a gasp; Tamani managed to keep a straight face, barely.

"Sorry. I know you tried to warn me," she said shakily.

"Okay, he's just letting himself sink until you take over. We'll bring him up in fifty minutes for a fresh tank." Tamani glanced over at Lenore, trying to see if there was any visible sign when she took Shawn's will. He'd only really watched Shar work a couple of times, and nothing Tamani did was ever this precise.

Lenore stared at the computer and took a noisy breath before settling into preternatural stillness, her eyes fixed on the screen.

And then Shawn started swimming.

Shawn had been more right than he could have known when he said Tamani should use him. Not only was Shawn a good swimmer, he'd gotten scuba-certified the previous summer. Tamani and Lenore could easily have recruited any human with adequate skills, but they would have needed to make sure no one became alarmed at their absence, then erased memories of the experience. With Shawn, the only effort required was a few minutes of Tamani's time—and Enticement—to convince the high school advisor that Shawn had been accepted into an advanced oceanography research internship. This not only got Shawn excused from school for a week, it would look great on his college applications.

As a willing and able participant, Shawn had suggested that there was no need for Lenore to take control of him at all, but he hadn't considered the consequences of actually running into the sea faeries. Tamani actually suspected that Lenore might be powerful enough to wrest Shawn's mind away from any sea fae that might attempt to control him, but he knew from experience that it was far easier to maintain control of an existing thrall than to seize control from someone else.

Besides, Tamani had a few ideas for finding and catching the sea fae that might require some large-scale undersea Enticement—something he had reason to suspect would be difficult, if not impossible. Today wasn't just about reconnaissance; it was also a test run of Lenore's powers in an unfavorable environment.

So here they were in a rented boat, with top-of-the-line scuba equipment, all courtesy of Avalon's overflowing coffers. On deck, Lenore concentrated on the monitor as if playing a video game, with Shawn as her avatar—except, of course, there was no controller in her hands.

"What's that?" Tamani said, pointing to a line of darkness at the edge of the screen.

Lenore's head ticked to the side and, several fathoms below, Shawn turned his head, shining a powerful light into a shallow, shadowed valley.

"Nothing," Tamani said. "Onward."

As the minutes ticked by, with little to see but long stretches of mud and algae, Tamani tried very hard to keep his expectations low. Laurel's Mixing had enhanced his resistance to the salty sea air, but could give him no special insight into what went on beneath the waves. Tracking quarry through a forest was a matter of spotting signs of passage; under the sea, that kind of evidence wouldn't last ten minutes.

The only real hope Tamani had—beyond the possibility that Shawn could function to attract the sea fae like a worm on a fishing line—was that exploring stretches of ocean near where humans had been abducted or abandoned might turn up a clue to the sea fae's whereabouts or intentions. An artifact, a temporary shelter; *anything*, really. He knew it was a long shot. But they had to do *something*, and there were worse ways to spend their time than testing their magic and getting their sea legs.

He was so focused that the beeping of his timer made Tamani jump. "Reel him in," Tamani said, shaking a stiffness born of stillness from his limbs.

Lenore's hands clenched, and then her entire body relaxed as she rolled her neck. "He'll come up on his own."

Five more times they repeated the exercise, switching out oxygen tanks and giving Shawn time to drink and snack to keep his strength up. Aside from occasional flora and fauna, their most noticeable encounter was with a barnacle-encrusted sheet of aluminum. Tamani wasn't surprised, but as he directed the boat back toward the dock where they'd rented it, he felt disappointed anyway.

"What's it like?" Tamani asked as Shawn was peeling off his gear.

"Less invasive than I was afraid it would be. That time at the boardwalk was like being *possessed.* I wasn't … it was like watching a cheesy horror flick where you're like, 'Stupid guy! Don't go into the dark woods alone after that strange noise!' But they go anyway." He dropped his wetsuit on the deck with a soggy splat. "Down there today? I felt the *moment* Lenore took over."

Shawn's eyes darted over to Lenore, who was silent and brooding enough to give his touchy twin sister a run for her money.

"But it was a completely different experience. Not like being a puppet at all … more like she was an angel on my shoulder, telling me what to do, and I was happy to do it. Though if I tried to fight it—and realized I couldn't—probably it would have felt much different."

"But you didn't fight. Not even to test it?"

"Didn't want to. It was weird. But not unpleasant." He grinned. "Plus I've never gotten to scuba for so long in one day. It's gorgeous down there."

Tamani wasn't sure he'd seen anything he'd describe as

gorgeous today, but perhaps the video feed didn't do it justice. "Will you be up for it again tomorrow?"

"Oh yeah."

***

It was a strange feeling to have her boyfriend not texting her, but regularly texting her uncle. Rowen flinched when Tamani's phone chimed a second time as she was slipping out of the car. To his credit, Tamani didn't check the message in her presence, but they both knew who it was. Laurel was in Avalon—not a place known for getting great cell service—and even if Lenore were prone to text, she was in the car with them. After Rowen got out, Tamani was going to pick up Shawn for another day of scuba diving, and that was certainly him letting them know he was ready.

For Rowen, the scuba trips simply resulted in a long and lonely week. Lenore assured her that it was dull work, and even if Rowen had a role to play on the boat, Tamani only had so many potions to help himself and Lenore endure the salt-laden sea air. So Rowen continued going to dance class, where Meghan continued to ignore her, and her phone continued to remain utterly Shawn-free.

Rowen was grateful for her rehearsals. She could lose herself not just in the beautiful music and choreography, but the exhausting effort that left her too weary to think very hard about the collapse of her first romance. He hadn't formally rejected her—yet—but his continued silence was a sharp pain in her chest that only dulled when she pushed herself past her limits on the dance floor. She wore herself out so completely that a night of sleep often didn't feel like enough. The exhaustion helped her feel better. Or maybe it made her *not* feel, and that was simply better.

"Rowen."

Rowen turned, but the only person she saw who was paying any attention to her was Meghan.

Meghan?

Rowen peered warily at her. "Me?"

"Yes, you. Come here."

Rowen drew near, feeling like an insect approaching a Venus flytrap, and Meghan tipped her head toward one of the smaller studios. "It's empty."

Rowen preceded Meghan into the small dance classroom and waited for Meghan to speak.

Except Meghan didn't speak. She just stood there, hands clasped in front of her—

And Rowen understood. Shawn had sent his sister to formally end their relationship. It was so incredibly insulting that for the first time since Shawn had walked away from her, Rowen wasn't sad.

She was mad.

She was *furious*.

She hitched her rucksack higher on her shoulder. "You tell your brother to do his own dirty work," she snapped. "This is beneath him." She brushed past Meghan, heading for the door.

"Wait."

Rowen turned, but kept her hand on the doorknob.

"This isn't about him." Meghan's brown eyes met Rowen's light green ones. "At the auditions, on the last lift, Thomas set me down too hard. Or maybe I landed too low on my heel. Doesn't matter—it's no one's fault. The point is that I hurt my Achilles."

Rowen had no idea what an Achilles was.

Meghan's eyes dropped to the floor again and she shrugged, as if to belie the tension so thick in the air. "I hoped it was the sort of thing that you ice over the weekend, pop some Advil the next couple days, and then get over it."

"But it wasn't."

Meghan shook her head. "It got worse. I think I knew even then. The moment it happened. You know, that bone-deep instinct that you can't shake no matter how hard you try?"

"Like how I felt the night we went to the boardwalk and I knew I wasn't supposed to be at the beach?"

"Oh man," Meghan said, breathing a humorless laugh. "Good thing you didn't listen to that one."

Rowen scrunched her eyebrows together. She'd have thought Meghan would love to take back *everything* that happened that night.

"I don't know if it's just Achilles tendonitis, or if I strained it, or if I actually ruptured it; what I know is that I've been fighting the pain since auditions, and trying to hide it, and it's just been getting worse."

Given the events of the past week,Rowen actually *could* blurt out that she had no idea what Meghan was talking about because she was clueless about human biology, but she sensed this was a moment to stay quiet.

"Last week I broke down and admitted to myself that I was going to have to tell someone, or I was going to hurt my leg so badly it was going to ruin my career. *Worse* than not dancing in the Nutcracker after getting cast as the lead was already going to." She chuckled dryly. "And then Shawn told me he liked you. That you guys were *together*, and all I could think was that you were going to get to dance my part after all, because I was going to have to drop out. You were going to get everything."

Now Rowen understood. This Achilles thing was like getting a warped stem, or a gnarled foot. Long-term and not always fixable. A long recovery at the very least.

"And then the riot happened and I didn't get a chance to confess to anyone and I came back to school and …"

Meghan paused and swallowed several times and Rowen had to blink at what she was seeing. Was Meghan tearing up?

"And I procrastinated. I thought, I'll get through warm-ups first. I'll tell them at break. And I started warm-ups and it didn't hurt. So I didn't say anything. I went to *pas de deaux* class, and still, no pain. I went to Nutcracker rehearsal after lunch and I've never danced so well. And then I figured out what happened." She fingered the skin around her neck, as if feeling invisible bruises. "Your uncle said that blue stuff fixes everything. *Everything.* I didn't even think about my Achilles. I mean, bruises are one thing. Blisters on my feet, really the same thing. But a major injury? I didn't think it was possible."

"Hey, if my aunt can't make it, it must be really great stuff," Rowen joked, and then quieted when Meghan remained grim. Meghan was staring at her so intensely Rowen had to stifle the impulse to check behind her to make sure no one was standing there.

"Whatever you say you are, Rowen, I don't care. I'm okay with it. And I will keep your secret for the rest of my life and still consider myself in your debt."

"It was nothing," Rowen mumbled. She couldn't take credit for Tamani accidentally fixing a problem no one knew Meghan had.

"No," Meghan said. "It was *everything.* Thank you."

The human girl stepped forward and threw her arms

around Rowen and somehow, against all expectation, Rowen was fairly sure she'd just made a new friend.

The door burst open behind and they turned to find Mitchell and Thomas staring at them.

Mitchell backed out of the studio, looked both ways down the hallway, and then stepped in again. "Did I just walk into the Twilight Zone? No, I'm serious," he said when Meghan tried to protest. "Shawn and Rowen have been avoiding each other for a week, and I walk in and find the two of you hugging? Something is happening and I have *not* been kept in the loop. Somebody better start confessing and now."

Rowen looked between Meghan and Mitchell several times before Meghan put an arm around her shoulder and beamed at Mitchell. "Nope, we girls have to stick together. If you can't figure it out on your own, that's your problem."

And as the door started to close behind them, Mitchell said, "Then I have got a very big problem."

TWENTY-NINE

"WE CAN'T DO *ANYTHING* IF WE CAN'T *FIND* them," Tamani said to Lenore after Rowen left for Scazio the next morning. He unrolled the bathymetric chart that the cashier at the boating shop had assured him would be extremely helpful for his "upcoming deep-sea scuba trip," but he wasn't nearly so optimistic about its usefulness.

Lenore leaned over the parchment, squinting at the densely-packed, multicolored lines. "Does this mean something to you?"

"Sadly, no. But I was hoping between the two of us we could figure it out."

"Well," Lenore said, peering at the right bottom corner. "Judging by the writing over here, it's upside-down."

Tamani blew out a noisy breath and roughly spun the map until the key was legible. "Of course it is. I've studied human culture for decades—lived among them for almost fifteen years. Why do I still feel so ignorant?"

"Because you can't read an obviously complex map?" Lenore waved an arm obliquely at the empty air surrounding the balcony. "I bet almost no one out there could do it, either."

Tamani grinned. It was funny, and not a little sad, how much talking to Lenore felt like chatting with Shar. He cleared his throat. "I was hoping to mark off the places we've been and check for any obvious places to look next."

"Is it easier to read the map here than it would be on the boat? I don't understand why we're not heading out there right now."

Tamani sighed. "We've kept Shawn out of school for week already. If I felt like we were making progress, maybe … but no. We can try again over the weekend."

"But we told his … teacher, or whoever—"

"Yes, but we can't let him get behind. He actually needs his education to succeed in his future."

"Truly?" Lenore asked.

"It's different here."

"Clearly." She shrugged. "We could use someone else."

"We could, but that has its own drawbacks. Plus, I only have a few bottles of the salt potion left. I've got to make a trip up to Orick—to Avalon, really—to get more." He leaned over the map again. "I'm just not sure it's worth it. I knew it was a bit of a long shot, but I'm starting to get the idea that calling it a *long shot* was wildly optimistic."

"Surely it's just a matter of time."

"Time is something I'm not sure we have."

"I mean—before they attack."

"That's what we're trying to *prevent*," Tamani said, unsure what Lenore was getting at.

She peered at him steadily. "Wouldn't them attacking be of benefit? Then we'd know *exactly* where they were."

Tamani shook his head. "Their methods have been evolving—escalating. I'd like to stop them before they can escalate things further. Besides, if we're not already nearby when it happens, we might not be able to get there in time to be useful. We'd need to … I don't know, take a helicopter right from the top of this building." He paused. "Though I guess that's within the realm of possibility."

"So it's in everyone's best interest to go on the offensive before they can strike again."

"Ideally, yes. But we can't do anything until we locate them, and they're hiding in a substance that covers seventy percent of the earth, that neither of us can even enter." He flopped down on the chaise. "Forget a seedpod in a stack of acorns, it's like finding a grain of salt on a sandy beach, in the dark."

"They're staying close though," Lenore said, leaning against the balcony railing. "They must be. All of the attacks have been along the coastline in … whatever this city is called, right?"

"San Francisco, and yes."

"And the riot was here, too?"

Tamani nodded.

"So this is their testing ground. It stands to reason it'll also be their attack point."

"Why wouldn't they go somewhere else? I would."

"But you *know* humans. If you were a faerie whose people had literally turned into a completely different kind of faerie over the last few thousand years, would *you* trust humans to be the same everywhere in the world?"

"Good point." And it was. Again, like Shar, she saw strategic elements he simply didn't.

Lenore went back to studying the map, her brows deeply furrowed. "Where are we right now?"

"On the map?"

"Yes."

"We're not. This is just the water."

Lenore threw her hands up. "Humans are crazy."

But when Tamani opened his compass app and started seriously trying to figure out the map, Lenore joined him, and it didn't take them too long to find the dock where they rented the boat. Armed with two different colors of markers, they did their best to color in the areas they'd already searched.

"Day four we found this ravine," Lenore said, pointing. "It was so deep we used up a whole air tank checking it out."

"I should've thought of asking for a map before we started," Tamani grumbled. "This is just topography. If it were dry land, I'd want to put sentries here," he said, pointing. "Or here. Maybe here."

"I see what you mean," Lenore said. "But underwater they'd want coverage from above, and wouldn't care much about anything from this angle," she said, pointing.

Tamani straightened, his arms crossed over his chest. "Look at what we've covered. It's like less than a hundredth of the ocean on this map. And the only day we really searched what I would consider strategically viable terrain was when we scoped out that ravine."

"Live and learn," Lenore said.

Tamani kicked a pillow against the railing. "I don't have time to live and learn."

"It sounds like what you need is someone who can find the sea fae for you."

Lenore and Tamani whirled at the sound of the unfamiliar voice, knives leaping to their hands from hidden sheathes. He didn't know Lenore even *had* a knife!

Marion smiled as if amused. "Please," she said, strolling toward the open balcony door. "As if either of you could harm me."

Tamani had some definite thoughts about just what he *could* do to a Winter faerie—especially here in his home, where he'd already prepared a variety of nasty defenses against a wide array of possible threats. But he lowered his weapon and saw Lenore doing the same out of the corner of his eye. Was her diamond-edged blade bigger than his?

"How did you get in here?" he asked, not bothering to conceal his irritation.

"Human locks are no obstacle to me."

"At least not when there are plants on the other side of the door," Tamani guessed. "How did you even know to come here?"

Marion continued to look completely unperturbed. "You're the one who told me about your troubles in Scotland. Don't act like this is a huge secret."

"I meant, this apartment. This building," Tamani said, trying to hold back his temper. "Who did you contact?"

The former queen laughed a deceptively carefree laugh. "Please. I'm a Winter faerie, and you're a plant in the middle of a barren stone jungle."

"I can't believe the sentries let you near the gate," Tamani muttered, sheathing his knife. "Unless you forced your way through," he mused—child's play for her, but still an act of aggression. How would Queen Yasmine respond to *that* news, he wondered?

"Gates? Please. I took a plane. Ghastly experience. They call *that* first class?"

Tamani blinked several times, trying to imagine the former faerie queen of Avalon on a commercial transatlantic, transcontinental flight. Even he had never done such a thing. It was beyond his ability to comprehend.

"Are you telling us you can find the sea fae?" Lenore asked. Tamani mentally kicked himself for not zeroing in on the most salient point more quickly.

"Practically done already. There's a large contingent of them—two to five dozen, I could only estimate at that distance. I sensed them as the plane was swooping in to land. Completely harrowing, by the way, I recommend you never try it. If faeries were meant to fly, the Goddess would have given us wings."

"Is this a trick?"

Marion straightened and glared at Tamani as though he'd questioned her ability to rule. Again. "Of course not. Do you think I'd go to all this trouble simply to have a laugh at you? You overestimate your own value."

"Prove it."

The two stared hard at each other until Marion nodded.

"All right. Let's see. The sea fae are that way."

She gestured haphazardly, and though she did point in the direction of the ocean, Tamani wasn't certain it wasn't dumb luck.

"Oh, you have a map. I just need to orient myself on it." She glanced at Lenore. "Where are *we*?"

A smile twitched at the corners of Lenore's mouth. "On the map?"

"Yes."

"We're not," she said carefully. "This is just the water."

Tamani couldn't hold back a snort and Marion turned, glaring daggers at him. "I fail to see the humor."

"Never mind," Tamani said. "Truly, we meant no offense." That was a blatant lie. "However, if the map extended, we would be approximately here." He pointed at a spot on the table, a few inches beyond the edge of the map.

Marion nodded and grabbed a marker. After lining up the map and double-checking the directions with Tamani, she drew two lines, diagonally out into the sea. "They are somewhere between these two lines. I can't tell how far out from this distance, and there are a great many plants between us. Everything grows more specific with closer proximity. Naturally," she added dryly when Lenore gave a skeptical hum. "Don't your own abilities grow stronger and more precise the closer you are to your thralls?"

Lenore's expression turned into a glower, but she didn't respond.

Tamani studied them both for several seconds and then

asked Marion, "What did you have in mind?"

"While in Scotland I've observed a great deal of fishing—those are smelly water creatures that humans, for some reason, like to scoop up and eat—"

"I *know* what fishing is."

"—and I thought we could arrange something similar."

"I don't think they're going to snatch bait from a hook," Tamani deadpanned. "They're as smart as any of us."

"Not that kind of fishing, Captain."

"I'm not a captain anymore."

"If you don't want the title, then she should have it," Marion said, her eyes moving to Lenore for the barest instant. "You are both his protégés."

Tamani suspected Lenore's stony expression was reflected in his own.

"I was thinking of net fishing. I suggest we find their camp, drop weighted nets between two boats, and drag them onto the shore."

Tamani paused, considering the efficacy of such a method, then asked, "And then what?"

"Oh, I'm sure I don't know. That's your job, isn't it?"

It was, but Tamani hated admitting she was right. That she was creative and efficient.

That she could do things he simply could not.

"Why are you doing this?" he asked softly.

"Doing what?"

"Helping us."

She smiled, the expression wholly patronizing. "You've never understood my commitment to Avalon, Tamani de Rhoslyn. That we disagree about what's best for her doesn't change the fact that there's nothing in the world I want more than to protect my homeland."

Tamani was quiet for a long time. Marion's arrival was … disturbing. As a Winter faerie, locating the sea fae was the *least* of what she could do. Probably she could kill them all at a distance, or control their movements in a rough imitation of the control Spring fae had over humans. She might not even need to interrogate them, if she could read the minds of other fae the way Yuki and perhaps Jamison had been known to do. And all that was only accounting for things Tamani *knew* about the Winter fae—the spells of Winter had been known to accomplish stranger things, too, from time to time. Like placing a golden key and the stunning possibilities it represented into the uncomprehending hands of a distraught sentry.

As disturbing as these thoughts were in isolation, it occurred to Tamani that he didn't even know which would be worse: if Mischa had arranged Marion's arrival, effectively assuring victory—whatever that might be—for the Unseelie, or if Marion had arrived to *oppose* Mischa in some way, placing

Tamani in the middle of an inevitable collision.

As he pondered, he could almost hear Shar laughing at him. *Solve the problem in front of you first*, he would say. *Or you'll never even get to the one you're worried about.*

"Fine," Tamani said at last. "Don't tell me. I'm desperate enough to take help from any quarter at this point."

Marion rolled her eyes, but didn't snap at his bait. "You have a guest room, do you not? I suggest you go off and make your preparations while I rest." She yawned, covering it delicately with one hand. "We have a big fishing trip ahead of us."

THIRTY

TAMANI TOOK IMMENSE SATISFACTION FROM poking his former monarch in the arm, waking her up a few hours after dark.

"Come on," he said when she opened her eyes. "We go *now*."

She sat up, blinking in the dim light that spilled in from the hallway. "At … night?"

"If we did this during the day, there wouldn't be enough memory elixir in all of Avalon to keep it secret." Not even with Lenore's assistance—not that Tamani intended to mention the apparent extent of her abilities to Marion.

"You have a Summer faerie," Marion argued, sounding decidedly jet-lagged. "Have her put up a screen. There's no need make anyone forget something they never even saw."

"She'll have her hands full enough with the humans we're using on the beach," Tamani answered coolly. "Unless the sea fae are waiting for us ten feet into the water, we'll have two boats out for everyone to see, dragging a net between them and approaching the shore. Trust me; the Coast Guard would be interested in that."

"But what are the humans on shore doing?"

"No time to waste," Tamani said, turning toward the open door. "Be ready in five."

It took ten. And Marion grumbled the whole time, but soon the whole party—dressed in black from head to toe—was headed down the elevator.

"Where's Lenore?" Marion asked, glaring accusingly at Tamani and Rowen, as though they might have done something to her.

"Waiting with the boats, at the shoreline," Tamani said, forcing himself to remain completely calm. Where Marion was concerned, if you let your temper override your good sense, even for a second, you were beaten. "Shawn is down there with her," he added, more to Rowen than Marion. But Rowen simply nodded, eyes downcast.

Marion took a deep breath and whispered, disapprovingly, "Boats."

"There's no reason you should have to touch saltwater at all. We're trying to be accommodating."

"Of course you are."

"Here," he said, holding out a hand to her with two small

vials in it. "These will help."

"What are they?"

"Energy and improved resistance to the unavoidable salt in the air."

With a fractional twitch of her brows, Marion smiled wanly. "The scion's work, I presume. Clever. Who's Shawn?"

After a long pause, Tamani answered simply. "A human who's helping us."

"In Lenore's thrall."

"No." Had he answered too quickly? "Not most of the time, anyway. His family was attacked by the sea fae. He volunteered to help us."

"Ever the vengeful creatures, your humans," Marion practically purred. "I'm not sure I'd care to rely on the hot-headedness of such a short-lived species, myself. It seems a flimsy support."

"You won't have to be on his boat—you can be on mine." She thought *Shawn* was flimsy? Marion was the one Tamani hated to depend on. Her motives were rarely clear, but inevitably self-serving to some degree. Between her plotting and Mischa's, Tamani couldn't really feel comfortable with any of his choices at this point.

But if there was another way, he couldn't think of it.

"Anyway I don't trust my strength to keep him free of the siren song while I'm focused on other things. And as powerful as Lenore is, she'll be too far away."

"Far away!" Marion snapped. "Why won't she be with us?"

"She'll be needed on the beach."

"What's going to happen on the beach?"

"As you so recently reminded me," Tamani said with a grin, "that's my job."

***

As they climbed from Tamani's car and approached the dock—and Shawn—Rowen wasn't sure if she dreaded or longed to see him more. Meghan hadn't offered up any advice, and Rowen certainly wasn't going to *ask*. Their tentative truce improved her time at Scazio immeasurably, but an association with Meghan automatically involved Shawn, just as being with Shawn had necessitated involvement with Meghan. It was surreal how quickly their roles in her life had reversed.

Except for Lenore and Shawn, the dock was deserted. At the first glimpse of Shawn's face in the dim lights, Rowen froze; Tamani's hand at the small of her back was all that kept her moving forward.

"Courage," he whispered.

Rowen straightened her spine and stuffed her hands deep into her pockets, trying not to look at Shawn as the five of them huddled at the end of the dock.

"Alright," Tamani said softly, "everyone knows

the plan—"

"I don't," Marion interrupted, an unmistakable sulk in her voice.

"—except Marion," Tamani continued smoothly, as though she'd said nothing. "I'll fill her in on the way. The rest of you, remember to keep in regular radio contact. Let's go." He straightened, breaking up the huddle, and inclined his head up the dock. "Marion?"

"We're going this way," Lenore said, tugging on Rowen's arm. The Spring faeries had obviously been busy while Rowen was in dance class, gathering resources and scouting terrain. Rowen had been busy, too, after a fashion—mostly, busy trying not to go completely mad with panic. It wasn't that she didn't trust her uncle; his competence was legendary. But the first time Rowen encountered real danger in her life, she'd lost her parents. The second time, she'd nearly lost Shawn and Meghan—and some humans had actually died.

She couldn't help but wonder who she would lose tonight.

"Okay," Rowen said softly. *I won't lose anyone,* she promised herself. *Whatever it takes.* At that her feet totally started to move in the direction Lenore was heading, but her eyes locked on Shawn's and she couldn't look away. His black hoodie was pulled up around his face, but the shadows weren't deep enough to hide his eyes.

Shawn took a step toward her and opened his mouth, so

Rowen resisted Lenore's grasp, waiting for words. But his mouth closed again, lips pursed, and he turned away.

"We have to go," Lenore said calmly, still tugging Rowen along. "Come on."

Defeated, Rowen followed her oldest friend.

"Are you okay with a short jog?"

"I'm a dancer, Len."

"I know, but it's dark, and we need you at your strongest."

"I'm good." And she was, at least in terms of energy. She'd spent the afternoon in the sun, downed two cans of Sprite, and at the last second opted to try a trick some Sparklers swore by as their prep for a big light show: maple syrup shots. She even had one of Laurel's perk-up potions, just in case.

If only Laurel made antidotes for heartbreak and fear, too.

They ran along the shore in silence until they reached the cove where, if all went according to plan, they would put an end to the sea fae murders, saving San Francisco and, if the human oracle could be believed, many other cities besides. It was a good-sized cove, kept mostly private by a series of rock outcroppings, which, at the moment, were dimly lit by the fires and flashlights of a smattering of humans enjoying an evening at the beach.

Lenore approached each group and couple in turn, whispering a few words and sending them on their way.

When they were alone with the waves, Rowen only

squirmed against the silence for a moment before realizing she had something to say.

"Sorry I left Avalon without—"

"I knew," Len said. "Even before I heard you'd actually gone, I realized. It was nice, to know you knew me well enough to be certain I would understand. Thanks for trusting me."

Rowen smiled and scrubbed a tear from one eye. "Thanks for … well, everything."

Lenore nodded. She seemed different than Rowen remembered—stronger. Grimmer, maybe, though she'd never exactly been a ray of sunshine in the first place.

"I don't think it would be good for me to live around humans the way you do, Row," Lenore said, as if reading Rowen's thoughts. "It's too easy. I'd have to think about *not* doing it every moment of the day. My—" Her voice quavered. "My father warned me. But I didn't truly understand until I came here."

"You've … been around humans before?" Rowen asked, surprised.

"Only for training purposes. Not casually and certainly not fully immersed like this."

It was Rowen's turn to nod silently.

"Do you need to do anything to prepare?" Lenore asked, changing the subject with all the subtlety of a rampaging bull.

"I'm alright. I've got an energy potion and some maple syrup, but at the moment either one would be overkill."

"Did you get a salt potion?"

"Yeah." The ocean here certainly *looked* the same as it did in Avalon. Rowen—of all fae—knew better than to be taken in by appearances. Yet somehow she couldn't shake the conviction that a massive body of poisonous water ought to *look* different from its clean, life-giving counterpart.

"I like Shawn."

Rowen let out a strangled laugh.

"No, I mean it. I've been in his head a lot the last ten days. He's a good person, and he really likes you. He just conflicted about—"

"No," Rowen said, cutting her off. "You can't tell me things you learned through Enticement. It's not fair to him."

Lenore looked like she wanted to argue, but after several seconds she shrugged and turned back to the waves. Neither said anything until the low growl of a large vehicle drew close, obviously heading their way.

"Ah," Lenore said, a grin lifting one corner of her mouth. "Our army."

When an actual army truck pulled into the tiny parking lot and soldiers in camouflage fatigues started jumping out, Rowen's mouth dropped. She'd seen soldiers like this in human movies, but they seemed somehow much … *larger* … in person. "I didn't think you literally meant 'Army.'"

"Tamani's idea," Lenore said, smirking. "We went to something called an *army base* and he had me convince the person in charge that we needed two dozen heavily-armed soldiers for a top secret mission tonight. They'll go home with no memory of what they did and a strong recollection that it's top secret anyway."

Rowen watched as the humans lined up according to the barked orders of one very loud man. She'd been told that humans had a way to make their guns quiet, so she hadn't worried much about the fact that her illusions couldn't cover sound, but if the loud man kept this up, they might attract passers-by. "Why not just people off the street? Wouldn't that be easier?"

"One thing I've learned from working with Shawn is that whatever I'm making someone do, either they need to know how to do it already, or I need to. I don't know how to work human weapons." She pointed at the soldiers. "They all come with weapons they know how to use, so all I have to do is tell them to use them. Or not use them," she added when Rowen's eyes widened. She smiled and patted Rowen's shoulder. "I have to go take control. Radio Tamani," she said over her shoulder. "Tell him the cavalry's here."

THIRTY-ONE

"EVERYONE'S IN PLACE," TAMANI SAID, STOWING the handheld radio he'd procured for the occasion. According to the human who sold it to him, it would keep his conversations private and had ample range for use on the open ocean. It wasn't as convenient as cell phones, but though humans apparently had ways to make those work while out at sea, Tamani hadn't really had time to shop around.

Too much improvisation, he chided himself. *So many ways this could go horribly wrong.*

"You're certain this vessel is seaworthy?" Marion asked, hands clinging to the rail of the immaculate Bayliner, procured at great expense for this single voyage. Of course Tamani might have simply Enticed the human into just giving him both boats, but that would have been needlessly cruel.

"Absolutely certain," Tamani drawled as he and Shawn untied the lines and tossed them aboard. "You ready?" he asked the young human.

"Ready as I'll ever be. I've gone over it in my head a hundred times."

"Good. Keep your radio handy, at least until the earplugs go in." Assuming the siren song was the sea fae's only method of Enticement, they probably wouldn't be able to snare Shawn as long as he was above the water and they, below, but Tamani wanted to leave as little to chance as possible.

He really would have preferred Len be aboard Shawn's boat, but she was needed on the shore, both to coordinate the soldiers and to handle any passers-by that Rowen's shield failed to deter. There was a lot of beach in San Francisco, but there were a lot of people too, and pulling this off without sparking a larger incident was going to be tricky.

Besides, if the sea fae *did* have some other method of Enticement, well … that was why Shawn was the only one on his boat. Perhaps the sea fae could cause him to hurt himself, but Tamani had been very clear about the risks as well as the unknowns, and Shawn seemed to understand. It would've been nice to generate a plan from more information—if the sea fae had a pet kraken, for example, then the three of them were almost certainly speeding toward certain death—but Tamani had done all he could think of. Sometimes all you could do was plant the seed and hope.

With a nod of encouragement, Tamani pushed on the hull

of his boat and jumped on as it floated away from the dock, watching out of the corner of his eye as Shawn did the same. As they eased into open waters Tamani brought Shawn up on the radio. "Follow us with as little wake as possible."

"Aye, aye, Captain," Shawn said, and Tamani rolled his eyes and released the talk button.

"Where to?" he asked Marion. He braced himself for resistance; some new demand or rhetorical barb.

The deposed monarch simply pointed out to sea.

"How far do you think?" Tamani asked, setting their course.

She tilted her head to the side, as if listening to some faint, distant sound. "Not far. Half a mile, perhaps? It's hard to tell in the water." She gave him a stern look when he made a strangled noise. "The closer we get, the more I'll know."

Tamani clamped his mouth closed and lined up the boat in the direction Marion had pointed, hoping he'd made the right choice putting his trust in her.

"I was a good queen, you know."

Did she just read his mind? The extent to which Winter faeries could and could not do that was just nebulous enough to make Tamani jumpy. "Were you, now?" he drawled.

"I was. The desires of the common fae outpaced me in the end, but until then, I was a good queen."

Tamani held his tongue for a long time before bursting

out, "I don't think you were. I was *there* the day you took a crippling number of Ticer sentries into the already unbreachable Winter Palace, for no other reason than to protect yourself."

She laughed. "Only myself? You've been inside the Palace; you know what manner of things are kept there. And don't forget that I also took Yasmine, your current oh-so-beloved queen."

"That was an excuse and you know it."

"Was it?"

In two words she had him questioning himself. "Yes," he said, before he could get very far down that path. "You thought of yourself and nothing else when you barred yourself in that Palace and nothing you say can convince me otherwise. You might have other justifications, but you were thinking of *you.*"

"Because Avalon would certainly have survived if it lost its Winter faeries," she said, and Tamani wondered where she had learned something as plebian as sarcasm.

"You weren't in any real danger," Tamani scoffed.

"I didn't know that then, did I?" She studied him, lit dimly by the half moon hanging above them in the sky. "Civilizations without leaders fall apart. All of history bears me out. Say what you like, if Jamison had died that day and I'd protected myself and my heir, Avalon would have survived. But if Callista had proven more deadly than she was—"

"She was more dangerous than you were ever willing to admit. Without Laurel, we'd *all* be dead, and Avalon with us."

Marion nodded, conceding the point, which made Tamani strangely uneasy. "But suppose the scion succeeded only after the renegade destroyed the court. How would rebuilding have proceeded without us? Who would keep the peace? There are yet Unseelie lurking on the fortunate isle, you know. And the humans—would they have been willing to follow in Arthur's footsteps? Or would they have cut down the gates?"

Desperately, Tamani struggled to keep his thoughts *away* from the key dangling against his chest. "You seem pretty confident that Avalon would collapse without your benevolent leadership."

"You have no idea what being without a leader can do to a kingdom. I worry about Yasmine already. No, I do," she said to Tamani's snort of derision. "She's young, healthy, strong—but she's only one *Bender*, as you call us when you think we're not listening. Avalon needs another."

Is this your angle, Marion? Are you helping in hopes that I'll plead your case to Yasmine? That seemed to be happening a lot lately. "You said you'd only come back as queen."

But apparently he'd misread her intent. "I don't mean me; I won't fight the will of my subjects. But if there isn't a new Winter sprout in the next twenty or thirty years, I worry for the survival of Avalon." She hesitated. "Haven't you got a sprout arriving soon?"

"No," Tamani said simply. No need to elaborate on that particular truth, not to this woman.

"Oh—I thought I'd heard—well, never mind."

Remembering what Laurel had told him about non-Fisherian organisms, he said, "I suspect nature will provide a Bender when Avalon needs it."

"That's true," Marion replied, and it didn't sound like a concession. "Nature, left undisturbed, does tend to provide. We're here."

"What?"

"We're here," she said again. "They're below us."

***

Rowen stood with her feet hip-width apart, her hands splayed slightly out from her sides, not because her posture made her magic do anything different, but because it helped her to visualize. Large-scale illusions were a regular feature of stage performance in Avalon, both for the décor around the coliseum and the backdrop on the stage. Every Sparkler learned how to do it as part of their general training, but only those who didn't excel in the performance arts were expected to do it often—so Rowen hadn't been trained beyond the basics.

Fortunately, it *was* quite basic—hiding the beach from nighttime hikers and privacy-seeking lovers was more a question of stamina than precision; a large-scale bending of not a lot of light. Three months ago she'd have said that was just what she *wasn't* good at, but coming to San Francisco and dancing day in and day out without the sun overhead had increased her stamina in ways she would never have bothered pursuing in Avalon.

The humans on the *inside* of the illusion might have been dismayed by the distortions Rowen's efforts manifested in their surroundings—eddies and swirls of darkness seeming to flow between earth and sky—but Lenore was already in complete control of the entire group. They were standing at perfect attention, their weapons on their shoulders: oversized dolls in military attire.

Rowen wondered if that was how Lenore thought of them. Lenore was far more used to humans than most young faeries, having been raised by a human-side gate sentry Captain, but over the years they'd had dozens of conversations about humans, and most of them ended with stories of sharp-toothed humans devouring faeries alive, or clever faeries leading hundreds of humans to the top of a cliff and sending them over the edge to die.

"Len?" The air was so still, with no sound except the crashing waves, that Rowen almost felt like she should whisper. "Don't let them shoot each other, okay? We want to return them all alive."

"I'm not so unfeeling," Lenore said.

"I know. I didn't mean …" But she *had* meant that. She meant exactly that, and Lenore knew it.

"I don't … feel the way you do," Lenore continued after a tense moment. "But my father never taught me mindless slaughter."

Rowen felt a little ashamed, but at the same time, the humans needed *someone* to advocate for them, didn't they?

"It wouldn't have to be forever, you know. With Shawn."

Rowen groaned and made herself focus on her illusion. She could already feel the drain. Not that she was running low; just how much this was going to take. "Not again."

"I'm not telling you his thoughts—I can't read minds," Lenore said with a grin. "Precisely. I'm just saying, both of you should realize that saying yes now isn't the same and saying yes forever. And that's not a bad thing."

"I'm not the one saying no," Rowen said softly.

"You're not the one reaching out making it easier for him to say yes, either."

Rowen opened her mouth to argue, but Lenore put up a hand.

"Someone's coming."

Rowen listened, then heard a shout from behind her.

"Rowen! Shawn!"

Her eyes widened when the names were repeated. "It's Meghan," she said in confusion. After looking up at the bright moon she had to blink a few times to make out Meghan's tall, lithe form standing at the edge of the small parking lot. Shawn must have told her where they were going. No reason not to, she supposed.

"Do I need to send her away?" Lenore asked, sounding uncertain for the first time that night.

"No," Rowen said hesitantly. "I don't think so. Meghan," she called out. "Walk toward my voice. I know you can't see me, but just come this way."

"You sure?" Lenore whispered. "I bet she'd turn around and go if you just asked her to."

"She's proved herself," Rowen said. "If she wants to be a part of this after all, she can."

"I'm not going to run into anything, am I?" Meghan asked, edging forward. She was inching her way along the beach, clinging with both hands to the strap of the large bag slung over her shoulder. From her perspective, Rowen knew, the night would seem unusually dark, and a massive stone outcropping would appear to bar her way. But from the inside of the illusion, Meghan just looked like a girl who'd never seen a sandy beach and found its existence completely perplexing.

"No," Rowen shouted. "The way is clear. Just walk

forward. Maybe close your eyes?"

Meghan took a deep breath and practically leapt forward a few feet. Then she was through the illusion and Rowen could only imagining what it must look like to suddenly have a huge swath of beach appear before your eyes, when you didn't believe in anything remotely supernatural two weeks past.

"That is the freakiest thing that ever happened to me and after the last couple weeks I think that is really, really saying something," Meghan said in a rush. "That is … I want to say *amazing* but it feels more *wrong*, you know. I feel like I should be looking around for the hidden cameras right now."

Lenore's blank expression probably mirrored her own and Rowen smiled to cover it up. "Yeah, it's probably a lot to take in."

When Meghan's gaze fell on the stiff, completely-still soldiers, her mouth dropped open. Rowen needed to act fast.

"Why are you here, Meghan?"

"Oh, I was home, well, obviously I was home. And I went in the garage and I saw this thing, and I just kept thinking about how your uncle said that you guys were actually plants, and Shawn said something about this being harder for you at night, and I just … I thought it would help and I couldn't stay at home when I really thought I'd found something that would help." She finished her meandering tirade with her arms folded across her chest in oh-so-classic Meghan style, as though waiting for an argument.

"What did you find?" Rowen asked, thoroughly confused.

Meghan dropped her arms. "I'll show you." She set the big duffel bag down on the sand and pulled out an odd-looking lantern. "Grow lights!"

Lenore and Rowen exchanged a quick glance. "What are grow lights?"

"Lights that make plants grow," she said, like it was the most obvious thing in the world. "When I was really little we lived in Montana. It's winter there like six months out of the year—I am *so* glad I don't remember it—and Mom used to grow seedlings in her garage under grow lights, so when the snow finally melted they'd be big enough to plant outside." She paused, clearly waiting for a response, but Rowen still didn't understand. "It's like a little sun," Meghan said.

"Oh. *Oh!*" Rowen said. "I didn't know there was such a thing. Does it work?"

Meghan shrugged. "It works on other plants."

Lenore grumbled something that sounded suspiciously like "human magic" and turned her attention back to her soldiers.

"I also have…" Meghan dug around in her bag. "A big portable battery, to plug it in."

"Seriously?" Rowen didn't actually know what that was, but it sounded very technical.

Meghan only sighed. "With Dad being an engineer we

have weird shit like this all over the house. Give me a sec and … there!"

Meghan flipped on a small lamp and held it up to Rowen. First Rowen grumbled and blinked at the bright light in her face, but after Meghan apologized and aimed it a little lower, a strange sensation crept over her skin.

"Song of the Goddess," she said softly. "It *is* like a little sun!"

Meghan beamed, clearly exceedingly proud of herself for having helped.

Marred by static but unmistakable, Tamani's voice sounded from the radio clipped to Rowen's pocket. "We found them."

It took Rowen a moment to remember which button to press before saying "Okay" into the thing Tamani assured her was *not* a phone, but only something *like* a phone. She looked at Meghan, then Lenore. "They'll be here soon."

Lenore rolled out her neck and, in eerily perfect synchrony, all twenty-four soldiers did the same. With a smile, she whispered, "*En guarde.*"

THIRTY-TWO

"YOU READY?" TAMANI ASKED SHAWN OVER THE radio.

"I am."

"Cast in three... two... "

Marion had given him the idea of net fishing, but Tamani had run with it on his own. The huge commercial fishing net, known as a Danish seine or "poor man's trawl," hadn't actually been cheap—especially on short notice. But it was manufactured from carbon fiber right here in San Francisco, and Tamani had Enticed the old sea dog at the warehouse to tell him everything they could possibly want to know about net.

It was wide, with weights on the bottom and buoys on the top to hold it open as it scraped the sea floor, then pulled closed like purse strings. Tamani had originally wanted a circle net, but the human fisher had made it clear that such nets were meant to catch stupid fish whose only instinct was to swim upward or outward.

Unfortunately, they were *not* dealing with brainless fish.

This net relied on momentum to scoop up fish and then close before they could swim against the drag and pop out the front. Shawn and Tamani had spent much of the afternoon altering it to better catch the sea fae unawares: adding weights so it would sink faster and removing half the buoys. Tamani was pretty sure the modifications were illegal; they were going to tear up a strip of ocean bottom and all the flora and fauna that went with it. Sadly, it was a price the human race was simply going to have to unknowingly pay.

Probably the sea fae would be unable to cut their way free from the carbon fiber webbing. *Probably* their group would be unable to resist the pull of the high-powered speedboats, too—a larger vessel would get beached long before reaching the small, shallow cove where Rowen and Lenore waited with borrowed soldiers. *Probably* the sea fae weren't keeping some kind of abominable ocean pet on hand.

This whole endeavor was a bit like cutting a trail through unfamiliar forest, and all Tamani could hope was that he wasn't about to stumble blindly over a cliff. They'd speed like hell for the cove as soon as the net reached the ocean floor—speed like hell, and hope.

The cable spooling out into the black water slowed

suddenly.

The net had hit ground.

"Lock and go!" Tamani shouted into the radio, wedging a heavy pin into his own spool. He ran to the controls and tossed a warning to Marion before opening up the throttle, urging the boat inland. He hardly dared look over at Shawn's Bayliner as his own took up the slack and then began pulling the net. Were they moving fast enough? Had they cast wide enough?

Tamani could hear the engines on his boat groaning as they worked, but they kept the boat moving at an appreciable clip. After about a minute the drag lessened and Tamani knew the top of the net must have pulled closed, lifting the weights up from the thick silt along the ocean bottom. Their speed crept slowly higher.

Above the roar of the engines and wake, he shouted to Marion, "Are the sea fae traveling with us, or are they getting farther away?"

She smiled easily, but maintained a white-knuckled grip on the armrests of her seat as she struggled to stay upright. "Oh, you got them."

***

"I hear them," Lenore said.

When she listened for it, Rowen could also make out the

faint whine of an engine, and it did seem to be getting closer. "I think you're right."

"What should I do?" Meghan asked, voice trembling as she straightened her shoulders, trying to look brave.

"Sit right behind me," Rowen said. "You'll still be in the illusion and my back can photosynthesize just as effectively as my front."

Meghan retreated behind her and they all stared out at the ocean, listening to the sound of the engines and the surf.

"They're going too fast," Meghan whispered to Rowen, as the seacrafts' silhouettes came into view, solid black shadows against a rippling field of darkness. "They're going to beach the boats."

"That's the point."

"They'll ruin the engines!" Meghan sounded personally offended.

"It's necessary."

Meghan didn't say anything else, but maintained an expression of horror.

The labored whine of the boats grew louder and louder and Rowen felt her throat tighten. It did look like they were all about to get run over by two boats. Tamani had assured her that between the drag of a net full of sea fae and the resistance of the sand in the shallows, there was no way the boats would clear the waterline, much less run up on the beach and hit them.

But then he'd erased any good that statement did by adding that they should probably be ready to dodge anyway.

Abruptly, the roar of engines grew noticeably louder—they seemed to be struggling. The boats slowed dramatically and, just as Tamani had predicted, shuddered to a halt well short of the tideline, hulls submerged in less than three feet of water.

"Lenore! Pull them in!" Tamani's bellow was loud through the crackling radio and immediately the soldiers jogged into the water.

Someone jumped off one of the boats; Rowen assumed it must be Shawn, because as soon as he landed he moved deeper into the salty water to grasp the end of the rope protruding from the back of his boat. A group of human soldiers joined him, and it became impossible to tell one laboring shadow from the next.

So Rowen watched as Tamani climbed carefully over the side of his own vessel—he'd obtained something he called *waders* from people who sold him the fishing net. They looked neither comfortable nor flexible, but apparently he'd been assured they were watertight. Once in the water, Tamani turned back to the boat and Rowen couldn't help but feel a little resentful as he took the traitorous former queen of Avalon into his arms and carried her toward the shore. He had just set Marion down on the beach when a huge, wriggling bundle of … *something* … emerged from the waves.

***

Tamani could hardly breathe as the soldiers—stubbornly assisted by Shawn—dragged the huge net up onto the shore. The water churned with the thrashing of the sea faeries, and high-pitched squeals split the air like lightning. Tamani approached as the human soldiers dragged the net up the beach to where even the most determined of waves wouldn't reach them.

They were *not* happy.

After a quick glance at Marion to make sure she was out of harm's way—as though a Bender couldn't protect herself—Tamani crossed his arms over his chest, as much to keep the sea faeries' attention off of Lenore as to assert his own authority. *She* was the powerful one, but it was best for everyone if they didn't know that.

"That's far enough, men," Tamani barked, though, of course, the order wasn't for them at all. The soldiers all backed away from the squirming lump and retrieved their guns, establishing a perimeter around the captured fae.

Free from the ocean's drag, the sea fae had little difficulty extricating themselves from the net—though by the way some of them were moving, Tamani could guess that a few had broken stems along the way, either from the inelegance of his plan, or attempts to escape it. No songs of Enticement rose from the group; in fact, the sea fae seemed almost oblivious to the humans surrounding them.

Tamani said nothing; he stood silently, waiting to see what would happen. For the first time tonight, he didn't feel as though he were in danger—everything had gone as they'd hoped, or close enough.

But the strange faeries still had their weapons—and their secrets. Though Tamani doubted they'd last long against armed, battle-hardened humans, he wanted to avoid further bloodshed if at all possible.

One faerie, a little taller than the others, stepped away from the huddled group, a grimace of disgust contorting its features. As it moved toward Tamani, he grew, much the way Tamani had observed that fateful night, months ago—a lifetime ago, it felt. This was their shapeshifter, assuming a roughly human guise—the face and features of a middle-aged man. He spoke, his voice pitched almost painfully high, but Tamani didn't understand.

Except … no. Tamani definitely knew *that* word. His mother had rinsed his mouth with cleansing serum for saying it when he was little boy. The creature was speaking Gaelic, or something very like it. Thousands of years separated from the Avalon fae had apparently changed their dialect.

If he kept his vocabulary simple, would the sea fae

understand? Tamani held up a hand as the shapeshifter took another step forward. "Halt. Now," he commanded in Gaelic.

The faerie snarled more epithets and continued stalking toward Tamani.

"Warn him," Tamani said, still speaking Gaelic—Lenore would understand, even if the sea fae didn't.

Sand burst from the ground in front of the shapeshifter; the crack that accompanied it, echoing off of the surrounding rocks, seemed to get the message through. He halted, perhaps ten steps from Tamani, but by this time he towered over Tam by at least twelve inches.

Tamani was unfazed. "I will kill you if you come any closer." He spread his arms wide. "Now, we parlay."

The sea faerie shook his head. "You can't stop us. No human can stop us."

"Good that I'm not human, then."

The sea faerie hesitated—and, for the first time, Tamani saw something other than malice in his eyes. But only for an instant.

"Please," Tamani said, before the other faerie could speak again. "Let's talk."

One side of the shapeshifter's mouth twitched up into a malevolent grin. Jauntily, he intoned, "I am as happy to kill you after talking as before."

Tamani raised an eyebrow, ignoring the jibe. "Why are you

here?"

The sea faerie gestured toward the fishing net, shoulders raised in what Tamani could only assume was a gesture of puzzlement. "You tell me."

Tamani almost laughed. It had been a long time since he'd last interrogated someone he couldn't simply Entice. "Why are you killing humans?"

"They destroyed our home; we're going to destroy theirs."

"Your home?"

"Our reef."

Reef?

"We walked seafloor in search of a new reef, a place with no humans, but they are already here! All across the ocean, there is nothing but sand and trash and impure waters!"

"The Great Barrier Reef?" Tamani asked, incredulous. "In Australia?" Had these creatures actually *walked* all the way from Australia? The famous reef there had been dying for years. And humans *were* to blame.

"The cursing of the waters and the death of our reef robbed us of our queen. Others died also." He held his arms out, indicating the beach and the visible bits of trash strewn about, even in this small cove. "And we come to this! It's *worse* than the reef. The humans are destroying the oceans and we will not stand by and let it happen."

"You can't just kill them," Tamani said, unable to

contradict the shapeshifter's claim. It was true; even the humans knew it. But it would be pointless to tell the angry faerie that the humans were at least trying to fix what they'd done.

"They killed us."

"War won't bring your reef back."

"I think you are wrong," the faerie snarled, sounding more feral than fae. "If we kill enough humans, the reef will survive."

That was … startlingly accurate, actually, but Tamani got the feeling that this faerie had no idea just how many humans there were in the world. He also got the idea that it wouldn't matter; the sea fae would try to kill them all anyway, and die in the attempt. He help up his hands, desperate to placate the warrior. "I understand, I do. But you can't kill an entire race out of spite."

"And who will stop us?"

"I will."

The sea fae laughed, a bubbling, melodic sound. "I don't think so."

And then the fae behind him began to sing.

The night Tamani had seen the sea fae lure the human girl to her death there had only been a handful of the faeries. Tonight there were about forty, and the song they sang was not beautiful. It was a haunting, savage melody that rang with pain and misery and death. Raw emotion gripped Tamani by the throat, not because he was at all subject to their Enticement, but because he understood their story and their song. He understood their desperation. They were facing extinction because humans had realized too late the devastating impact they sometimes had on the world around them..

But war would only hasten the genocide of the sea fae. Tamani understood—and he had to find a way to broker peace.

Before he could move, however, the song of the sea fae crescendoed and lost its sadness, turning instead to a clanging melody of wrath. The shapeshifter donned a grimace of rage and, even as Tamani opened his mouth to order the sea fae to stand down, their leader whipped a knife from his belt and hurtled at Tamani.

Tamani dodged backward, barely keeping his footing in the soft sand, but the shapeshifter was on top of him, swinging another knife in a wide arc—

And with the retort of gunfire, the shapeshifter was reeling backward, stumbling into the sand. The sharp sound and the obvious wounding of their spokesperson sent the sea fae into a frenzy. As one body, they rushed the soldiers, knives out, pointed teeth barred. Shots erupted from everywhere.

"No!" Tamani shouted. But he saw that several of the shots had simply gone into the sand, and others into feet and ankles. Lenore was doing her best to preserve lives. The soldiers were fighting with their guns, cracking rifle stocks against the heads of any fae who drew too close. Screams and shrieks filled the air and Tamani looked into the chaos. He had to stop it. He had to make peace, and he couldn't do that if they were all dead.

"Shawn!" Rowen's scream pierced the air, drawing Tamani's attention. She looked ready to break into a run, but froze as her eyes locked with Tamani's.

"Hold," Tamani shouted. "Just hold. I got it!"

Tamani kicked away from the wounded shapeshifter—hoping its powers didn't make it *too* resistant to gunfire—and ran toward the shore where he'd last seen Shawn. He found the human boy at the waterline; someone had gotten him with a knife and blood was trailing onto the wet sand in a long line as a handful of sea fae tried to drag him to the waves.

"Shawn," Tamani yelled, whipping a diamond-edged *kunai* through the air; one faerie staggered away from the struggling human, clutching at her shoulder, but two more replaced her. *We should have tied them up immediately*, Tamani chided himself, collapsing another green-skinned siren with a sharp kick to the head. They weren't great fighters—not on land, anyway—but trying to *subdue* them without killing them was difficult when they exhibited such surprising disregard for their own safety.

By the time Tamani managed to drive off Shawn's captors,

the human was on his hands and knees in six inches of surf. Tamani vaguely felt the sting of saltwater on his arms as he reached down to help him. "Can you stand?"

Shawn nodded, clutching at the shallow score across his ribs—at a glance, Tamani could tell that it looked much worse than it actually was. Had to sting like crazy in the ocean spray, though. Another faerie rushed them as Shawn climbed to his feet; Tamani landed a vicious blow to the creature's temple and began working his way back to the tall shapeshifter.

Shawn stuck close; though the song of the sea faeries had faded, their fighting spirit hadn't. Disarmed, wounded, oozing sap onto the sand, still they fought; when they lost their knives, they used their teeth and claws. Those shot in the legs bit at the ankles of the human soldiers. Those shot in the arms or shoulders screamed and kicked and did what they could to trip the soldiers. No matter how amazing Lenore was, hobbled by Tamani's pacifism there was only so much she could do.

And in the midst of it all, the shapeshifter laughed.

"Stop this," Tamani growled, grabbing the leader of the sea faeries by the front of his toga-like robes. "I offered parlay. You can't take the humans from our control; we've more than proved that. The only reason your faeries are still alive to fight at all is because I haven't ordered the humans to kill you. Call them off and help me find a solution."

But the sea faerie continued to chuckle. "Death is the only

solution. I see now what you've done. You've taken control of this army, but there are few of your kind here. We've discovered much about the humans lately. We'll go to all their shores, steal their minds, turn them on each other. You can't stop us. You can't be everywhere at once, and my school is but the tip of the spear." The shapeshifter leaned closer and grinned. "We will kill every human on earth or die trying."

School—like a school of fish? And *tip of the spear*—there were other groups like this one, poised to strike. If they attacked in places without faerie protectors, the amount of human blood spilled would be apocalyptic. The human oracle hadn't been exaggerating—not even a tiny bit. Tamani's hands shook as he maintained his grasp on the faerie's seawater-drenched clothing. He needed to know more about their plans, and the only way he was going to find out was by hearing it from the sea fae themselves. But they refused to abandon their rage.

Across the sandy battlefield, Tamani caught Lenore's eye and knew what she was thinking: she wasn't going to be able to subdue this group any longer without using lethal force.

She was waiting for permission.

His permission.

Tamani closed his eyes and thought of Avalon and the Manor, of Chelsea and Jason. Mostly, he thought of Laurel and Sharlet and the safety they could never enjoy with such bloodthirsty faeries at large in the world. Killing this group wouldn't end the threat, but it would be a start.

Tamani opened his eyes and met Lenore's. "Do it."

With a tense nod she turned, and all twenty-four of the soldiers turned with her, raising their guns.

"I think that's enough fun for one day," said Marion, and somehow, though she did not shout, her words reached everyone's ears. Then, at the sound of a single clap from the deposed Queen of Avalon, every faerie on the beach, from ocean and island alike, went still.

THIRTY-THREE

"GUNS DOWN, LENORE," MARION SAID SHARPLY, smiling in a way Rowen didn't understand. "No one's going to misbehave."

Lenore glowered at the Winter faerie, but after a long silence she lowered her hands. The human soldiers lowered their guns.

Shawn was the first to break the tableau by running toward Rowen and Meghan. Blood streamed from a cut along his ribs, but seeing him alive was enough. Rowen lowered her eyes, not wanting to know if he was running to her, or to Meghan—who was standing *behind* her.

He stopped in front of Rowen.

"Don't," she said shakily, cursing the timing of the universe as he raised his arms to hug her. "I have to hold this illusion and if … if—" A sob overtook her, but she managed to maintain the illusion hiding the cove rather than drop the shield and crumple into his arms. Barely. If this was the last opportunity she ever had to be in Shawn's arms and she missed it, she was never going to speak to her uncle again.

But miss it she did, as Meghan stepped around Rowen and threw her arms around her brother, pulling back when he groaned.

"Are you okay?" she asked, but Shawn shushed her, eyeing Marion.

The deposed queen strode forward and Rowen moved only her eyes to take in the beach. A handful of the sea faeries were lying in the sand, groaning.

But many weren't.

Some of the human soldiers had sustained injuries—knife wounds, mostly, with a smattering of bites and bruises. None of them were dead, but Marion was apparently in a position to kill them all, if that's what she wanted.

With a chill, Rowen realized no one ever really knew what Marion wanted.

"Now," Marion said, her tone patronizing, "we've all shown how big and strong we are and how willing we are to destroy one another. I hope that was sufficient playtime because now we must think of our futures."

"You think this is some kind of game?" Tamani growled, and Rowen could tell the words came through clenched teeth.

"An *exercise* is not the same as a game, Captain."

"Exercise!" he shouted. "You could have stopped them at any time! People are *dead!*"

"Not *any* time, Captain," Marion said cryptically, eyes scanning the shoreline. "There were things for you to accomplish, first. And some of them *are* dead, I grant you. Practically threw themselves on their own knives though. Couldn't be helped. But your crew?" She glanced at Rowen, Meghan, Shawn, Tamani and Lenore, each in turn. "Let's be honest, they were never in any real danger."

Rowen's mouth dropped as she thought of the way Shawn had fought for his life *mere minutes ago*. She managed one halting step forward, hand rising to strike the Winter faerie for her outrage.

But one step was all she managed to take.

"Temper, temper," Marion said, the corner of her mouth lifting in a grin.

Struggling against Marion's magical constraint, Rowen almost didn't hear Meghan whisper, "Girl, I got your back."

As smoothly and gracefully as any dancer in the history of all the world could possibly having managed, Meghan punched Marion in the face.

The Winter faerie staggered backward with a gasp and, though Tamani stood within a few feet of her, he didn't rush to assist.

Marion glared at Lenore. "You *let* that happen."

Lenore looked away, shrugging one shoulder. "I'm a little busy."

Marion gingerly touched the skin around her eye, reassuming the haughty air that so defined her. She glanced at Meghan. "I suppose allowances must be made for humans and their tendency toward brutality. Are you quite finished?"

Meghan crossed her arms over her chest and raised her eyebrows.

"Thank you." Marion turned away from them and back to the struggling sea faeries. "My name is Marion d'Avalon, Winter faerie, former queen of the realm of the fae, and I believe we can find an answer to your problems that will satisfy everyone without further conflict."

Rowen expected the brash leader of the sea fae to immediately argue, but instead, he dropped to one knee and bowed his head. Every sea faerie who still could did the same.

And Rowen remembered what Avalon had been like, not so many years ago. She felt sick.

As the sea fae rose, Marion spoke loud enough for the entire assembly to hear her. "The way I see it, the humans have robbed you of your home, and your queen. I propose to give both of those things back."

Murmurs of surprise rippled across the beach.

"Just how do you propose to do that?" the shapeshifter asked, clearly angry despite his continued deference.

Marion glanced at the soldiers. "I think this is faerie business and we should send the humans home," she said. "Besides, our Summer faerie is exhausted."

Rowen bristled, but she couldn't deny the truth. Her own nervous energy had burned through far too much of her reserves in the last ten minutes and she could feel her stems starting to quiver.

"Take care of your own," Marion added to the shapeshifter, her words dripping with a compassion Rowen felt certain was completely feigned.

It took a surprisingly short time for Lenore to dismiss her soldiers, wiping the night's events from their minds and sending them away in their intimidating vehicles. Tamani watched the operation from start to finish, looking angrier that Rowen had ever seen him, with the possible exception of the night she'd almost flung Chelsea's baby to the floor. Only once the truck was out of sight did Rowen let the illusion fall—and as soon as she did, her knees buckled.

Shawn caught her.

"I'm, okay," she muttered, though her legs were determined to make a liar out of her.

"I've got you," Shawn whispered near her ear.

Giving up, Rowen sagged against him, letting herself close her eyes and rest. A little.

"I was wrong," Shawn said.

"What?"

"I've been trying to find a good way, a good time, to tell you. For days. But there is no perfect time for something like this." He lifted her chin with one finger so he could see her face. "I know there's no time to talk now, but I was wrong to avoid you for so long. You trusted me and I threw that trust back in your face." He looked up as Tamani approached. "Soon. Can we talk soon?"

Rowen nodded, tears welling up in her eyes. Whatever happened next, she could get through it if she knew Shawn was going to stand with her.

"Shawn," Tamani said, holding out one hand. "You were an incredibly ally tonight. I don't say this lightly: I couldn't have done it without you."

Shawn took Tamani's hand, giving it a firm shake. "I sense a *but*," he said dryly.

Tamani grinned, nodding. "The fighting is over, but the negotiations have only just begun. And I'm afraid it's faerie business."

"But—"

"*Not* my rule," he said, glancing toward Marion. "I'm afraid when a Bender speaks, we have little choice but to at least listen. I suggest you get home and patch yourself up. And you, Miss," he said, addressing Meghan for the first time. "Some ice on those knuckles will help."

It was the first time Rowen had noticed Meghan was cradling her right hand.

"I've never done that before," Meghan said.

"I'd never have known," Tamani said. "Good form." And then, in a move Meghan could not have fully appreciated, he bent at the waist, giving her a small bow.

With a pleasantly quizzical smile, Meghan made the motions of a curtsy in return—though she had no skirts to spread.

Tamani stood beside Rowen and watched as the human siblings picked their way over the rocks at the edge of the parking lot and got into their car. "He's a good one," Tamani said earnestly. "I've really enjoyed getting to know him this week."

"Is this your stamp of approval?" she asked, with more than a hint of sarcasm.

"Your parents aren't here to do it."

Rowen was quiet for a long time before whispering, "Thank you."

***

Tamani felt more than a little suspicious as the sea faeries gathered around a small phosphorescing flower Marion had gotten from Goddess-knew-where. Rowen had been given one of Laurel's energy potions and a few minutes to rest, but all she really had to do now was a small-scale illusion and she'd promised Tamani she was well up to that.

All that remained was to learn the terms of Marion's plot, whatever it was.

The former queen stood while everyone else sat, and Tamani just shook his head at the transparency of her power play.

"The Great Barrier Reef will never be what it once was," Marion said, and the grumbles of the sea faeries sounded ominous. "But, I can make you a new home. A new reef."

"Why would you do that?" the shapeshifter asked.

"Because, like you, I've been pushed out of my home."

Tamani opened his mouth to defend his new queen, but was silenced by Lenore's hand hard on his arm.

"Patience," she whispered.

"I would like a new home, and a new start, and if you will let me, I propose to be your queen."

Tamani wanted to laugh. Loud and long and hard. For a moment—a moment—he'd thought she might actually be protecting Avalon from the threat of the sea faeries via the humans. But no. She was self-serving to the end.

"I can assure you the purest, cleanest water you've ever seen, and keep you hidden and safe from humans and their nature-polluting ways."

"A reef is not a plant," the shapeshifter argued. "You can't simply command a reef into existence, Bender or no."

Tamani thought it interesting that the more vulgar caste names had apparently been around so long they'd survived millennia of linguistic evolution.

"No, but I can manipulate the environment in such a way that the reef will grow faster than you could imagine." Her eyes sparkled even in her flower's dim light. "I've been studying."

"You couldn't live there," the leader of the sea fae pressed. "You cannot tolerate our salt; we cannot live without it."

"All I need is an island—a small one. The reef will grow around it. I will be close, if not entirely among you."

"You're not young," the sea faerie said, looking her up and down with a critical eye.

"Nor am I so old," she retorted, sounding miffed for the first time. "Once you have a home you can plant sprouts again. When you have a young Winter faerie, bring her to me, and I will train her in the Winter ways, to replace me when I am gone."

"And if there isn't one?"

"I have a century of life left in me. I believe in you," she said, almost saucily.

Silence weighed heavily as sea fae glanced at each other, saying nothing.

"I'm offering you a new world," Marion said. "All I ask is that you let me share it. You'll have to give up your plans of revenge, of course. But in return, you'll be pardoned the atrocities you have already committed. Isn't that right, Captain?"

Tamani bristled, as much at her continued insistence on calling him "Captain" as at the audacity of making such an offer without even consulting him. But these were desperate times if ever there were. So he gave a sharp nod, and held his tongue.

"We must consult," the sea faerie said.

"Naturally."

The sea faeries walked down toward the waves. As they disappeared beneath the ocean, Tamani couldn't help but feel a pang of regret that the sea fae were headed right back to where he had worked so hard to drag them from—a bit diminished in number, a bit worse for the wear, but free to flee if they so chose. He doubted even Marion could stop them, once they put a few thousand gallons of saltwater between themselves and the woman who now aspired to rule them.

Marion gave a sigh and sat herself beside Tamani on a driftwood bench. "There will be much work to do. I'll need the Manor's cooperation in finding a suitable island and securing transportation to it."

"The Manor's assistance?" Tamani asked in disbelief. "In setting you up as a rival queen?"

"Absolutely not," Marion snapped. "*Joint* queen. Of a far

smaller population, I might add."

"They haven't agreed yet."

"They will."

Tamani wanted to argue, but it would only be clashing for the sake of clashing. It was a perfect solution. It served everyone. The benefits to the humans and sea faeries were obvious, but it helped Avalon too. By getting a disgruntled but immensely powerful Winter faerie not only out of their way, but in their debt. He knew it was a good solution, but he hated the way they'd all arrived at it.

When had Marion known what she was going to do? How long had Tamani been her pawn? He knew he'd never get those answers.

"You will talk to Yasmine?" Marion asked.

Tamani let out a long sigh. "I will. She'll be wary."

"Of course she will. That's why you'll propose that Lenore serve as ambassador between the two kingdoms."

"Lenore?" Tamani asked in shock, eyes sliding over to where the young Spring and Summer teens were conversing, heads close together, several yards away.

"What is the sea faeries' greatest power?"

Tamani shook his head, already seeing the end of this argument. Then he answered anyway. "Controlling humans. But they're not as good at it as Lenore. If Lenore is your ambassador, she'll always be available to put down any possible revolt. It essentially keeps the sea faerie population under Avalon's thumb."

"Good. Perhaps you're Shar's protégé after all."

Tamani gazed at Lenore from across the beach. "But Lenore may not want to be your catspaw. She's not just powerful; she's every bit as clever as her father was."

"I'm well aware."

Tamani was beginning to see the outline of a pattern and he didn't want to lose the thread. He kept talking. "Not just her father. Her grandmother, too. When I went to the Unseelie, Mischa asked if I knew how powerful Lenore was. I suspect Mischa was similarly powerful."

"Not was—is. It runs in the family."

Tamani turned to Marion, eyes wide.

Marion faced him, unruffled. "About a hundred and fifty years ago, when Jamison was young, there were two Winter faeries who decided to throw off tradition and have a seedling. They theorized that two Winter faeries would have an even more powerful Winter sprout." She smiled wanly. "Imagine their dismay when the seedling showed signs of opening in the spring. A *Spring* faerie child of Winter royalty." She shook her head. "It was unacceptable."

"What did they do?"

"They passed the child off as someone else's. Washed their hands of her. Which likely would have been the end of it, had a certain political faction not gotten wind of the possibilities."

"Mischa." It made terrible sense.

"Our origins are written in our cells. Mischa always knew she was created for something bigger. Her embrace of Unseelie principles and her ultimate rebellion were, I think, inescapable. But her power and her plots live on in her descendants."

"How do you know this?" Tamani didn't get the impression that this was one of those secrets the Winter faeries kept amongst themselves; he felt certain Jamison would have at least hinted about it if he'd known.

No, this was *Marion's* secret.

"Twenty years after their failure, the Winter court tried again." She smiled. "That's how I came to be. No one suspected who my true parents were, because all Winter fae are raised in the Winter Palace."

Tamani felt sick and strangely elated all at the same time. "You're Mischa's *sister*?"

"And Lenore is my last remaining kin in Avalon." Marion glanced over at the young faerie. "I *will* see her raised up. One way or another. My parents told me of Mischa's existence as a cautionary tale—to warn me against certain courses of action, given that success was far from guaranteed. But in their very telling they created something they never intended."

"And what would that be?"

"A bond. If a strange one." Marion looked out at the sea.

"There's little on Earth more important than family, Captain. They cause you to do things you could never justify otherwise. To make irrational decisions, take unnecessary risks. Whether you want it or not, there's loyalty there—no matter how unlovable and imperfect one's family may be."

When Tamani scoffed, she shot him a knowing look.

"You're telling me you didn't think of *your* family, a breath before you ordered Lenore to slaughter dozens of justly-aggrieved faeries?"

When Tamani didn't answer, Marion merely smiled. She rose to her feet and dusted off her hands. "This has been a good night's work. We're all to be congratulated."

THIRTY-FOUR

THE FOREST WAS STILL DARK WHEN TAMANI pulled into the driveway of his empty house in Orick. He hadn't slept, but that seemed unimportant as he leapt from his convertible, slipped around the house, and headed down the trail into the woods, sprinting for the gate to Avalon with Lenore following close behind.

"I'm not ready to see the queen yet," he told Lenore, gaze focused on the path ahead, wanting so badly to be back with his loved ones. "I have to see my family first. Talk to Laurel. You can go straight to Yasmine, or go see your mother—the choice is yours."

"You'll have to see her for at least a few minutes," Lenore said.

Tamani hesitated. He really *was* tired—he'd failed to guard his tongue. But he truly *wasn't* ready to see Yasmine yet. He needed to talk to Laurel, get her advice; she was often so much wiser than he. "No, I won't," he said softly.

He interrupted whatever Lenore might have said next when he waved to the sentries guarding the tree that masked the gate. For several minutes they waited in tense silence as the sentries assembled, got into formation, and the transformation of the tree unfolded before them. Once the gate had appeared, the sentry captain asked if Yasmine would be coming to open the gate for him.

"I've already contacted the queen," Tamani lied.

As he and Lenore walked forward the sentries faced away, ever vigilant against dangers ancient and new. This gave Tamani the few moments he needed to pull out his key. He stared hard at Lenore, who glared unblinkingly back. "You're going to be trusted with a great many secrets in the future, Lenore."

"Are you questioning my—"

"No," Tamani said, cutting her off. "Merely informing you that this is the first."

Lenore nodded sharply, but still looked confused.

Tamani turned to the gate. He *could* call Yasmine, but if he did, he'd have no reason not to take the time to debrief her. But he longed to be with Laurel. With Sharlet. With his *family*. At this moment he would rather trust his best friend's daughter with the greatest secret in Avalon than postpone his visit with his partner and child for even that small amount of time.

Marion was right; family made you do things you could never otherwise justify.

Tamani pulled the chain up through the neck of his shirt and, with Lenore looking on, unlocked the gate into Avalon. Lenore gave a quiet gasp, but said nothing until they had stepped through and the gate was closed and dark again.

"Where did you—"

"Even here we don't talk about it," Tamani whispered. "Ever."

Lenore straightened and nodded.

"You were excellent tonight, Lenore. Your father would be proud."

"No one will know, will they?"

"What you did? No. It's safer that way."

Lenore smiled sadly. "I always hated that no one ever knew the great things my father did."

"I knew."

"But more importantly, *he* knew."

Tamani laughed softly and nodded.

"I saved a lot of lives tonight, Tam."

"Millions," Tamani agreed. "If not billions."

"It feels good. I don't need anyone to know." She was silent for a long moment, then shrugged. "I guess he didn't, either."

"The greatest acts of heroism are ones no one will ever

know about." He touched the key under his shirt. "Including this one."

"Will you tell me someday?"

"I can't promise that. But the day may come."

"Good enough."

"And now, I have a beautiful woman to kiss." With a respectful nod, he turned and sprinted away.

The distance between the Gate Garden and the Summer quarter had only felt so long once before, back when he and David had made the trip carrying Jamison, rushing to save Avalon from Klea. Tonight, the fight was over, but the intensity of Tamani's desperation was the same. The sun was just rising over the horizon and a handful of faeries were out beginning the work of the day, but Tamani had eyes for nothing but his mother's house in the expansive hollow of the broad-leafed tree a long-dead Winter faerie had once made for her. Perhaps Marion and Mischa's mother, Tamani realized.

Without knocking, Tamani burst through the front door and Laurel's shriek of surprise was the sweetest sound he'd heard in a very, very long time. He threw his arms around her and held so tight she made a strangled sound—playfully, he expected, but regardless, he couldn't get his arms to let go.

Not until he felt a tugging on his pants. "Papa?"

"Sharlet!" he bent and scooped up the tiny girl and held her against his chest, then pulled Laurel close again, his arms encircling his whole world. He kissed one cheek then another, and back and forth until both of them were giggling. "Did you miss me?" he asked with a grin.

"Every minute," Laurel said. "What happened? Did—"

"Kisses first," Tamani said, capturing her lips. He felt like a cactus in the desert, her kisses like rain. He'd gotten so good at putting everything out of his mind during battles, but now that he was with them again, he could hardly comprehend how close he had come to losing them. He almost forgot his tiny daughter until she pounded at his chest, getting smooshed between her two parents.

"I missed you too," Tamani said somberly, letting Laurel pull back so he could hug Sharlet gently before returning her to the floor.

"What happened to your hands?" Laurel asked, looking at the brown, flaking layer of skin on his arms and hands as he made sure Sharlet was steady on her feet.

"Seawater. It'll heal."

"Let me look at it," Laurel said. "I'll get my kit. I—"

"Later," Tamani said, pulling her close again. "I told you, kisses first."

Laurel was laughing as Tamani kissed every part of her skin he could reach while not so subtly steering her backward toward the room they always stayed in at Rhoslyn's house. "Tamani, you have to answer my questions. Where is Rowen?"

"I left her in San Francisco. She has some making up to do with her boyfriend."

"How did he—"

"Later." More kissing; more steering.

"You left them there alone?"

"They'll be fine."

"But—"

"I seem to remember you and I hooking up at about the same age."

"We were older."

"Not in human years."

"They—"

"Later."

They were in the doorway of their bedroom now and Laurel had grabbed onto the doorframe, laughing and giggling empty protests. "But Sharlet," she said with wide, melodramatic eyes. "Don't you want to spend some time with Sharlet?"

"Desperately. Later." He took her mouth in a particularly deep, hungry kiss, so she didn't notice when he peeled her fingers from the doorframe and got her all the way inside the bedroom.

"But she learned to walk while you were gone," Laurel said, her protests breathless now. "Don't you want to see?"

"Try harder. She learned to walk the day she came out of

her pod. Hey Sharlet," he called out. "Your grandmother has a treat for you." He waited only long enough to hear his daughter's soft "Yay!" before he backed Laurel up one more step and kicked the door closed behind him.

***

A dozen candles were glowing around the apartment when Rowen opened the door to let Shawn in.

"Candles?" he asked.

She shrugged. "I saw it on Netflix. And while I don't find fire romantic, I thought you might." She hesitated. "Do you?"

"It's great."

She stepped around him to close the door and then leaned against it, facing him. The moment was heavy and awkward until Shawn held out his hand, holding a pink glittery bag tied with a curling ribbon. "Peace offering," he said. "Meghan wrapped it. She said it was romantic, too. Is it?"

Rowen grinned and parroted his words. "It's great." She looked inside the sparkly pink bag. "What is it?"

"Well, I tried to bring you chocolate and you said you couldn't eat it, and Tamani told me that it was because of the fats and oils in chocolate. So I brought you something with no fat."

Rowen just stared down at the bright red fish. "Is it candy?"

"Gummy candy. They're called Swedish Fish and they have three different kinds of sugar in them." He grinned. "Which I guess, for you, makes them health food."

Rowen pulled one out and sniffed it suspiciously, but it seemed fine. She raised an eyebrow and popped it into her mouth. "Oh, those are good."

"As a bonus, they're a favorite of mine too. Something we can share."

Rowen beamed. "Thank you. I'll … just …" She gestured toward the kitchen with the bag and slipped by him, setting the gift on the kitchen counter. When she turned around she found herself trapped, Shawn's hands braced on the counter on either side of her. "I missed you," he said softly.

"I missed you too," she confessed in a whisper.

"I was surprised that I missed you so much, actually. I mean, because we hadn't been dating that long, and I'd just found out you were a whole different species, and … all that. But I missed you."

He touched the tip of his nose to hers and a low rumble escaped her mouth when his rubbed up and down the bridge of her nose. "I missed this," he whispered. His lips met hers tentatively, his mouth soft against hers. "But not just this," he said, his lips so close they tickled hers as he spoke. "I need you to know that."

"I do." Her gaze dropped to the floor. "I knew it would be

hard for you to accept what I am. Honestly, it took me a really long time to accept what you are. You just didn't know it at the time."

He laughed, then lifted her hands to his mouth and kissed each one before holding them against his chest. "I spent a lot of time with your uncle this week. He told me things." He shrugged. "I asked a lot of questions. It felt a lot less … awkward, asking him."

"Well, you weren't thinking about having kissed him."

Shawn laughed. "No, no I wasn't." He sobered. "But he also told me some things about your country. Avalon. About how he grew up in the … lower class, I guess. It felt really familiar. To be judged for what you're born to, instead of the person you choose to be. I got that. Mostly when I was little. It's been better since I got big. Now I'm the tall black guy everyone picks to be on their team in PE. Too bad for them I'm not much for sports."

He rubbed her hands, looking at the floor, and Rowen realized he was trying to collect his emotions.

"But just when it stopped affecting me so much, it started affecting Meghan *more*. It's really hard for her in ballet. Things are improving—they are—but ballet is still mostly a world for rich, white girls. And Meghan is neither. I'm not sure anyone who isn't a twin can completely understand how much you feel every victory and failure in this other person. It broke my heart to see her work so hard and get so little credit for her efforts. And then you came in—a rich white girl—and I judged you for that."

"But you wised up," Rowen said, desperate to make him feel better. To remove that haunted look from his eyes.

"Eventually. With a little scolding," he added with a self-deprecating smile. "But when I found out you weren't human, I slipped right back into it. Judged you for *what* you are, not who."

Her own feelings of guilt surged up. They had not only both made mistakes, they'd made the *same* mistake.

"I of all people, should've known better," Shawn said.

"It was bigger than that," Rowen said, sliding her hands around his waist. "You didn't just have to accept that I was different—I think you would have been okay with that. I kind of changed your *reality*."

"Yes, you did." He paused, dipping his head to rest, brow to brow, against hers. "But I've accepted it, now. I just hope I'm not too late."

"You're not too late," she whispered.

When he brushed her hair back from her face, his fingers were trembling. "I should have said something sooner. Texted sooner."

"You were busy."

"But I hurt you."

"Then you should kiss me better."

"Mmm, yes ma'am." He paused, his mouth a fraction of an inch from hers. "Is Tamani here?"

Rowen couldn't hold back the laughter that rolled from her. "No. He and Lenore both headed back to Avalon a couple of hours ago. My aunt, Laurel, and her new baby haven't seen Tam in two weeks."

"She had her baby?"

"Three weeks ago."

Shawn peered at her oddly. "You told my parents it was too soon to know when she was having a baby and she had it like a week later?"

Rowen put both hands on Shawn's chest. "Trust me; don't ask that question tonight. I'll explain it all another day. The point is, Tamani is gone, he's going to be gone for a while, and you're supposed to be kissing me."

"You know me," Shawn said, wrapping his arms around her and lifting her up to sit on the counter in front of him. "I always do what I'm supposed to."

EPILOGUE
Six Weeks Later

ROWEN HAD NEVER, EVER BEEN THIS NERVOUS before a performance in Avalon. It didn't help that she was offstage until well into the second act, so she'd already sat through the first hour of the performance, cheering on her friends and listening as the audience applauded for them.

"Come here," Mitchell whispered in her ear, tugging at her arm. She followed him up a metal ladder and across a narrow walkway, into a section above the stage that she'd never been to before. "You can see the audience and the dancers," Mitchell said, showing her where to crouch.

"Won't they see me?"

"You're right behind the lights. You'll be nothing but a patch of blackness to them—don't worry. I found this spot when I was twelve."

Rowen crept out on the thin walkway, enjoying an aerial view of the dancers. Every time the girls spun, their skirts flared, making them look like perfect little pastel circles.

After a moment, however, she looked out at the audience. Most of them were strangers, but her eyes quickly found familiar faces. There was Shawn, of course, who was there to see not only her and Meghan, but Thomas and Mitchell and the dozens of other dancers who he'd become friends with through his sister. Next to him were his parents, who Rowen was getting to know better—they were warm, hard-working, amazingly caring people, and Rowen found it impossible to imagine that she'd once suspected all humans of being barely more than monsters. Seated beside them were Tamani and Laurel, with little Sharlet on Laurel's lap.

They'd gone back and forth on that. Sharlet looked like a one-year-old human—fae infants never really looked like human babies—and spoke like a human four-year-old. But she'd wanted to come see her cousin—another of Tamani's human family words— dance so badly that Tamani and Laurel had made her swear not to say a single word. Rowen worried that her announcement to Shawn's parents would make it impossible for Laurel and Tamani to bring eight-week-old Sharlet anywhere near them, but Tamani assured her that humans rarely asked awkward baby questions to your face.

Manners, he'd said.

Human etiquette: Rowen had given up on it.

Rowen smiled warmly when her eyes lit on the people

sitting next to Laurel: Chelsea and Jason. Their children, being actual human babies, were not trusted to keep their mouths shut, so they'd been left with something called a sitter. But the adults had both come. It had been more than two months since Rowen had apologized to them, and Rowen was still mortified at her terrible mistake. But they'd come, and she loved them for that.

And beside Chelsea, Lenore. Lenore, who had already been given assignments to complete in her new role as ambassador to the Sea Kingdom. She seemed to revel in the responsibility, and Rowen didn't think it was just the job. Lenore seemed more positive, more fulfilled than when they'd parted in Avalon almost six months ago. She'd let go of much of her bitterness. Rowen had asked about it, but in response Lenore simply shrugged and smiled. Whatever had provoked the change, Rowen was glad for it.

Rowen felt tears gather in her eyes as she looked at the row of people who loved her. Six months ago she'd felt so alone. Even four months ago, when family had been invited to watch auditions, there'd been no one in those seats for her. Tonight, she was going to dance for the most important people in her life, and she couldn't wait.

As if reading her thoughts, Mitchell poked her and whispered, "We should go warm up."

Rowen took a slow breath and tried to calm her nerves as

they limbered up and marked their way through their *pas de deux*.

Then it was time.

As they waited in the wings, Rowen peeked out at Meghan, sitting on a throne next to the Nutcracker Prince at the top of the stage. She glowed with a happiness that went far beyond mere acting as she lived her dream of playing Clara before an audience for the very first time. It was a huge night for Meghan and Rowen couldn't have been happier for her.

"Watch out," Mitchell said, pulling her back a few inches as a crowd of younger dancers exited the stage to the sound of applause. "Ready?" Mitchell whispered as the first strains of their music filled the auditorium.

"To dance with the best partner in the world? Yes," Rowen said affectionately, and Mitchell grinned and dropped a quick kiss on her cheek.

The lights came up, the orchestra sounded her cue, and Rowen stepped onto the stage.

THE END

BEAUTY.
BLACKMAIL.
BETRAYAL.

"The Palace of Versailles gets a darkly twisted, modern-day makeover that **had me hooked from the heart-pounding opening scene.** *Glitter* is a thoroughly **inventive, genre-bending tale** that delivers on every level!"

—ALYSON NOËL,
#1 *New York Times* bestselling author

Art copyright © 2016 by Erin Hize
Photo of powder copyright © Shutterstock/artjazz.

CPSIA information can be obtained
at www.ICGtesting.com
Printed in the USA
LVHW090801090222
710672LV00007B/19